Silver Moon Books of Leeds and New York are in no way connected with
Silver Moon Books of London

If you like one of our books you will probably like them all!

Write for our free 20 page booklet of extracts from early books - surely the most erotic feebie yet - and, if you wish to be on our confidential mailing list, from forthcoming monthly titles as they are published:-

Silver Moon Reader Services

c/o DS Sales Ltd.
PO Box 1100 London N21 2WQ
http://www.limitededition.co.uk

or leave details on our 24hr UK answerphone
0181 245 0985
International acces code then +44 181 245 0985

<u>**New authors welcome**</u>
Please send submissions to
PO Box 5663
Nottingham
NG3 6PJ

Your Obedient Servant, Charlotte
by
Anna Grant

All events and characters, in this story, are entirely
ficticious and any resemblance to real people and events
is co-incidental

Chapter One

Ellie had been naughty, very naughty, but she still had to serve the guests. She had upset our mistress, but she still had to be of use to her. So that was why she stood, bound but useful, desperately hoping to get back into her mistress's good books. She could not see anything, because she wore the leather hood; in fact she was deprived of most of her senses. However, she knew that if she failed her mistress one more time today, she would really be in trouble.

Her elbows had been forced to within inches of each other behind her back, by a broad leather belt, but her wrists were pinioned to her sides and joined with leather cuffs and a short chain across her flat stomach. A thin rope had been attached to the chain, dragged between the lips of her exposed pussy, and then pulled up, viciously tight, between her buttocks and tied to the belt. A four-foot spreader bar, attached to her ankles splayed her legs wide apart and her torment was completed by pegs, linked by a silver chain and dangling painfully from her nipples.

She was naked, apart from high-heeled ankle boots, hold up stockings, short leather gloves and a studded dog collar. In her hands she held a glass tray with empty champagne glasses on. It was heavy and difficult for a girl in her predicament to hold, but she dare not drop it, for if she did, the price would be far too high to pay. She was strategically positioned in the entrance hall, by the wide staircase, in order that the guests could be furnished with champagne as they arrived at the party. The hostess of the party, a certain Miss Francesca De Grace, had ordered me to place Ellie there and then to replenish her tray, when the glasses had gone, as well as placing the guests' coats in one of the bedrooms upstairs.

It had been me, who had bound my friend in such

a cruel way, not because I wanted to, but because I had been ordered to by Miss Francesca, our stern and harsh mistress. I would never have done that to lovely Ellie, unless I had been ordered to, but I knew that if I did not obey, then it would be me, Charlotte Fen, who would be confined in that painful and humiliating way instead of Ellie. In fact, I was relatively free; free to serve, that was. My mistress had told me to wear my French Maid's outfit, which consisted of a very short black dress, with puffed shoulders and a frilly petticoat, black seamed hold-ups, five-inch heel court shoes and white frilled apron and cap.

The dress fell short of my stocking tops and I had not been allowed to wear any panties, which meant that I was still very exposed myself, especially when I had to bend over to retrieve things from the floor. Even before the guests began to arrive, I knew it would be a long night, with me being at everyone's beck and call and dressed in such an inviting and revealing fashion. However, my position was not as bad as poor Ellie's. Her evening would start badly and get worse as the time passed. She was to be the central attraction at the strange party, which was about to begin. It could have been me, but it was Ellie who had upset our mistress and so it would be Ellie who would have to pay.

You see Ellie had been summoned to attend Miss Francesca that morning and that usually entailed bathing and dressing the mistress and then bringing her breakfast to her chamber. Ellie had gone, dressed in her maid's outfit as I was now, only she had been permitted to wear small white satin panties. This was what we usually wore around the house, as Miss Francesca thought that these were fitting garments for housemaids. Ellie had run a bath, wrapped Miss Francesca's silk gown around the naked body of her mistress, and led her to her en suite bathroom.

Ellie had then slipped off the robe and assisted

her mistress into the soapy bath, which had been scented with perfume and treated with essential oils. She had proceeded to bathe her mistress's voluptuous body, soaping her back and her breasts, down her long legs to her dainty feet and washing her long, raven black hair. She had even been allowed to rub her flannel across the top of Miss Francesca's thighs and between her legs, a rare honour indeed. After the bath, she had dried her mistress off with the kind of luxurious smooth towels that we were not allowed to use, put the robe back on and led her mistress back to the bedroom. Then she had scampered off to bring the breakfast, which I had prepared, pausing briefly to tell me of the joys of bathing our mistress, in an effort to make me jealous.

I had just smiled and sent her on her way with a loving pat on her bottom. Ellie was a little younger than myself and had not been with Miss Francesca as long as I had and, consequently, she was still trying to prove herself, both to me and our mistress. She went off, her lovely pert bottom wiggling as she walked with a tray filled with fresh orange juice, lightly buttered toast, coffee and the morning post, which was Miss Francesca's usual morning repast. She went up to Miss Francesca's chamber, knocked on the door and entered, at her mistress's command. She had approached the bed and curtsied, as she had been taught to, but unfortunately for her, she had lost control of the tray, spilling the coffee onto the bed and the orange juice onto Miss Francesca.

She had stood up and stared at the mess that Ellie had created and then at her trembling slave. Ellie fell to her knees, put her forehead on the floor and kow-towed before her mistress. Miss Francesca was a stern, but fair mistress, but Ellie knew that, this time, she was furious with her slave, and that all the slave could do now was keep silent and prostrate herself. And indeed Miss

Francesca was furious, punishment was inevitable, but not immediately. She did not want to let her anger cloud her judgement and her enjoyment and, besides, there was the possibility that she would be too hard on the girl in her present, enraged state.

There was also the party that evening and she had been struggling to think of a theme for the event. Perhaps the punishment of Ellie would form the perfect centrepiece for her guests and she knew that I could handle the meal by myself. So Ellie had been banished to the tiny cupboard under the stairs. She had simply been told that she was to be the star of the show and then she had been left to worry.

In the meantime I had cooked the meal, set the huge table and prepared the guest bedrooms, for some of the Miss Francesca's friends were due to sleep over, after the party and the games. Hard work, but better than having incurred our mistress's wrath and crouching in a tiny hole, with hardly enough room to breathe, let alone move around. When six o'clock came everything was ready and Miss Francesca walked into the kitchen to inspect my efforts. She looked stunning, for she wore a sleeveless evening dress of the finest quality, with her hair piled up on top of her head and held in place with a jewelled comb.

The dress was made from black silk and extended to the floor, but was slit to the top of her left thigh, revealing her stocking top. She wore black patent leather court shoes with extremely high heels and straps buckled around her ankles. She also had on full-length opera gloves, with diamond bracelets on each wrist and exquisite make-up on her face, which she had put on herself. She did not trust anyone else to do her justice. She was drenched in her favourite AnaÔs AnaÔs and smelt absolutely divine and, as she approached me, I curtsied, holding the hem of my meagre dress out to the sides, drinking in this vision

8

of beauty and power before me.

Casually, she acknowledged my gesture of sub-servience and began to examine the food. It was unlikely that she would eat much, for she never did, always concerned about keeping her perfect size twelve figure, but she had to be sure that the guests would be happy with what they were served. If they were not happy, it would reflect badly on her and be even worse for me. Luckily, she was satisfied with the food and went on to thoroughly inspect the rest of the house, which she finally pronounced as being ready. It felt good to please my mistress, for I hoped to be rewarded later. She might even allow me to sleep with her this evening, but even if she did not, at least I would not be punished for being lazy.

She then ordered me to release Ellie from the cupboard and get her ready for the dinner party and her ordeal, in the way that she had previously described to me. Ellie was so grateful to be set free and tried to kiss my hands, but I would not have it. I did not want to upset Miss Francesca and so I led her to the foot of the stairs. She hobbled along, stiff from her confinement and wincing with every step, but we could not dawdle. When the mistress wanted something doing, you had to do it straight-away, or suffer the consequences. I did not even allow Ellie to speak, although I did whisper an apology to her, as I stripped her of her uniform and bound her as I had been ordered.

The final binding I applied was the cruellest of all - the rope panties. I knelt before my friend and pulled the rope down towards her pussy. She was already wet, despite the tight and painful bondage she found herself in, and the pungent smell of an aroused female filled my nostrils, so I looked round and checked whether I was being watched. Finding that I wasn't, I quickly licked Ellie's pouting and helpless lips. As I ran my eager tongue along the groove of her pussy, I savoured the taste that I knew so well and loved so much. My nipples hardened beneath my dress and I rubbed them briefly, excited by own touch and by my proximity to the triangle of short hair framing the top of Ellie's spread legs.

I had gagged her, before fastening the hood around her head, but I could still hear her muffled moans of pleasure as I worked. However, I dared not linger and so I withdrew my tongue, separated her pussy lips with one hand and fed the coarse rope through with the other. I then pulled it up between her naked buttocks to the belt holding her elbows. As I pulled as tight as I could Ellie winced again and I felt a pang of sympathy for her. I had been bound in a similar way several times and knew how painful it could be, but I could have no mercy on Ellie, for if I did, Miss Francesca would have no mercy on me. And so I tied the final knot and left poor Ellie by the main entrance and that is where she stayed, until the guests arrived.

I ran off upstairs to prepare myself, which meant putting on make-up in the way Miss Francesca had taught me and ensuring that my seams were straight. As I bent over to smooth round my stockings, Miss Francesca entered my quarters and walked over to me. I straightened up and curtsied, bowing my head and looking at her shoes; we were not allowed to look her in the eye without permission. I smelt the AnaÔs AnaÔs again, a fragrance which I had learned to associate with both excruciating pain and delicious pleasure, depending on the mood of my mistress. This smell always made me reminisce about times I had shared with Miss Francesca and to fantasise about other times to come. However, my dreams about my mistress in her beautiful dress were interrupted.

"I just wanted to come and compliment you on your work today," said Miss Francesca, "that silly girl really upset me this morning, but you have come up trumps. I can usually rely on you."

"Thank you, mistress," I stammered, falling to my knees and reaching for her hand, in order to kiss it to show how grateful I was. Ellie and I rarely received compliments from Miss Francesca and when we did, we were invariably overcome with gratitude and felt compelled to show it any way we could.

"It's alright, my child," said Miss Francesca, patting my head with the hand that I wasn't kissing. "Stand up and kiss me on my mouth, but not too passionately, I don't want you spoiling my make-up."

What an honour, to be able to kiss my mistress on the mouth. A very rare event, I must have pleased her. Slowly I rose and tentatively approached the object of all my love, putting my hands on my head and spreading my legs obscenely wide, as I had been taught to do. I closed my eyes and kissed my mistress gently on her lips, totally awed by being so close to her. She reached down and grasped my naked bottom under my dress; firmly squeezing my buttocks and making me swoon with desire for her. If only she would let me fall back to my knees and serve her, she would soon learn how well I could work between her legs.

"What is that taste on your lips, Charlotte?" asked Miss Francesca, breaking into my wildest fantasies.

"I don't know, mistress," I replied, suddenly scared of discovery.

"It tastes slightly salty like...I know what it is," she said, staring at me with accusing eyes, "It's the taste of young Ellie. You have abused the position of power I placed you in and licked her pussy, haven't you, you naughty girl?"

"Yes, mistress," I said, dropping once more to my knees, this time absolutely terrified. Licking another girl's

11

pussy, without Miss Francesca's permission, was a heinous crime, punishable with a severe beating and long periods of confinement.

"Why have you committed this crime?" asked Miss Francesca, with a dangerous edge to her voice. "Did I not make you work hard enough with your little tongue last night?" I had been ordered to my mistress's bed the previous night and had licked her pussy for almost two hours before being bound and gagged at the foot of her bed. I had worked hard, but I had not been able to resist tasting Ellie's pussy and alleviating her suffering a little. I had to think of something fast.

"I am sorry, mistress," I began tentatively, "but I was having difficulty forcing the rope between her sex lips and I knew you wouldn't be happy with a poorly done job. So, I decided to lick her, to make her wet and make it easier to force the rope further inside her. As you have seen for yourself, mistress, my plan worked."

"And no doubt you enjoyed carrying out your ingenious plan, didn't you?" asked Miss Francesca, a slight grin appearing on her gorgeous face.

"Please forgive me, but you have taught me, mistress, to appreciate the things I have in common with other women and, although none are as beautiful as you, I confess that I do love to serve those of my sex." I hoped that my words would appease her, for it was not too late for me to replace Ellie as the centre of attention at the party.

"You have answered well, little one," said Miss Francesca, now laughing at my attempts to prove my innocence, "and you have worked so hard today and tied poor Ellie so efficiently. You will be rewarded for your efforts, but I will have to punish you for licking pussy, without seeking permission first. Don't worry, you naughty little slut, it won't be too severe. Just enough to stimulate us both!"

12

"O, thank you, mistress," I sighed, kissing her feet out of sheer relief.

"That's alright," replied Miss Francesca, "but if I catch you licking pussy again, without my express permission, I will string you up and give you stripes like a tiger across your pretty back, do I make myself clear?"

"Yes mistress, O yes," I assured her, now slavishly licking my mistress's shoes, to show my utter devotion to her.

" Get up, before you take the leather off my shoes," she said, smiling at me, "and go and pour out the champagne. My guests will be arriving soon and I want everything to be ready for when they do."

"Yes, mistress," I said, standing up in front of her. I curtsied and turned to leave my room and, as I left, Miss Francesca slapped me very hard on my exposed bottom. I yelped, involuntarily, and trotted off.

"You'll scream louder than that if you're naughty again, young lady!" called Miss Francesca after me.

"Yes, mistress," I shouted back, already halfway down the stairs. I ran past the stricken Ellie towards the kitchen. I grabbed a bottle of Don Perignon from the fridge and brought it back to Ellie.

"Here's the champagne, Ellie," I said, "It'll make the tray heavier, but the guests will be here soon and they'll take the glasses from you."

I wanted to try to reassure Ellie, but she could only moan into her gag as I poured the champagne. I held the tray underneath, but Miss Francesca saw me as she descended the stairs, her make-up perfect once more, restored after her brief dalliance with me.

"Do you want to be naughty all the time, little Charlotte?" she asked, realising that I was trying to make things easier for Ellie. "Have I not warned you about disobeying me? Are you sure you wouldn't like to 'meet the tiger'?"

"I'm sorry, mistress," I offered, letting go of the tray, "it won't happen again!"

"It had better not," said Miss Francesca, "I have some important guests coming tonight and I need at least one of you to be on their best behaviour. Ellie is already being punished and there is more, much more to come. Do not interfere any more and get on with you work."

"I apologise, mistress," I said, finishing pouring the champagne and then walking briskly off to the kitchen.

Miss Francesca had tried to foster a sense of rivalry between us, so we would compete for her affections and, to a certain extent this had worked. There was nothing that Ellie and I craved more than to spend the night with our mistress and we worked as hard as we could to earn this privilege, but we had grown to love each other as well. Consequently we humble slaves looked out for each other and showed our affection for each other as often as we could. However, our mistress always had to come first and if that meant forsaking a fellow slave for the evening, then so be it. I would make it up to Ellie, somehow.

When I reached the kitchen I threw myself into my work and wondered what was in store for young Ellie.

The ringing of the doorbell brought me back to my senses and sent me trotting off past her to answer the front door. As I opened it I saw a tall blond man wearing a dinner suit accompanied by a girl with dark hair, wearing a short, low cut taffeta ball dress. They were both younger than myself, but barged past me, the girl handing me her cashmere shawl and the man a cravat and gloves.

"Dispose of these, my dear," said the man, arrogantly, slapping my bottom as I took the items of clothing and turned to go upstairs. I heard the girl laugh, a pretty laugh, as I ran upstairs, obviously showing off the fact

14

that I had no panties on. I placed the clothes on one of the guest beds and ran off back downstairs, to find the couple staring at poor Ellie.

"This is fantastic," said the young man, looking at her like a small child staring at the last chocolate bar in the sweet shop. "Perhaps I should do this to you! Or, perhaps I should ask Miss Francesca to do it to you, for all the guests to see!"

"No, Jeremy, please don't," pleaded the girl, I'll do anything you want, but please don't do that!"

"Anything?"

"You know I'll do anything," replied the girl, putting her arms around the young man and pressing her slender body against his. He took his eyes off Ellie at this point and began to kiss the girl, full on the lips. I decided to offer them champagne at this point and to usher them into the lounge to meet my mistress.

"Well, if that's all you're offering, then that's all I'll take. But later on......well we'll see." The man said breaking off the embrace, but keeping his hand firmly on the girl's bottom. "Maybe a threesome."

"Jeremy!" The girl sounded shocked and I felt she was very ill disciplined. Suddenly his hand went to her hair and he pulled her head back violently. "Any whining from you in front of my friends and I'll flog you raw! Understand?"

I saw the girl swallow nervously but push herself against him, obviously caught in the classic slave's dilemma of fear of punishment and love of domination.

"Yes sir." she whispered, and he relaxed his grip.

"That's better," said Jeremy and, turning to me he added, " pass me my champagne, and lead me to Miss Francesca."

"Yes, sir," I said, hastily handing the couple their champagne and leading them into the living room. I to-

15

tally approved of discipline but couldn't help feeling a bit frightened of the violence I sensed in Jeremy.

I was to find out how right I was to be frightened very shortly.

As we entered, Miss Francesca rose from her plush seat to receive her guests. My heart skipped a beat, as it sometimes did when I saw my mistress at her radiant best.

"Jeremy, darling, how lovely to see you, and your beautiful little slave, er..."

"Rachael," said the girl.

"Don't insult Miss Francesca," said Jeremy, "You know that she likes to be called Mistress, especially in her own home. Go on, address her correctly, or we'll talk to her about the Champagne Girl."

"Rachael, mistress." Said Rachael, staring at the floor.

"Now be a good girl, Rachael and get on your knees before me and kiss my feet."

"Jeremy..." pleaded Rachael, turning to her boyfriend for support.

"Sir," said Jeremy, firmly, "and obey your mistress, before you make us both cross!"

"But, Jeremy..." begged Rachael.

"Sir!" shouted Jeremy, "And get on your knees, now!"

"Yes, sir", whimpered Rachael dropping to her knees to kiss my mistress's feet.

"She needs much more beating yet." Jeremy sighed.

I wondered why I felt a pang of jealousy at the sight of another beautiful young woman serving my mistress, but as I thought about this, the door bell rang and I was forced to tear myself away to answer it. When I reached the door, I opened it to reveal two women, both a little

16

older than Jeremy and Rachael. One had short-cropped dark hair and was wearing a very short party dress, with a studded dog collar, similar to the one Ellie was wearing. Attached to the collar was a chain lead, which was being held by the other woman, who had long blonde hair and was wearing a tight black leather dress, extremely high heels and full length leather gloves. Neither seemed to have a coat, so I showed them in and led them over to Ellie.

"Would you like some champagne, madam?" I asked.

"The slut won't have anything," said the woman, presumably referring to the slave girl, who stood with her hands behind her back, "but you may give me one. What a splendid way to serve champagne, I must compliment your mistress on her style. Where is she?"

"She's in the living room, miss," I said.

"Well then," said the woman, "lead me to her, my girl!"

"Yes, mistress," I said, going in front of the pair. I remembered the couple now, from the last party. I opened the lounge door and stood aside for them and, as they passed, I realised that the slave girl had handcuffs on and was forced to keep her hands behind her back.

"Darling, Olivia," cried Miss Francesca, looking up from the prostrate Rachael and recognising her friend and rival coming through the door, "and you've brought your slut with you."

"Yes, Francesca dear," replied Olivia, "The last time she got so lonely, chained up in her kennel outside, that she cried all night and kept me awake when I did get home. Anyway I thought she might prove to be a useful addition to the proceedings this evening."

"Yes, you're right, my dear," said Miss Francesca, "but I'll have to get Charlotte to set another place at the

17

table."

"Oh don't worry," said Olivia. "Young Julia never eats at table. We'll put her in the kitchen with your servants, and she can eat from a bowl on the floor."

"Very well, Olivia, have it your way. Have you met Jeremy and Rachael?"

At this point, the doorbell rang again, so I curtsied and left the room to see who else had been invited. I opened the door and found another couple on the doorstep, but this time there was a tall man with dark hair, also wearing a dinner suit, but the girl with him, a blonde in a kingfisher blue cocktail dress, was knelt at his feet, with her back to me. Her head was moving at just below his waist level.

"OK, Cindy, up you get," said the man, looking at me straight in the eye and zipping up his flies, "the maid has arrived and we should go in now. There'll be plenty of time for this later."

"Yes, master," said Cindy, getting up from her knees and turning to face me. She was quite stunning, with blue green eyes and it made me go weak at the knees, thinking of her kneeling at my feet. However, she looked straight through me and stalked past me into the house, followed by the man.

I followed them into the hall and offered them champagne.

"Yes, but take my jacket away first," said the girl, handing me a tiny blue jacket the she had been wearing, "and be quick about it!"

"Now, Cindy," said the man, "remember your manners, or we'll have to do something about it."

"But, master," complained the girl, "She's only a slave, like me. Why should I be polite to her?"

"Because, you naughty little slut" answered the man, pointing to poor Ellie, "You might end up like this

18

specimen here. Now, be civil to the maid here and accept your champagne with grace."

The girl turned to me, took the glass I offered her and apologised.

"That's alright, miss, I'm used to being treated that way," I responded. I was impressed; the young man did have her under control.. He accepted his champagne and I turned round and ran upstairs with the jacket. When I returned, I found them both looking at Ellie. It was plain to see that she was already a hit with the guests and they would certainly enjoy whatever my mistress had in store for her later on. Finally, I broke them away from the object of their desire and led them into the living room, whereupon Miss Francesca turned away from the conversation that she was having with Olivia and said, "Martin, darling, how are you?"

"Just fine, thank you, Miss Francesca," he replied, taking her hand and kissing it with all the elegance of a duke.

"And, Cindy, how are you, my dear?" she asked, with slightly less enthusiasm.

"Very well, thank you, mistress," said Cindy, curt-seying and bowing her head.

"Very good," said Miss Francesca, impressed by Cindy's tone of voice and her actions, "I see you've been working on her."

"I have, I certainly have," said Martin, full of pride at his efforts, "She's been over my knee many times since we last met Miss Francesca, and I think she's finally getting the message."

"That's the ticket, my dear," said Miss Francesca, "I told you all she needed was a very firm hand. Now, Cindy, let's see if you can be as well behaved as Rachael here. Come here and show me the same deference as she is doing."

Cindy looked at her master briefly, but he just nodded encouragingly and pointed to the grovelling form of Rachael, who was still licking Miss Francesca's shoes. She walked over to the spot where Rachael's bottom was sticking high in the air as testament to her efforts at Miss Francesca's feet. She assumed the same position as Rachael and began to kiss the Mistress's shoes.

"Very good," said Miss Francesca "Now they look like a couple of bitches, eating out of the same bowl. Perhaps young Julia should join them, before she has to have her supper in this way."

"Maybe later," said Olivia, "but she will serve as my footstool for the moment."

And, with that she sat in the nearest chair and clicked her fingers, whereupon Julia got down on to her knees in front of her mistress and then put her face to the floor. This was quite difficult, as she could not support her body, her hands still being cuffed behind her. Olivia then placed her legs on her upturned bottom and made herself comfortable in the chair. I also knew this position very well and had often spent whole evenings as a footstool for my mistress, whilst she read a book or watched her graphic videos of girls being subjected to the same treatment as Ellie and myself, no doubt looking for other ways to degrade and punish us.

Once again, the ringing of the doorbell interrupted my dreaming and I scampered off, wondering who it could be.

Miss Francesca was quite fond of entertaining and these strange gatherings were nothing new to me, but I hoped that one of the guests might bring a male slave. They had sometimes in the past, and although it was arousing and interesting to see attractive girls kneeling before their masters and mistresses, I always found it stimulating to see a male slave abase himself to his mistress. Be-

20

sides, on occasions Ellie and I had been given to male slaves and it made a refreshing change, however much in love we were with women.

I sighed to myself quietly, I just didn't know which way to turn these days, for my mistress had introduced me to so many fantasies and ways to make love, with both men and women. What was a girl to do?

When I opened the door this time an even stranger sight met my eyes, because standing there was a large man, who had the figure of a rugby player, crammed into an evening suit. But it was what he had with him that attracted my attention, for stood at either side of him were two of the prettiest girls I had ever seen, wearing identical black leotards, hold-up stockings and thigh length boots. Their gloved arms appeared to be positioned behind their backs and each had their ankles joined together by cuffs and a short length of chain. However, strangest of all was the fact that they were both wearing horses' bridles, complete with thick bits and huge black plumes of feathers, which seemed to be sprouting from the tops of their heads.

"Welcome, sir," I stammered, "Won't you come in?"

"Don't mind if I do," replied the man, "Now come on, my beauties, let's go and see Auntie Francesca."

With that the man tugged on the reins, which were attached to the girls' bits and led them into the hallway and, pausing only to glance at Ellie and whistle his appreciation of her predicament, wandered off towards the living room, with girls in tow.

"Be a sweetie, would you my dear," he called over his shoulder to me, "and bring me some of that champagne that your friend is holding so precariously. Just the one, though. The fillies here won't be needing any. They've been watered already this evening, haven't you, my beauties?"

21

"Yes, sir," I replied, reaching for a glass from Ellie's tray.

He had a pleasant voice and I recognised him from some of my mistress's other parties. He was obviously not pleasant to his 'horses' though, for I noticed that their elbows were bound and cinched together behind their backs with rope and I knew, from personal experience, that this was cruel and painful constriction. Their breasts were thrust out by the way that they had been bound and they were finding it difficult to move with the leg-cuffs on. But, despite this, they trotted ever so prettily, behind their master. What a parade of unusual beauty we were being treated to this evening, accompanied by such powerful masters and mistresses.

"O, Rupert, you are so naughty," said Miss Francesca, as the man made his grand entrance with his menagerie, "You know it's supposed to be evening dress, even for the slaves!"

"Hello, Miss Francesca," said Rupert, going over to my mistress and kissing her offered hand, "This is evening wear for my slaves, especially when they have drawn my carriage to the ball."

"You haven't come in your rickshaw, have you?" asked a surprised Martin.

"Of course," replied Rupert, "I only live down the road, so why should I bring my car or walk? No point in having dogs and barking yourself, is there?"

"Quite right," said Olivia, approvingly, "but how did you get away with it, without being seen?"

"Well, I cheated really," admitted Rupert, with a cheeky grin, "you see my land is adjacent to Miss Francesca's and there's an old track that I can run my carts along, isn't there darling?"

"There certainly is," replied my mistress to her charming guest, "In fact, Rupert's always trotting along to visit me in his carriages, pulled by various charges. And, speaking of charges, who are these two beauties? I don't think I've met them before."

"Ah, these are twin sisters, Portia and Hortia," he said, patting each of the girls on their bottoms as he introduced them, "I've borrowed them from a friend of mine at the club. They have to go back next week, but I thought I might use them for racing before then. You know you really ought to bring your fillies round to race against mine. I have a couple of spare carts and traps and plenty of gear and tack."

"I am sure you do, and yes, I might consider it one day," said Miss Francesca.

I shuddered at the thought of racing, because Rupert meant racing pairs of pony-girls, attached to traps, around the track that he had created in his grounds. Ellie and I had not yet been drafted into to pull Miss Francesca in a trap in races against Rupert's teams, but Rupert could be very persuasive. And it seemed like such hard work in the hot sun, encouraged to greater effort by all manner of whips and crops that Rupert no doubt had at his disposal. I hoped that my mistress would go off the idea, for Portia and Hortia looked mightily uncomfortable in their tight bondage. Imagine pulling a cart wearing all that!

At that moment, the doorbell summoned me yet again and so I left the room, quite relieved to escape all the talk of racing pony-girls and pulling traps. I tried to expel all those disturbing thoughts of being trussed up like Portia and Hortia and opened the door to the latest guest.

A very handsome young man stood before me. He had blond hair and light blue eyes, which I found completely captivating. I stood and looked into those eyes for what seemed an age, until he finally broke the deadlock.

"Er...Hello," he said, giving me a smile which turned my knees to water, "is this the house of Miss

Francesca De Grace?"

"Yes, sir," I replied, gathering my wits once more, "Please come in. Can I take your coat?"

"Yes, please," he said, looking at me as though I had three heads. I don't think that he had ever seen a girl dressed as I was. He took off his coat, handed it to me and watched me walk over to the stairs. It was at this point that he spotted Ellie, still standing resolutely at her post. I glanced over my shoulder as I climbed the stairs, slightly disappointed that his gaze was now on Ellie, rather than being fixed on my exposed bottom, as I thought it should have been. How strange that I should now want another man to see me, especially as I had been so full of apprehension at how exposed I would be in my maid's uniform earlier on.

But, being a slave had done strange things to me over the last twelve months. I had changed from being a shy wallflower to being an open, passionate slave, fully attuned with all my needs and desires. I put the coat on the bed and walked quickly back downstairs, looking at the young man in the hall. He was still staring in awe at Ellie, which annoyed me, but gave me the opportunity to study him a little more. He had broad shoulders, but slim hips and he fitted his evening suit perfectly. His short blond hair was swept over to one side, revealing his beautiful, clean-shaven face. In short, he was lovely.

He noticed me on the stairs and, pointing to Ellie he asked, "who trussed her up like this?"

"Me sir."

"And why?"

"Because she's been clumsy sir. And my mistress ordered me to tie her up and await punishment."

"Ah, I see." He examined Ellie some more and even felt how tight some of her bonds were. He seemed to feel some sympathy for her and I warmed to him even more, conscious of the fact that where the warmth was coming from was only very slightly hidden by my tiny skirt.

"Still," he said at last, "I suppose neither of you would have it any other way." And he smiled at me again. I was immediately aware that I was beginning to blush furiously, this strange young man, with apparently no slave of his own had hit the nail on the head. He understood instinctively the submissive mentality, the constant entanglement of fear and love, of pain and pleasure.

"No sir." I said and tried to hide my confusion by giving him a curtsey.

The living room door was thrown open just then and my mistress strode into the hallway.

"Ah, Steven, my dear boy," she cried, "what has been keeping you? Not this little slave of mine, I hope? If she's been slovenly in attending to you, I will have her beaten for you."

I cringed, in fear of the punishment I would surely receive if the young man revealed that I had been talking to him. He looked at my face, noted the fear in my eyes and turned to Miss Francesca, saying, "Not at all, Miss Francesca. I was simply admiring your handiwork here."

"Ah, yes," said Miss Francesca, glancing at Ellie, "Charlotte bound her for me, at my instruction. Young Ellie has been very naughty and you will see her punished for it this evening. Now, come in and meet my guests."

"Of course, I'd love to," said Steven, walking towards the living room, but winking at me as he walked past. I went weak with relief and stared after his muscular and tight buttocks. I was alarmed to find myself thinking that if I had to be beaten for anyone, I wouldn't mind being beaten for him......and my mistress of course. But how could a man like him not have a slave of his own?

"What are you staring at, my girl," asked Miss

Francesca, making me jump, "so, you think he's attractive as well do you. Well, so do I and I fully intend for us both to get to know him better."

"Yes, mistress," I replied. What did she mean? Would he be another rival for my mistress's love, or would he become a lover of mine? Who could tell? However, before I could think about this further, my mistress spoke again.

"Steven is the last of the guests, so you may begin serving the first course. I will bring the guests through to the dining room in about ten minutes. But, before you go, take the tray from Ellie and release her arms. Just handcuff her wrists behind her back and remove her nipple pegs and the rope from her pussy; I want her fully recovered for the ordeal she will have to face after the meal. Take her to the library and leave her in front of the fireplace. Now, carry on."

"Yes, mistress," I said, watching her walk back to the living room. I turned to Ellie, took the tray from her and removed the belt from her elbows and the cruel rope panties. Every kindness I did for her caused her to wince and moan into her gag, as the removal of tight bonds can create more pain for the victim when the blood starts to flow again. I put the leather cuffs back on her wrists, this time with the short chain taut across her lower back. Gently, I removed her pegs, causing her to release a muffled gasp and so I quickly bent over and licked her throbbing nipples, hoping to ease the pain a little.

This was another punishable offence, but I didn't think that I would be caught. She seemed to relax as I licked and I felt my own nipples hardening, as I worked on my friend once more. I could have continued serving Ellie for quite some time, but I had work to do, so I led my friend by the arm, into the library. I had to release her from the spreader bar for the short walk, before I re-tied her.

As instructed I placed her in front of the large fireplace, in which apple logs burnt brightly, giving off a delicious heat and a wonderful aroma. Before I left her to wait, once more, I stroked her bottom.

"Don't worry, my sweet Ellie," I said softly to her, "You'll survive tonight and I promise I'll look after you, later on."

I knew that she had heard me, despite the leather hood, for she sighed and leant her head against mine. As I turned to leave I thought about Ellie and me and what the evening would bring. But also I found my thoughts turning to the last guest; Steven. What part would he play?

Chapter Two

Miss Francesca De Grace lived, with us her two slaves, in a large house called Gilbert Manor, which was set in extensive grounds in the heart of North Yorkshire, not far from Ripon. She was the only child of a newspaper owner, who had died at a relatively young age and who had left her a fortune and the Yorkshire estate. She had left the small London flat that she had been living in and moved to Gilbert Manor almost immediately, realising that there were unlimited possibilities to live the way she wanted to up here.

It was difficult to accommodate the kind of parties that she wished to hold, in the two bedroomed flat in Chelsea for, even though daddy had never left her short of money, there had never been enough room to swing a cat. And it certainly wasn't the feline variety that she was interested in, especially as she was a member of the RSPCA. No, cruelty to animals was not on, but cruelty to humans was fine, in moderation of course and she needed room to swing a cat-o-nine tails. There was plenty of room at Gilbert Manor, and plenty of rooms for that matter and so she gave up her job as photographer with her deceased father's newspapers and prepared to move north.

And that was when she invited me to live with her.

I had met her while out clubbing with girlfriends, who were trying to cheer me up after my last boyfriend had dumped me. She swept me off my feet. She radiated self-confidence; she was outgoing and strong and beautiful. That very first night I drank too much and we ended up in bed together. Francesca was experienced with female lovers and guided me, gently at first. She could play on my body with her tongue and fingers like no man had ever been able to and drive me to multiple orgasms time and again. As quickly as I could I learned how to do the same for her and was pathetically grateful when she told me that I pleased her. In a matter of weeks she came to dominate my entire life; and my body. She introduced me to the delights of SM, and I could clearly remember the first time she put me over her knee, raised my skirt, pulled down my panties and delivered a spanking with her hand which left my buttocks blazing and my sex on fire. I loved every second of it, the way the pain and shock had given way to the most delicious white heat which had consumed my whole body, and how the thought of my helpless submission to her had flooded my pussy with juices. And when she finally stopped beating me she had pushed her fingers straight into my eager vagina and laughed.

"Well my little Charlotte. I think we understand each other now," she had said. And it was no more than the truth, we were mistress and slave from then on.

Inevitably we graduated to stricter bondage and harder forms of punishment. My bottom and back became accustomed to, and responded to, the strap, the whip and the crop. Eagerly we explored the heights of pain and pleasure I could be driven to and I soon reached the stage where I couldn't get enough of my new mistress.

At that time I worked as a secretary in Kensington, but could only afford to live down in Wandsworth, commuting up every day through the busy West End traffic. I worked for a lecherous boss, who was always staring at my full breasts and making risquÈ comments about what he wanted to do with my body. I was desperate for a way out and my mistress suggested that I work as her assistant. I jumped at the chance and was soon working with her on her photographic assignments, travelling all around the South East of England. I still retained my flat in Wandsworth, because I wasn't sure that we could survive in the small attic flat in Chelsea, but I spent a lot of my time there, almost every night in fact. Some nights my mistress would allow me to sleep with her, but most nights I would be bound at the foot of her bed or strung up by my wrists in her wardrobe.

My life began to revolve entirely around my mistress, who I had come to adore. She could do what she wanted to me and I did not mind, for she took me to new levels of ecstasy, almost every time we were alone together and sometimes when we were not alone.

There was one occasion when she had pushed me off a well-trodden path in Richmond Park and found a secluded clearing. She had that light in her eye, which told me, she had something in store for me and I wasn't disappointed. Almost breathless with excitement herself she had told me to take off my blouse and bra. Caught up in excited anticipation of what she was going to do to me, I shrugged them off, for the first time feeling how the cool air of the outdoors blew across my already hardening nipples and made them stand out rigidly in tightly throbbing nubs. Francesca produced handcuffs and tied me with my back to a tree, my wrists imprisoned behind it. The rough bark chafed at my skin but I welcomed the discomfort as proof of her power over me. My bondage meant my breasts were pushed out towards her and she caressed them roughly, tweaking and twisting the nipples and watching me close my eyes and moan with pleasure at the pain, but then she bent her head and began to nip at them with her sharp teeth, while her hand went up my skirt to trace the puffy groove of my sex lips as they pushed against my sodden panties. I began to cry out, not caring whether anyone heard us, but Francesca stopped and laughed at my frustration.

"Now let's get you home where I can beat you to my heart's content and you can scream your head off," she whispered in my ear. To her delight I came in a long shuddering climax just at the prospect.

I loved everything she did to me, however dangerous, however painful and we decided that we would pool our resources and find a larger place for us to live in, together. So, when the news of the death Francesca's father arrived, it came as a bittersweet pill. Shared sadness, but with hope that out of the grief would come a golden opportunity for us to cement our love in a new place. I did not have to think for a long time before I decided to accept my mistress's offer, give up my flat, pack up and move north.

My mistress had decided to carry on with her photography career and I would devote myself to serving her, full time.

And that life of service began after we had completed the six-hour journey to Ripon, with me driving most of the way and my mistress explaining to me how our lives would be. It would certainly be different, for I was to be her slave and she would be in total control of me. I would not eat or sleep or do anything without her express permission and there would be a book of rules, that she would write and that I would have to learn, off by heart. Any infringement of the rules would result in severe punishment, as would any failure to obey her commands or carry out her orders. I would have my own servant's quarters, but my nights would be spent entirely at my mistress's disposal.

And I accepted everything that she demanded. Every petty rule, every discomfort and every punishment, and she certainly meted out plenty of those as I was trying to learn the ropes. At first, she seemed to make the rules up as she went along and I would be beaten if I could not remember them, even if she had changed them overnight. The standard punishment, in those early days, was for me to bend over one end of the large kitchen table, spread my legs and hold on to the sides. I would then have to beg for forgiveness and my mistress would come and pull down my panties, if I was wearing any, and proceed to give me seven strokes across my bare buttocks with a riding crop, which she had made me purchase for her from a local tack shop.

I was also made to wear the French maid's uniform right from the beginning, as we found that it excited both of us and that it was, somehow, appropriate attire for my position as her slave. I cleaned the large house, which was already full of antique furniture, cooked the meals and generally took care of the housekeeping. I was allowed to do the shopping and that invariably meant keeping on my maid's outfit, with no panties and putting on a raincoat, so as not to give the whole game away. It was always embarrassing for me and I was sure that everyone in Ripon knew that I was a slave, out shopping for my mistress. Just simple actions like reaching up to pick items off supermarket shelves, or squatting down on my heels to get things off bottom shelves constantly reminded me of my nakedness as cloth moved across my bare buttocks and I felt every current of air brush my pussy, which became quiveringly aroused. Inevitably I arrived home in a state of acute embarrassment and excitement, but if Francesca was in a good mood, I was allowed to masturbate while she watched.

However, life settled into a pattern and Miss Francesca, as my mistress soon decided to call herself, began to work in the studio and darkroom that she had built. She took pictures for various newspapers and magazines and built up a reputation for herself as an excellent photographer. I helped her as much as I could and, when she was developing photographs, she took to stringing me up by my wrists in the dark room with her. She stroked and fondled me whilst the pictures appeared in the trays of liquid, usually reducing me to a hysterical and highly aroused state before she would break off to complete her job, leaving me hanging, and very much unfinished.

Eventually, my mistress decided to photograph me and send the pictures off to various magazines down in London. She ordered me to strip to my shoes and stockings and then tied me, spread-eagled and face up on her four-poster bed. She then photographed me from every possible angle and went off to develop the prints, leaving me helpless and excited. After an hour, she returned with the pictures, which she showed me. I had to admit that I looked pretty sexy, with my long blonde hair splayed out under my head and my arms and legs stretched tight, away from my helpless body.

There were several pictures of my blonde bush, cropped short at my mistress's request and the sight of my pussy lips, boldly standing out amongst the short hair, turned me on even more. Miss Francesca had not bothered to untie me, even when she had returned, and so I strained against my bonds and begged my mistress to kiss me. Finally, after another hour of looking at those highly erotic pictures and me begging for all I was worth, she took her clothes off, climbed on to the bed beside my defenceless, but desperate form and kissed me on my mouth, running her soft hands all over my body. Even then she managed to keep me from having an orgasm for a long time, first sitting on my face and making me eat out her wide open pussy. I loved the way her coral pink inner lips were crushed down onto my mouth and as she moved on me I was able to rasp my tongue over her hard clitoris and listen for her groans of pleasure before I plunged my tongue deep into the musky depths of her channel, staring up at her buttock crease and seeing the tight little anus, which, once she had finished she would allow me to lick as well. And only when she was fully satisfied did she probe and rub with her fingers at my soaking vulva until wave after wave of joy made me buck and strain in my bonds while she relentlessly rammed her hand into me and I came in a long frozen moment of ecstasy.

That episode marked the beginning of my career as a model for my mistress, appearing in various publications devoted to the sadomasochistic scene. My mistress would photograph me tied up in many different positions and wearing costumes of all descriptions. I was a bound nun, a helpless whore, a handcuffed policewoman, a trussed up harem slave and, of course, a restrained maid. Sometimes my mistress would set the timer on her camera and appear in the pictures as the one binding or torturing me. She never showed her face, of course, but did occasionally reveal her breasts and it was during one tricky session, where she had to set the camera and run to pretend to be tying me to a chandelier, that she fell and hurt herself.

That was it. Neither of us could cope with her not being in full control. We needed another model, one who could appear in the pictures and could be photographed spanking or whipping me for the corporal punishment magazines. And that was where Ellie came in. She responded to an advert that we had placed in one of the magazines in which we published our pictures. She came up from Leeds and was an instant hit with both of us at her interview and began work straight away, taking it in turns with me to play the dominant or submissive roles in our pictorial scenarios. From the first pictures, of me as a naughty schoolgirl and her as a strict young teacher, caning my bare bottom, Ellie entered her roles with enthusiasm.

And then, during one session, the inevitable happened and we took one of our games in front of the camera too far. I had been bound by my mistress in the cellar, because it looked a bit like a dungeon and we used it for variety. I was stark naked and spread between two posts, arms stretched above me and legs tied to the wooden bases. Ellie was dressed in a tight leather corset, thigh length boots, leather gloves and a leather facemask. She carried a cat-o-nine tails and proceeded to beat me with it steadily and slowly, whilst my mistress took pictures. Ellie paused from beating me to rub the red stripes that she had put on my back belly and buttocks, causing me to cry out even more with pain and pleasure.

I was highly aroused and my pussy was soaking wet. Ellie's gloved hand strayed from my belly down between my legs. Swiftly she put a finger inside me, wriggled it around and withdrew it. Slowly she brought the offending finger up towards my mouth, tracing it over my taut stomach and between my breasts, and finally offering it for me to lick. Immediately I strained my head forward and put her leather clad finger in my mouth, sucking my own juices from it as I did so. This was in the script, but then Ellie began to kiss me, her tongue desperately searching for mine. She put her arms around me, dug her nails into my weals and pulled me in tight and continued to kiss me. I responded, forcing my helpless body against hers, moaning with pure pleasure all the time. This was certainly not in the script and my mistress knew that something was wrong.

Jealousy made her angry and she told Ellie to leave the cellar and to wait for her up in the lounge. I watched Ellie go, disappointed, but scared of the wrath of my mistress. I knew that I had done wrong, but I could not help myself. I tried to tell her that I could not get away and that I was at Ellie's mercy, but my mistress knew that there was more to it than that. She left me bound between the posts, telling me, in a chilling voice, that she would deal with me later, but that first she had to deal with Ellie. I spent the next two hours wondering in fear and anticipation what was going on and what my mistress would do to me. I was sure that she would whip me, and much harder than Ellie had done during the session.

I was frightened, but used to waiting for my punishment. Miss Francesca had done this to me on many occasions, sometimes making me wait up to three hours for my comeuppance, bound and anxious. This time I felt that I had waited for an age, thinking about what I done and what my mistress might do to me, but also about young Ellie and how she had turned me on.

Eventually, my mistress returned, but not alone. Ellie was with her, wearing the same outfit, but with her hands cuffed behind her back. I began to beg for forgiveness from my mistress, in the hope of reducing my punishment. But my mistress smiled and explained the she and Ellie had had a little chat and come to an agreement.

It seemed that Ellie wanted more than just a professional relationship with us and that she actually wanted to join us. She had not dared to approach Miss Francesca and so had hatched a plan to trick me into making love to her, in front of my mistress to set up a confrontation.

The plan had worked and, during the course of the conversation upstairs, Ellie had offered herself to Miss Francesca as another slave. My mistress had accepted on the basis that Ellie subject herself to her in the same way that I had, living at Gilbert Manor as an equal slave, with no rights. Ellie had accepted and, apparently to seal their pact, my mistress had stripped off, put handcuffs on Ellie and ordered her to lick her new mistress's pussy. Ellie had obeyed and, because Miss Francesca was so aroused by what Ellie had done to me, she came with such ferocity as to exhaust herself, so she had fallen asleep on the floor in the lap of her new slave.

That was why they had taken so long to return to the cellar, but my mistress said that session alone between the posts was good discipline for me and punishment enough for responding to Ellie's advances. I was very relieved, but a little apprehensive about sharing my mistress with another slave. We continued the photo shoot and Ellie whipped me again and again, the whip smacking across my already striped back until I came repeatedly whilst my mistress captured the scene on celluloid forever. Eventually, she was satisfied with the results and she went off to develop the pictures, telling Ellie to release me. After our mistress left, Ellie continued where she had left off, before we had been interrupted.

She put her arms around me again and kissed me on my mouth, but she did not linger there long, knowing that she did not have much time. Instead, she kissed down my neck and onto my shoulders, then down to my breasts. I was in ecstasy, urging her on with her efforts and beg-

36

ging her to make me come again. She paused at my nipples, biting them briefly causing me to gasp and then she moved on with her tongue, over my belly and then down to my sodden bush. At this point she fell to her knees, pushed her face into the midst of my pubic hair and licked my pussy, swiftly and expertly swirling her tongue round my achingly erect clitoris and delving with her fingers.

I came almost immediately, screaming out loud in the throes of one of the most intense orgasms I had ever experienced. I did not stop screaming until the last shudders of my orgasm had ripped through my straining body. I whispered my thanks to Ellie and she stood and held me for a short time, stroking my hair and telling me that everything was going to be all right. Then she released me and helped me back up to the lounge where we sat and I recovered from my wearing ordeal. As we waited for Miss Francesca to return with the pictures I began to think that it might not be too bad, having young Ellie around and that we might become close friends, even lovers.

And so it was that Ellie joined our household as a slave, just like me, both serving our mistress and hoping to get into her good books. It was difficult for me at first, for I was used to being Miss Francesca's only slave, but eventually I got used to the idea, and there were advantages to the arrangement. With there being two of us, there was a chance that I might not be punished quite so often as in the past. In fact Ellie was punished more times than I was, leaving me free to serve Miss Francesca. And then there were the times that Ellie and I stole moments of passion together, behind our mistress's back.

Some nights, when our mistress wanted to be alone and had left us in our chambers, one of us would sneak into the other's room and we would make love to each other until the early hours. We would get into one of our narrow beds, caress each others' bodies and kiss and lick each other, giving ourselves as much pleasure as we could in those few brief hours. Occasionally we would simply comfort each other by holding one another and trading tales of the harsh punishments that we had received and sharing slaves' secrets of terrible pain and blinding pleasure. These sessions would invariably end with each of us kissing the other slave's whip and rope marks, followed by more tender lovemaking.

Our pictures soon became a roaring success in London as well as abroad and our work was much sought after. Whether it was Ellie binding and beating me or me tying Ellie down and torturing her to within an inch of an orgasm, our prints could be found all over the world and our mistress, rich already through inheritance, became wealthier as commissions flooded in. And, as she amassed more money, her social standing increased and she was invited to more parties and, consequently hosted more parties herself. Parties like the one I had worked so hard to prepare for today and that Ellie would play a central role in.

It was even harder work than I had anticipated, serving at a dinner party by myself, for I was used to Ellie around to help me and there was Miss Francesca, and seven guests, to satisfy. Rupert had tied the reins of Portia and Hortia to the banisters of the main staircase and the pony-girls were left to stand in the hall. In addition to this, poor Julia had been led to the kitchen by Olivia and was eating scraps that I gave her from a bowl on the floor with her hands still cuffed behind her, just as her mistress said she would. Three less guests to look after, but eight people was more than enough for one slave to cater for.

And the guests seemed to like the food, but they also liked to grope me as I leant over the table to serve them or to slap my exposed bottom, as I bent over to retrieve things from the floor around the table. They also wanted the next course as soon as the last course was over and they felt that I was not serving then fast enough. I realised that this was reflecting badly on my mistress, but I was working as hard as I could. She knew that I was trying my best, but she also realised that I would have to be punished, in front of the guests for being slovenly at table, in order that she would not lose face.

"Charlotte," she said, irritably "You have made my guests wait too long during the meal. I realise that Ellie is not able to help you at the moment, but you should have tried harder. You will be punished by me, after we have dealt with Ellie. Now, clear the plates away and then join us in the library."

"Yes, mistress," I said, worried by the prospect of further punishment and saddened by the fact that my mistress had been manoeuvred into chastising me by the impatience and cruelty of her guests. As I began to pick up the plates Miss Francesca and the guests left the dining room and wandered off towards the library, where the unlucky Ellie was awaiting her fate. The last to leave was the young man, Steven. He came over to me and whispered, "You did fine and the food was great." And, with that he stepped up to me, kissed my forehead and walked off after the other guests. I smiled and continued with the task that Miss Francesca had set for me. I was right, he was nice and it would be good to get to know him a little better, that is if my mistress let me.

It did not take me too long to tidy up the dining room and I was soon back in the library with my friend, only this time the room was full of people and my mistress was holding court. Julia had rejoined the group, but was standing in the corner of the room, facing the wall. The other guests were sat in a semicircle around the fireplace and Ellie was still standing there in the midst of them, just as I had left her, only now she had an eager audience, waiting for her punishment to commence.

I had brought the brandy in on the tray Ellie had held and began to serve everyone. None of them thanked me, except Steven, who smiled at me and winked again, as he accepted his glass. He was definitely having a strange effect on me, and I wondered what he would be like to make love to. It was a good job that I could not be punished for my thoughts, or I would always have a sore bottom!

"Charlotte, stop staring at poor Steven, or he might think there's something wrong with him," my mistress had interrupted my daydreaming once again, "anyway, it's time for you to prepare Ellie for her punishment. You know what to do."

"Yes, mistress," I said, walking over to poor Ellie. I undid one of the cuffs that bound her and pulled her arms round to her front. I then dragged her wrists down to the spreader bar that was still keeping her legs wide apart, forcing her to bend over and expose her pussy to the eager crowd.

"That's a better view," said, Jeremy, "well done, Charlotte!"

"I love the way you make your fillies trim their bushes," said Rupert, approvingly, looking closely at Ellie's pussy, "the hair's not too long, but not shaved off completely, like some owners do to their slaves."

"Why, thank you, Rupert," replied Miss Francesca, "I try my best to maintain high standards here at Gilbert Manor." I had finished looping Ellie's chain under her spreader bar and refastening the open cuff onto her wrist, thus compelling her to remain bent double and at the mercy of her tormentors. I had taken up position at the side of the fireplace, to await my next orders. Miss Francesca looked around the group. She seemed to notice something for the first time and said,

"Rupert, darling, you don't have a partner, now that you've stabled your fillies. Perhaps Charlotte should sit on your knee, so as you won't feel lonely before the punishment."

"Why, that's very kind of you, Miss Francesca," replied Rupert, " I think I'll take you up on your offer."

"Go on then, Charlotte, what are you waiting for?" my mistress asked me, pointing to Rupert's lap.

Slowly, I walked over to Rupert, thinking all the while about the poor sisters, bound out in the hallway. It would be awful to be his slave and I hoped that Miss Francesca had no plans to hand me over to him. I sat in his lap, putting my left arm around his neck, whilst he put one arm around my waist and his other hand on my thigh.

"There, that's much better," Rupert said to me, "Now, before we start the punishment, why don't you tell us about that gag and hood that poor Ellie is wearing. I hear that Miss Francesca has her slaves gagged in a very special way."

I looked nervously at my mistress, but she nodded to me, to indicate that I should tell them about the gag and the hood.

"My mistress ordered me to gag Ellie in our usual way and to put the hood on," I began, tentatively, "So I took a pair of my panties and a pair of Miss Francesca's from the linen basket, as well as the large bit from the gag drawer. I crumpled my panties into a ball and forced them into Ellie's mouth and pulled my mistress's panties over her head, so that the crotch was over her nose," I was warming to my audience by now, "I then rubbed the bit part of the gag up and down my naked pussy, until it was wet with my juices, forced it into her mouth and fastened it tight at the back of her head. This meant that Ellie could not push my panties out of her mouth and could, therefore, not scream out loud. It also meant that my mistress's panties were secured against Ellie's nostrils."

"Why all the panties?" asked Jeremy, obviously new to the bondage scene.

"Because," I explained patiently, "when the hood is strapped on over the panties and the gag, all Ellie can taste is me, from my panties in her mouth and all she can smell is the leather and my mistress, from her panties. The taste of me constantly reminds her that I am free, whilst she is bound. The smell of Miss Francesca reminds her that she is Ellie's mistress and the smell of the leather reminds her of the punishment, which she is about to receive."

"Bravo, Charlotte, bravo," said Olivia, " an excellently concise explanation."

"Thank you, miss," I said, "But my mistress is a good teacher and I try to learn all that I can from her."

"Or else she'll punish you, no doubt," said Martin.

"Of course," I said, simply, "If a slave is badly behaved or lazy, then she must be punished. That is one of the most important rules, here at Gilbert Manor."

"Quite right," said Rupert, patting my exposed buttocks with the hand that he had had around my waist, "and, speaking of punishment, what about Ellie. Isn't it time she got her just deserts for upsetting you, Miss Francesca?"

Everyone agreed it was time to get on with the entertainment and I was sent to the downstairs punishment cupboard. There were several punishment cupboards around the house, all containing various handcuffs and whips that my mistress had purchased over the last year, but this was the one designed specifically for guests. I opened the cupboard and took out a riding crop, a cane, a paddle, a three-pronged tawse, a long handled wooden spoon and a wicked looking strap.

I also placed two dice on the tray and I realised what my mistress had in store for poor Ellie. It was to be the dice game, a devilish diversion, used by our mistress when she was bored with our usual punishments. It would be a long night for Ellie. Reluctantly, I entered the library, to find my mistress explaining to her guests what the wretched Ellie had done to incur her wrath.

"Then she spilled the orange juice all over me! Well, I couldn't let that go, could I?" She laughed, "Ah, there you are, Charlotte! Go and stand by the fireplace and hold the tray for us."

"Yes, mistress," I said, moving to my allotted position.

"And now, ladies and gentlemen, we will play the dice game."

"Ah, the old dice game," said Olivia, "I haven't played that for years."

"What's the dice game?" asked Jeremy

"Well, it's a way of punishing a slave, with an unknown number of strokes from unknown implements," explained Miss Francesca ."We all take turns at throwing both of the dice that Charlotte has brought us. The red dice will determine the instrument of correction to be used and the white dice will determine the number of strokes to be delivered."

"How will we know which number corresponds to which whip?" asked Martin, reasonably.

"Charlotte knows which number is which," said Miss Francesca, firmly, "we will throw the dice and she will tell us. Now, who wants to go first?"

"I will," said Rupert, "I'll show you how it's done."

With that he walked over to me and picked up the dice. He looked at me, shook the tiny cubes and threw them on to the tray. When they had stopped rattling around, the red dice showed three dots and the white dice showed three dots.

"Red three and white three, mistress," I said, "Three strokes, with the paddle."

"Only three strokes," said Rupert, with obvious disappointment, "hardly worth getting out of my seat for."

"We are doubling the white dice score, especially for this evening," said Miss Francesca explained calmly.

"That's more like it," said Rupert, seizing the table tennis bat shaped paddle from the tray and walking over to Ellie's left hand side, "six of the best!"

"Three from each side, Rupert dear," insisted Miss Francesca, "we want her to have an even tan, don't we?"

"Of course, my dear, of course!" said Rupert, pulling back his right arm and raising the paddle high in the air. "Here we go then."

And, with that he brought the paddle down onto poor Ellie's left buttock with a loud thwack. Ellie jumped, as far as she could, given the way I had bound her and let out a muffled cry of pain and anguish. I winced for her and looked at Rupert, pleading with my eyes for him to go easy on my friend. She had a lot more coming, and would go far beyond pleasure while enduring it. But he had no mercy on her and delivered the next two strokes with the same ferocity. He then strode over to Ellie's right hand side, took position, aimed and struck Ellie's right cheek, this time with a backhand stroke. The last two followed in quick succession, causing Ellie to scream into her gag every time.

By the time Rupert had finished and returned to his seat, I could hear that Ellie was crying, the pitiful sound smothered by my panties in her mouth.

"Well done, Rupert," said Miss Francesca, heartily, "Who's next?"

"Me," said Jeremy, rushing over to me, "it's my turn."

"Very well," said Miss Francesca, "go ahead."

He grabbed the dice and threw them onto the tray.

"White five, red two," I said, "and that means five, sorry, ten strokes, with the cane."

There was a murmur of approval from the guests and Jeremy grasped the cane with a wicked gleam in his eye. Poor, poor Ellie. This was going to hurt a lot and we had only just started. Jeremy moved to Ellie's left side, raised the cane high above her helpless bottom and, without pausing, struck her very hard across both buttocks. The cane came down with a terrifying whistle and the blow itself caused a mighty crack, which reverberated around the room. Even I jumped this time, because of the viciousness of the first stroke and poor Ellie remained silent for a second and then screamed, loud enough for all to hear. I looked at Jeremy, but realised that he would have no mercy either and, no sooner were the tell tale tramlines appearing across Ellie's bottom, than the second stroke landed, and the third, fourth and fifth.

Ellie was screaming continuously by this point. Jeremy moved to the other side and continued to thrash Ellie with all the venom of one who had been wronged personally by her. Ellie was still crying out when Jeremy had returned to his seat, his work well and truly done. Her bottom was covered with vivid, double red lines, crisscrossing the globes of her buttocks. He was not an expert, but even amateurs can be effective at dishing out pain with a cane in their hands.

Most of the guests remained silent after Jeremy had finished, so Martin stood up, nodded to Miss Francesca and walked over to me. He took the dice, shook them in his hands and threw them onto the tray.

"White two, red six," I called out, "Which means

four strokes, with the strap."

I think that there was a little relief around the room, that Ellie was only to receive four with the strap and thus have a bit of a break after Jeremy's excesses. Martin stood beside Ellie and delivered two quick strokes which slapped against her buttocks, causing the strap to wrap itself around her bottom. Ellie simply moaned and I knew that the strokes were not too bad for her, although she was probably still stunned from the caning. Martin moved quickly to the other side, slashed the strap down twice and returned it to me.

He then returned to his chair. Perhaps he had decided to be merciful or perhaps he preferred to watch others give the punishment, but I was grateful that he had not laid his strokes on too hard.

"After the next one, I think we'll have a break and, perhaps we'll allow Charlotte to lick Ellie's bottom as a reward for lasting out so far, "said Miss Francesca,. "So, who's next?"

"I'll have a go, if I may, mistress," said Rachael. She had been thoroughly turned on by the proceedings so far and wanted a turn herself.

"Of course, my dear," said Miss Francesca, impressed by Rachael's deference, "go and shake the dice."

Rachael came over to me and shook the dice as the others had.

"White four, red five," I announced, "which means eight strokes with the spoon."

"The spoon?" asked Rachael.

"Yes, my dear," explained Miss Francesca, "useful in the kitchen, but essential in the bedroom."

The guests all laughed and Rachael picked up the spoon and approached Ellie. I prayed that she would not be as hard on Ellie as her boyfriend had been and she wasn't. However, the spoon still whooshed down eight

46

times, slapping against Ellie's bottom, with a sound like a short, sharp handclap and Ellie still jumped with every stroke. But it was bearable and Ellie had survived half of the turns. Rachael returned to her seat, thanking her lucky stars that it was not her backside bared for punishment. Then Miss Francesca stood up to address her guests.

"Well done to those who have had their goes," she said, "and to those who haven't, it will soon be your turn. Charlotte will now provide us with refreshments. Coffee, anyone?"

Most of the guests announced that they wanted coffee, so I went off once more to the kitchen, pausing briefly to look at the pony-girls, who were still standing patiently, but in pain, by the banisters. I knew I was busy, but compared to Portia, Hortia and Ellie, I was having an easy time of it. I knew that I was to be punished later, but my mistress would not be too hard on me and she had also mentioned licking Ellie's bottom. I knew that I would enjoy that, so I returned to the library with a spring in my step, handed out the coffee and resumed my position by the fireplace.

"Now, Charlotte," said Miss Francesca, "I think that you should be a nice girl and give young Ellie some relief by licking her wounded bottom."

"Yes, mistress," I said. I walked round to Ellie's upturned bottom, knelt between her legs, put my hands behind my back and began to lick the tortured globes. Ellie had a lovely, pert bottom, but it was glowing red and covered in weals and the marks of her punishment. Jeremy's double ridge cane marks were still scarlet and stuck out from Ellie's usually smooth skin like parallel railway lines. They would take a long time to heal, even if my mistress used her special healing balm on them. As I licked the marks I could hear Ellie wincing and whining, like a scolded puppy, but she eventually calmed down and seemed to be enjoying what I was doing.

I could smell her pussy again and it was clear that she had been turned on by this outrageous treatment. How a girl could derive any pleasure from being tormented the way Ellie had, I just did not understand, but she was definitely not alone. I too had experienced the same arousal during some of the harsh punishments that I had received, whether from my mistress or Ellie herself. It just did not make sense, but there it was; pain and pleasure, who could explain it? And, even though my tongue rekindled the pain from her beating, Ellie responded to my efforts and actually began to moan out loud with pleasure.

"You're not licking her pussy again are you, Charlotte?" asked Miss Francesca, hearing the groaning coming from beneath Ellie's hood, "You know what I'll do to you, if you are!"

"No, mistress," I said.

"You may lick her anus, if you like, but not her pussy."

Yes, mistress," I said, immediately gliding my tongue across her left buttock and down into the cleft between both cheeks. I found Ellie's anus straightaway and began to lap it, gently at first and then more vigorously, savouring the little ridges of the puckered opening. Ellie began to moan louder, for she loved it when I did this to her. Miss Francesca thought that this type of activity would humiliate me, and she was right, I enjoyed it, especially if it brought Ellie to an island of ecstasy in the midst of this sea of pain.

"What ever are you doing, Charlotte," asked Miss Francesca, "I told you not to lick her pussy!"

"I am licking Ellie's anus, as you ordered me to," I insisted, "not her pussy."

"Well, stop it at once," ordered my mistress, "She seems to be enjoying it far too much. She is here to be

48

punished, you know. Now come and clear away these coffee cups, so we can get on with the chastisement."

"Yes, mistress," I said, reluctantly stopping what I was doing.

However, before I pulled my head back and stood up, I quickly licked along the length of Ellie's pussy, making her come and causing her whole body to shudder. Ellie had finally had some fun and my mouth was full of the delicious taste of her quim. As I stood up, I realised that Steven had seen what I had done, but he just looked at me and nodded his head in approval. He would not give me away, because he was a fair man and he knew that Ellie had desperately needed that break. I smiled at him, collected all the cups and took them back to the kitchen.

Steven did seem like a fair man, but he would have to take his turn at beating Ellie, like all the others. Would he be merciful to her, or would he lay on his strokes, for fear of offending Miss Francesca? We would find out presently for, as soon as I returned to the library, Miss Francesca would announce the commencement of the second half of Ellie's punishment.

Chapter Three

She did not have to wait too long. I was sent straight back to the fireplace and told to pick up the tray, piled high with those dreadful devices of torment and pain, in order to facilitate her correction. I felt a little aggrieved that the punishment, in this case had not fitted the crime and that my mistress was being too hard on her. However, I was simply a humble slave and there was nothing I could do, except be there for Ellie when it was all over.

"I think I ought to go next, Francesca darling," said Olivia, getting up from her seat and walking over to me, "After all, I'm an expert and will set the standard for the rest of young Ellie's chastisement."

"Very well, my dear," replied Miss Francesca, "help yourself."

And Olivia did help herself. She took the dice and threw a white five and a red four, which meant ten strokes with the tawse, that wicked leather strap that had been the scourge of so many Scottish schoolgirls. Olivia took Ellie's latest instrument of torment and, quickly and efficiently, slashed it down on to her bottom with hard, even blows, each one eliciting a loud slapping sound. Ellie moaned each time Olivia hit her. She was very good at it, allowing Ellie's body time to absorb the full pain of each blow before delivering the next. And her buttocks, soothed by my efforts with my tongue, were soon returned to a fiery hell, turning a bright cherry colour. Unlike Jeremy, Olivia was adept at causing pain and she really knew how to punish a girl. Poor Ellie was at the mercy of a real expert.

"There," said Olivia, when she had administered the last stroke, "that should do the trick. The girl won't sit down for a week now!"

With that, she returned to her seat, almost defying anyone else to do as good a job as she had just done. Miss Francesca looked round the group, to remind herself who had not taken their turn.

"Cindy, my dear," she said, "Would you like a go next?"

"Yes, please. Mistress," replied Cindy. Poor Ellie was in for it his time and I prayed that the dice would be kind to her, because Cindy certainly would not be. And, for a change, they were, for what Cindy threw was snake eyes: double one.

"Red one, white one," I announced, with what I hoped was not too much joy in my voice, "That's two strokes, with the crop."

"Only two strokes," complained Cindy, "surely there must be a house minimum number of strokes."

"There is, my dear, but only at my discretion," said Miss Francesca, "and I have decided that I will not let you, a lowly slave yourself, give more than two strokes to my slave."

"That's not fair," said Cindy, pouting like a spoilt child.

"If you wish to begin the game once more, only with you lewdly displayed and waiting for the dice to decide your fate, instead of Ellie, then carry on complaining. If not, then get on with it and return to your seat!" My mistress was angry now, obviously feeling that Cindy had presumed too much and had forgotten that she was nothing but an enslaved slut that Martin had brought to the party.

"I am sorry, mistress," said Cindy, suddenly remembering her place and fearing for her own bottom, "it's just that I wanted to show you that I am as good with a whip as Rachael was."

"Yes, well I'm all for a healthy rivalry between slaves," said Miss Francesca, "but you will stick to two strokes."

"Yes, mistress and thank you, mistress," said Cindy, seizing the crop from the tray and taking her position at Ellie's side. Briefly, she looked at Martin and brought the leather-braided crop down across Ellie's cheeks with surprising speed and force. Ellie howled into her gag and began to wiggle her bottom around in a vain attempt to avoid the next stroke. Cindy, totally ignoring

51

the suffering that she had induced in her fellow slave, walked round to Ellie's other side and delivered a similar blow, which whistled down and slapped Ellie's buttocks with just as much power as the first. Cindy then replaced the crop and sauntered back to her chair, looking very smug and pleased with herself.

"Well, it's just you and me now, Steven," said Miss Francesca, "and I think that you should go first, for I want this little slut to receive my personal punishment last of all."

"Very well, Miss Francesca," said Steven, graciously, "although I must protest and say that I believe that this girl has tolerated enough."

"You're not thinking of shirking your duty to our hostess are you, my boy?" asked Olivia, astonished that someone would think about turning down the opportunity to beat the bottom of a deserving slave.

"Of course not," said Steven, looking at Miss Francesca, "I will beat the poor girl as hard as the rest of you, in deference to you, dear lady, but I wish you to know that I do it out of duty and under sufferance."

"If you don't want to do it," said Jeremy, "I'll have another go."

"Certainly not," said Miss Francesca, firmly, "Steven will take his turn, like the rest of us, but I note his protest. Perhaps he has a point, but I am in charge here and I want Ellie punished."

Steven nodded graciously at Miss Francesca and walked over to where I was standing with the tray. I liked him even more for the stand he had tried to make, but I also understood that he had to carry out my mistress's wishes, for he was her guest and he did not want to insult her. Giving me an apologetic look he picked up the dice and shook them, perhaps hoping that fate would at least call upon him to deliver as few strokes as possible. However, neither he nor Ellie were lucky on this occasion for, when the dice came to rest the white one showed six spots and the red one showed one. If only they had been the other way round, for two strokes with the strap would have been fine. Instead, I had to announce a sentence that would make Ellie suffer and endure even more.

"White six and Red one," I said, sadly; "That means twelve strokes with the crop."

"Ah, the crop again," said Olivia; "What are the chances of that happening?"

"I know," replied Miss Francesca, "but it does happen occasionally and poor old Ellie will have to grin and bear it."

"Think of England and all that!" said Rupert, smiling broadly.

"Well, whatever she is thinking of," said Miss Francesca, "She will have to face what is coming to her. Now, come on young Steven, don't keep Ellie or the rest of us waiting."

"Yes, Miss Francesca," said Steven, taking the crop from the tray and walking over to Ellie's left side.

It was obvious that he did not want to strike Ellie at all but he did, with as much force as he dared, given that Ellie's bottom was already dark red and covered in whip marks from the efforts of the other guests. The crop repeatedly thwacked down on Ellie's bruised peaches with each lash making the flesh tremble and causing Ellie to jolt around and her muffled cries to grow in intensity. To begin with Steven derived no pleasure from what he was doing, that was obvious, but the other guests did. They found it highly arousing that Ellie was having to undergo all this after having already endured so much. And at last even he fell under the spell which any shapely bottom under full punishment casts. I could see his eyes were fixed on Ellie's tormented writhings and wriggling, and the way her buttocks shook at each Swish! Smack! of the crop. Steadily he increased the force of the blows.

But even after this, there was more to come, for the mistress of the house would be taking her turn next. I was well acquainted with the strangely erotic feeling of being bound and helpless before strangers, but I couldn't help feeling that this time the way Ellie had been treated was beyond the pale.

Still there was nothing that I could do about it and it would soon be my turn to feel the wrath of my mistress for upsetting her at the dinner table. Perhaps, if I took my punishment bravely, she would take me to bed once all the guests had gone to theirs, that is if she didn't end up in bed with one of them.

I knew that she had her eyes on Steven, as he swung his arm back to deliver his painful blows, his muscles rippling below his shirt. She wanted him and I could not compete with this polite young man although, for a few moments, I found myself wishing that it was me straining against those bonds and receiving the punishment that Steven was meting out. I began to feel horny again, with waves of excitement flooding from my already quivering pussy.

As I watched yet more stripes appearing on Ellie's buttocks I began to moan with pure lust, all the time hoping that the noises I was making would be covered by Ellie's anguished cries. The sheer cruelty of the spectacle over rode any qualms I might have. Whether I was watching or receiving a thrashing, I had to admit I loved them, feared them to start with certainly but eventually I couldn't help loving them. Suddenly, I noticed that the room had gone quiet, apart from Ellie's pitiful sobbing. I opened my eyes and saw that Steven had finished and that he was bringing the crop back to me. He looked a little relieved that his turn was over, but maybe there was a touch of surprise at how much he had enjoyed it. Briefly he touched my hand as he placed the wicked article back onto the tray, and the combination of his hand and the crop sent tiny electric shocks shooting up from between my legs. As he returned to his chair, my mistress rose to her feet and looked around the assembled guests.

"Well done everybody, you have all done a splendid job," she said, filled with pride that her party had been such a success; "By my reckoning poor Ellie here has received fifty-two strokes, with various implements. Now, I happen to think that she has received enough punishment for one day."

"You're not going to bend your own rules are you, Francesca?" asked Olivia, surprised at this turn of events.

"Yes, I'm afraid I am," said Miss Francesca, firmly; "I believe in punishing naughty and unruly slaves, but Ellie has been beaten enough. I will hold my strokes as a kind of suspended sentence and, believe me, if she upsets me over the next few days, she will be suspended, by her wrists, and beaten until she screams loud enough for the whole neighbourhood to hear."

"But we wanted to see you in action, Miss Francesca," complained Jeremy, thoroughly turned on by the things that he had seen so far and wanting more.

"I thought that you might say that," said Miss Francesca, wisely, "So I will beat Charlotte for you and then I will give one of you the opportunity to beat her."

"Which one of us?" asked Jeremy, eagerly

"You will all write your names on a piece of paper and then Charlotte will pick a name out of a hat - the name of the one who is to double her punishment," said Miss Francesca, triumphantly.

I had been happy that Ellie's ordeal was to be cut short, but was now I had been offered up as an alternative sacrifice. Who would it be and how hard would they hit me? If it was Jeremy or Rupert I was in trouble but, on the other hand, it could be Steven, an altogether different prospect. My fantasies of being at his mercy were interrupted by my mistress.

"Bring my special ointment, Charlotte," she ordered, "and you can put some on Ellie's cheeks here."
"Yes, mistress," I said, scampering off to retrieve the salve which would bring immediate relief to Ellie and begin to heal her wounds.

I grabbed a small bottle from the punishment cupboard in the lounge and ran back to the library, past the hapless pony-girls. They had been suffering bondage all evening and it would soon be my turn to suffer as I felt the lash, but that was preferable. I entered the library, and walked over to Ellie. Without waiting for further orders I dropped to my knees, unscrewed the top of the bottle and began to apply a little to Ellie's tortured flesh.

The balm was cool against her red hot skin and she jumped at first, but the soothing effect soon began to calm her and her breathing quickened as pleasure replaced pain once more. Slowly and carefully I covered her wounded bottom, lovingly tracing the stripes and weals, my fingers occasionally straying into the cleft between the ruby cheeks to her pussy, soliciting further moans and stifled sighs. She was beginning to feel better and, despite the pain from her beating, her quim was wet through, an obvious sign of her arousal. I was also enjoying myself and my nipples were rock hard and pushing their way through my flimsy uniform. My own pussy was thoroughly moist by now and I was just thinking of a way to bring myself to orgasm when my mistress broke into my thoughts again.

"Charlotte, you may stop that now," she said, perhaps sensing that Ellie and I were going too far and that I might bring undeserved pleasure to both of us. "Release her and take her to her chamber. Then, put her into bed with no clothes on and her wrists cuffed in front of her, then return here to face your punishment."

"Yes, mistress," I said, setting about the task of undoing Ellie's various bonds.

I unfastened one of Ellie's wrist-cuffs and helped her to stand upright once more. I then freed her ankles from the spreader bar, thus enabling her to bring her legs back together and regain a modicum of modesty. My final task was to refasten her cuffs in front of her and then to lead her away, out of the library and up to her room. Once there I removed her boots and stockings and proceeded to free her of her hood and gag.

I released the buckles of the leather hood and her collar and took off the restrictive items. Next came my mistress's panties, damp with Ellie's tears but still smelling of their owner and AnaÔs AnaÔs. I could not resist taking a quick sniff of them myself, before moving on to remove the gag and my panties from her mouth, both of which were sodden with saliva. I put the panties into Ellie's linen basket, tidied away the hood and the bit and helped Ellie into her narrow bed. As I covered her with her sheets, I looked at her face, tear stained and dishevelled but strangely elated, probably because she had survived her ordeal and had begun to work her way back into her mistress's affections.

I stroked her face gently and then left to return to the party to face my particular ordeal, one which had already been extended at the whim of my mistress and her guests. They would make me choose the name of my tormentor out of a hat, but what would they beat me with and would they expect me to be bound as Ellie had been? How many strokes would there be and would I be able to bear what was coming to me as well as poor Ellie had just done? All these questions raced around my head as I entered the

57

library to meet my fate.

"Ah, there you are Charlotte," said Miss Francesca, "Now come and pick three pieces of paper; one out of here and two out of here."

She pointed to two of her own hats, which she must have retrieved from the downstairs closet and which were filled with small pieces of paper, all folded neatly. They had been busy in my absence and now these slips of paper would decide how much pain I would have to take and who, besides my mistress, would be the architect of it. Hesitantly, I picked out one piece of paper from the first hat and two pieces from the second and made as if to hand all three to my mistress.

"No, Charlotte," said my mistress, firmly, "you read out what is on the papers for us."

"Yes, mistress," I said, looking at what was written on my chosen papers; "They say 'paddle', 'spoon' and 'Cindy', mistress."

"Well, Cindy," said Miss Francesca, graciously, "It looks like you will have the chance to make up for all those strokes that you felt you should have given earlier."

"Yes, mistress," said Cindy, enthusiastically, "thank you.."

"You will go first with the paddle, because Charlotte pulled the paddle ticket out first," said Miss Francesca, "and I will complete the punishment with the spoon."

"Yes, mistress" said Cindy, looking at me with a gleam in her eye.

"Now, Charlotte," continued Miss Francesca, turning to me, "remove your uniform and come and stand in the centre of the room. Keep your shoes and stockings on."

"Yes, mistress," I said, obeying as quickly as I could. When I had stripped off my uniform and folded it neatly on one of the chairs, I stood where Ellie had been bound, only ten minutes earlier, wrists crossed behind my back and legs spread as wide as I could. I was practically naked and vulnerable and still wondering whether I would be tied up myself when my mistress made it all clear for me.

"Now, Charlotte," said Miss Francesca, "fetch one of those chairs and then bend over it in the usual way. I will not bind you, for the moment. But if you move, in any way, during the course of your punishment, then we will tie you in that position and begin the flogging again. Do I make myself clear?"

"Yes, mistress," I said, scurrying off to grab one of the antique chairs, which were dotted around the library and bringing it back in front of the fireplace. I then draped myself over the back of the chair, spreading myself again and holding onto the seat with my exposed pussy facing the 'audience'. I pulled my head back and arched my back, as my mistress had taught me, and this thrust my buttocks even higher into the air, making them a very inviting target.

"You may begin, Cindy," said my mistress.

"Thank you, mistress," said Cindy, standing up and walking over to where I had left the punishment tray. She selected the paddle and assumed the position as she had done before.

"You will give her twelve strokes," ordered Miss Francesca, "and don't forget to distribute them evenly, six on each cheek."

"No, mistress," said Cindy, "I will not disappoint you!"

And, with that she brought the paddle down on to my proffered bottom with a resounding splat, followed by a blast of pain, for me. I had been paddled before, but the amount of discomfort that the seemingly innocent device could deliver always surprised me. I let out a small cry and it took all my self-discipline to keep my hands from flying back to soothe and protect my blazing left buttock. Cindy continued, undeterred by the anguished noises that I was making. The blows rained down alternately on my upturned cheeks and I could feel a crescendo of pain, spreading from my bottom throughout the whole of my body.

However, in spite of the increasing discomfort I began to feel a sensation that I had experienced so many times. The ultimate irony had started to affect me and Cindy's efforts to tan my backside created a warm glow, not only on her target area, but also between my legs. I quivered with excitement, at being at the mercy of this girl in front of an appreciative audience. I dare not feel myself, of course, but I knew that my pussy was already moist and becoming wetter with every stroke. Everyone would be able to see my moist lips filling and opening as my body lapped up the pain. I gripped the chair as firmly as I could and closed my eyes, relaxing into my punishment as I had done so many times before.

Every time Cindy struck me I took another step along my journey towards an orgasm. I settled down and really began to take pleasure from each blow that Cindy gave me. I breathed deeply and in time with Cindy's efforts drawing the delicious pain into me and I knew that it would only take one touch of either my pussy or my nipples and I would be gone. The tops of my thighs were damp with the juices seeping from my excited quim and I found myself thinking that, if this continued, my stocking tops would soon be drenched.

Sadly, it did not continue, much to my annoyance. I had not even realised that Cindy had changed sides and that she was standing at my right hand side as she finished chastising me. And she had finished, because she moved from her new position, returned the paddle to the tray and returned to her seat. She may have been thinking that she had made me suffer, but it was the fact that she had stopped that had really disappointed me and I groaned loudly, not caring who was listening. I had been so close to coming, but had been denied by the fact that the number of strokes had been limited to twelve. Another of life's little ironies for me to contemplate.

As my mistress approached the infamous tray, I wondered whether she realised that Cindy had taken me to the brink of an orgasm and then left me stranded. She probably did, for she was very wise in such matters and had often kept me from coming for what felt like ages.

The long wooden spoon was already in her hands and, without further ado, she took up position at my side and began to beat me with hard, regular strokes. Again it is such an innocent item, the wooden spoon, but it stings, not as much as other instruments of discipline but the effect accumulates slowly and surely. Miss Francesca knew how to use it. The spoon whooshed down and smacked hard across my buttocks, making the pain slam back into my confused brain, but also re-kindling the heat between my legs. As the pain grew, so did my arousal, each stroke from my mistress taking me higher and higher towards the ethereal heights of ecstasy. As she changed her position to my right hand side, she leaned forward and whispered in my ear.

"It's alright, my little slave," she murmured, reassuringly, "You may come; I will let you."

"Thank you, mistress," I said, not so loud as anyone else would hear.

As my mistress continued to chastise with that experienced, slow pacing of the blows to my shuddering cheeks, I closed my eyes, concentrating on turning my pain into pleasure. I would come if my mistress beat me hard enough and long enough. She was doing her part and I settled down to do mine. I had lost count of the strokes, but I realised I did not have a lot of time left.

As the wooden implement rose and fell with buttock-juddering force I pictured my mistress holding it in her gloved hands and applying it to my rear end. I thought about her supple, yet voluptuous body, encased in the silky black evening dress, her ample breasts straining against the luxurious material as she swung the spoon down. I imagined myself, after my punishment, kneeling at her feet, hands bound behind me, endeavouring to reach her pussy in order to serve her, but being denied access by a playful mistress. Eventually, she would let me lap her clitoris with my tongue and taste her honey pot. I would lick and kiss and nibble as well as I could and she would come, pulling my hair and forcing my face closer into her groin as she drifted off to heaven.

It was at this point that I followed the mistress of my imagination and came myself, allowing the waves of pleasure to flood through my body. I felt myself shuddering and could not help but scream at the top of my voice. Luckily my mistress was still beating me, for I had lost all sense of time and place, as I surrendered to my orgasm. . Miss Francesca returned to her seat before ordering me to put the chair back and to stand in front of the fire again, which I did, moving slower than I had before, as I was exhausted after my beating and my little trip to the stars.

However, I was not too tired to forget my manners and, as I came back and passed Cindy, I quickly fell to my knees, kissed her shoes and thanked her for my punishment, then I crawled on my knees to Miss Francesca and repeated my thanks, but adding that I was glad she had made me scream, I added the extra bit for my mistress because of where she'd allowed me to go during my beating. She knew exactly what I was thanking her for and nodded to me and smiled. I had pleased her, especially by remembering to thank her and Cindy and I was sure that I was back in her good books.

"Very well, my dears," said my mistress, looking around her guests, "I believe that this concludes the business of the day. However, before we all rush off to bed, in order to pursue whatever passions have been lit within us, there is something else that I would like to say."

Miss Francesca was well aware that only I had been allowed to have an orgasm so far and that the rest, including herself, were quite keen to join me in achieving that state of grace. However, it seemed that she had something to tell us.

"I have decided," continued my mistress. "that I would like to swap slaves for a while, perhaps a week at a time."

"What do you mean, Francesca dear?" asked Olivia.

"Well, for instance, I would exchange Charlotte and Ellie for young Julia for a week. You would deliver Julia, all bound and ready, here at Gilbert Manor and you would take my girls away, in any way you wished. You would be able to treat my slaves exactly as you want for the next seven days and Julia would be at my mercy," explained Miss Francesca; "The same would apply for you and Rachael, as well as the rest of you. I would even find a place for your fillies, Rupert, but you'll have to provide straw for them!"

Everybody in the group laughed delightedly, except me. My stomach lurched at the prospect of being at the mercy of Jeremy and being subjected to his cane, or being made into one of Rupert's pony-girls! However, there was the possibility of belonging to Steven for a week. He had not been too cruel and had expressed his concern about the way Ellie had been treated. He had also been kind to me and it might be worth suffering the attentions of the others, just to be able to spend a week at his place, wherever that was and be at his mercy.

"The only exception to this proposal is Steven," said my mistress, breaking into my thoughts and dashing my hopes of a week with him. "He has only himself to offer and nothing to swap; so I will accept his offer now and he will accompany me to my bed."

"Very well, Miss Francesca," he said, standing up and giving me a brief look.

He had obviously agreed on this course of action before he came, but his interaction with me had left him not so sure. Still, there was nothing that either of us could do about it. With a sinking feeling in my heart, I watched him walk over to my mistress, take her in his arms and kiss her on her full lips. She kissed him back and then turned to her guests.

"Charlotte will show you to your rooms and I hope that you all sleep well," she said, and then turned to me. "When you have finished, report to my bedroom."

"Yes mistress," I said, wondering why she would need me, as well as the handsome Steven - surely she would want to have him to herself alone.

"I'm going to go back to my place, if you don't mind, Miss Francesca," said Rupert, "got to get these fillies of mine back into their stable for the night, you know!"

"Of course, Rupert, I understand," said Miss Francesca, graciously, "I was going to discuss the details of the slave swap over breakfast, but I will forward the details to you, if that's alright?"

"Yes, that'll be fine. It's a great idea and I'll fit in with any week."

The others all seemed to agree and so, without further ado, I followed Steven and my mistress upstairs, leading the other guests to their rooms and then sneaking hurriedly off to Ellie's bedside.

She was sleeping peacefully, under her covers. She was exhausted, the poor little thing. She had done really well and, no doubt, our mistress would surely have forgiven her for her mistake earlier in the day. Kissing her on her forehead I left her room and went downstairs to check whether Rupert had left and to lock the door. He was not in the hall, so I looked outside and, sure enough, he was there, sat in a small two wheeled trap, attached to the shafts of which were Hortia and Portia.

They were standing patiently, as they had done all evening, waiting for the signal to set off and, with a crack of his long carriage whip, Rupert announced that they were going. At first the trap did not move, despite the fact that Hortia and Portia were straining to pull it along. Rupert slashed both pony-girls across their buttocks with the whip, which had a long braided leather handle and a long, wicked looking lash, also made of leather, with a knot tied at the end. A vicious instrument of correction or encouragement, which must have hurt, for the pony-girls finally got the trap moving and they were on their way.

As I turned to close and lock the door I heard Rupert shouting at the poor girls to get them to go faster and the cracking of his whip as he painfully underlined his commands. I shuddered, thinking of myself pulling his cart and hoping that my mistress would change her mind before Ellie and I had to spend a week with him. Hurriedly, I turned the key in the lock and ran upstairs, for I did not want to keep my mistress any longer than was necessary.

When I reached the door of my mistress's chamber I knocked timidly and waited to be told to enter. Eventually, my mistress ordered me to go in and, as I did, I saw the most stimulating sight of an evening which had been filled with unusual and exciting spectacles. My mistress's room was lit by about a dozen candles, which gave off a dim but pleasant glow, and laid on her huge four poster bed was Steven, hands behind his head, smiling nonchalantly. He was naked as the day he was born and his large penis was standing proud and erect for all to see.

He lay there quite still, not at all embarrassed by my arrival, simply waiting for whatever was going to happen next. It was only after I had stared at his hard cock for several minutes that I tore my eyes away and looked at my mistress. She had removed her dress and stood in her hold-ups, heels and gloves and was also looking at Steven's member, with a look on her face like a cat with cream.

"Haven't I done well, Charlotte?" she asked, not even bothering to look at me.

"Er...yes, mistress," I said, not entirely sure what she meant.

"And you shall stay and witness me claiming my reward for being such a good hostess this evening."

"Yes, mistress," I said, realising why I had been summoned to her chamber.

"Now, go and stand in the corner and I will string you up," she said, pointing to the corner of the room, furthest from the door, but nearest the bed.

I had been tied like this many times before, compelled to watch Ellie and my mistress having fun together. This time it would be my mistress and a man, Steven, who I had already come to like and desire for myself. Miss Francesca came over to me, tied my wrists in front of me and then hung them up from a hook set high in the corner. She went back to Steven, who was still erect and ready for her, evidently not put off by the fact that they were to be watched by me. I was left, standing on tiptoe, watching the scene unfold before me, highly aroused and desperate to join in, but resigned to the fact that I would not be able to.

I stared longingly at Steven. His broad chest was covered in a mist of blonde hair which any girl would love to curl up against, but rearing up above his taut and muscular stomach was his magnificent cock. It speared up from his tangle of fair pubic hair to a length which would surely fill any vagina, and its veined and massive girth promised ecstasy to any female lucky enough to be penetrated by it. The huge purple helm was already glistening and lubricated, at the slit I could see just a drop of pre-ejaculate, and licked my lips.

My mistress did not need much warming up after all the excitement of the evening and she simply climbed onto her bed, straddled Steven's body and kissed him on his lips. She did not immediately allow him to enter her, instead rubbing her wet pussy along his firm penis whilst gripping her hand around it to hold it vertical, thus continuing to stimulate herself, but denying him any pleasure. Pretty soon they were both moaning, her from enjoyment and him from sheer frustration. I was moaning with frustration myself, watching my mistress having her wicked way with Steven; it should have been me and not her, lying with him, but not to tease him.

"So, are you enjoying yourself, young Steven?" my mistress asked her plaything, pinching his nipples as she continued to torment his cock with her wet quim, causing him to cry out with shock and pain.

"Yes, Miss Francesca," replied Steven, pushing up with his strong thighs in a futile attempt to enter his new and demanding lover.

"Naughty, naughty," said Miss Francesca, pinching his nipples again, "not until I'm fully ready for you."

"But you're already wet, Miss Francesca," pleaded Steven, "you must want me to enter you!"

My mistress gave a husky laugh and in agonised envy I watched her raise herself and then push down to allow his shaft to sink into her; "Ah...that feels good!"

"O, thank you, Miss Francesca," sighed Steven, "thank you so much."

"Don't mention it," said Miss Francesca, beginning to rise up and down on his rampant member, "now let's go riding - giddy up!"

I watched helplessly as his shaft disappeared up into her and then re-appeared, shining with juices whenever my mistress lifted herself again. Slowly the rhythm of penetration and withdrawal speeded up as my mistress and Steven took each other to the heights of passion and pleasure. After only a few short minutes, which felt like a lifetime to me, the two writhing figures came, as one. They both cried out, their backs arched and after the spasms had run through them they lay still, Miss Francesca's arms around her lover. I was a seething mass of frustrated desire by then, being naked and strung up, forced to watch Steven and my mistress make love, and all I wanted was to join in. but, of course, I was not allowed to. Not, that is, until my mistress extricated herself from his embrace and came over to me, looking flushed and replete. She untied me and told me I was to clean Steven's cock and harden it up for her, then I could go to bed and leave him to her for the night.

Anything was better than nothing. I climbed onto the bed while he watched me and I knelt between his widely stretched legs, put my hands behind my back and began to lick his penis, which was not as hard as when I had first entered the room, but remained an impressive sight. Semen was dribbling from the end in a little white stream and the smell of his seed was mixed with the all too familiar odour of my mistress's pussy. I sucked the still partly engorged end of the cock, even though it was far from erect it nearly filled my mouth completely. I eagerly licked off the sperm and swallowed it then enthusiastically I licked the shaft, feeling the hardness begin to form under the soft skin.

"Why don't you use this to encourage her?" Miss Francesca asked Steven, from the corner of my eye I saw her take the long dressage whip from the wardrobe.

"But she's doing alright as she is," said Steven reasonably.

"She'll do better if she's whipped, believe me. Get your buttocks up higher Charlotte."

I obeyed, absolutely thrilled at the idea of being beaten by Steven while his member throbbed back to life in my mouth.

Suddenly I felt the lash trail gently down between my buttocks and I groaned with the desire to feel it lashing me properly while I sucked at this cock which was now stuffing my mouth so full I thought it would choke me.

"Don't tease the poor girl," I heard my mistress say, "she's dying for you to lay into her. Do it!"

"Alright, alright," I heard Steven say. And suddenly the whip cracked down on my defenceless bottom. Immediately I was off again on the painful path to coming under the whip. He continued to strike me and the pain grew and grew as I worked, but I welcomed it and drew it into me because it was Steven holding the lash and at that moment I would have been happy with him doing anything to me that he wanted to, just so long as I could serve him as I was doing now.

In addition to that the combined taste of Steven and my mistress was simply divine and I would have carried on lapping the growing penis forever if I'd have been allowed to. If only I was exciting Steven for my own benefit, but I knew that my mistress would continue to reward herself as soon as he was ready. As I worked, I could feel him hardening and was very pleased with my efforts, but I was not there to please myself; I was there to please my mistress and to prepare Steven to pleasure her. So I took what pleasure I could from holding the dome of his rigid member deep in my mouth, flicking and licking with my tongue across the slit, sucking hard on it and loving the smooth feel of the skin on the rock-hard shaft. It had been a long time since I had had a mouthful of cock, and I was surprised by how much I enjoyed it. But then the whip and the cock; I was getting both together and no slavegirl could ask for more. As soon as his member was fully hard, filling my mouth so completely that I was having to puff out my cheeks when he pushed it into me, my mistress interrupted my pleasure in order to seek hers.

"That will do, Charlotte, now go to your bed and leave us in peace."

As I left, I could hear my mistress giggling with delight and Steven moaning with desire as they both started their journey towards the ultimate satisfaction once more. Quietly I closed the door and walked along the corridor to my room and the sounds of Steven and my mistress were promptly replaced by the sounds of the guests, in their various rooms. My bottom still glowed pleasantly from the whipping and my mouth was filled with the tastes of male and female excitement, and I wanted to come very badly. To add to my woes, I could hear the guests in their rooms, there were groans of pain and pleasure made in time to the smack of leather on flesh, and there were abandoned cries of utter joy as one or other of the girls achieved a shattering orgasm.

Ellie was still fast asleep and I did not have the heart to wake her and ask her to ease my yearning and the dull ache between my legs. Instead, I removed my shoes and stockings, climbed into the small bed beside her and held her in my arms. As I listened to her soft breathing and watched her pert breasts rising and falling I realised that I was exhausted myself and it wasn't long before I fell asleep, still frustrated, but also strangely satisfied with my efforts throughout the day...

Chapter Four

Luckily for me I woke up before my mistress the following morning. If I had been caught in the arms of Ellie I would have found it hard to sit down for the rest of the week, and my back would really have been striped. But as it was I was able to slip into my stockings, heels and uniform while leaving Ellie to sleep a little longer. The house was quiet as everyone slept off the night's excesses when I made my way down to the kitchen to make the morning coffee. When I had the tray ready I went back upstairs and woke Ellie before the guests. She took some rousing, which was hardly surprising but when I left her she was hobbling stiffly over to the sink gently massaging her terribly bruised backside. Miss Francesca and Steven were still entwined in each others' arms when I entered her room, and immediately all the previous night's jealousy flooded back. They made a very handsome pair, the black hair and the blonde on the pillow, they stirred as I entered and breathed in the scent of sexuality which still hung in the air. My mistress gave me a look of such triumph as she let her hand stray down across Steven's stomach that my hands trembled as I served them, and when I left the room I had to take a deep breath and steady myself before serving the other guests. Normally I wouldn't have bothered what state the slaves were in, but if this 'swap' was going ahead then it concerned me very personally indeed.

In Martin's room, he and Cindy were sitting up in bed, and while I served them he played with her breasts. Out of the corner of my eye I could see how the soft flesh moved under his hands and how her nipples hardened and stood out proudly. However hard I tried I couldn't help being aware of how the sight was making my own nipples swell and press against the satin of my uniform. He grinned at me and turned Cindy by her shoulders a little to give me a glimpse of the traces left by the beating he'd given her the previous night. As soon as I saw the stripes I felt myself moisten and a flush of excitement burned my cheeks. Martin laughed when he reached out and ran his hand between my legs, finding my secret immediately. He would have me at his mercy very shortly. All thoughts of jealousy evaporated from my mind, just a glimpse of a whip-striped female back and I was juicing helplessly. I just had to face it, I was prime slave material, Steven belonged with the masters and mistresses, and I belonged to Miss Francesca.

In Olivia's room, Julia was hung by her wrists in a corner where she had obviously been all night, and she too showed the traces of a sound beating. But Rachael was faring the worst. She was tied in a crouching position at the foot of her master's bed. Her hands were cuffed behind her, her ankles were tied together and a strap round her back ran under her thighs and kept her bent double, her bottom in the air. Jeremy was whipping her and she grunted and moaned at each blow which made her buttocks ripple. It was obviously a regular morning workout for him and he didn't let me interrupt.

Full of foreboding I went downstairs. All three of them were going to be very harsh, but Rupert was probably going to be the worst of all. I found Ellie already preparing breakfast. Her lovely auburn hair was in a French plait and she looked delicious in spite of the night before, somehow she had even managed to cover up some of the worst bruises on her buttocks. I began to help her and told her all about the night's events, she was pleased for me that I had had an enjoyable beating, she told me that her own pleasure in being beaten had passed by the second dose, and from then on it had been pure exquisite pain, but even that had been arousing in its way.

I told her about the 'swap' and she was aghast.

"But I don't want to be anyone else's slave. I gave myself to Miss Francesca and I want to serve her!"

"We don't have any choice Ellie," I told her. "If we belong to Miss Francesca and she wants to lend us out, then she's quite entitled to. Just think of it as serving her, only in another place."

I sounded more convinced than I felt but we were interrupted by Olivia and Julia arriving in the dining room. I was told to bring Julia into the kitchen and feed her from a bowl, like the night before. I had to explain who she was to Ellie because she had been hooded for the whole evening. We watched as she knelt humbly and lapped at her food, a position we had both had to adopt on many occasions ourselves.

When I returned to the dining room Martin and Cindy had come down, she was fully clothed and allowed to sit beside her master. But when Jeremy and Rachael entered soon after, Rachael had only been allowed her high heels, stockings and suspenders. Moreover she was made to kneel beside her master, facing away from him so that everyone could see the marks of the crop on her buttocks.

I served everyone and was ignored so I was able to stand quietly and listen to the conversation. Olivia, Martin and Jeremy were all delighted with the idea of the swap. They felt Cindy and Rachael would benefit from Miss Francesca's discipline, while Julia would continue to receive the harsh treatment which Olivia said she revelled in. And I supposed she must, what strange creatures we slaves are, living in fear of punishment but welcoming it too and deriving pleasure from excruciating pain.

And of course all of them were looking forward to having a brace of well trained and pretty slave girls to play with themselves.

At that point Francesca entered dressed only in a flimsy nightgown and a diaphanous robe which was open at the front so the swell of her magnificent breasts pressed against the filmy material, her nipples turning it dark pink. She looked positively radiant and easily dominated Olivia, Jeremy and Martin. She bade everyone good morning and Martin told her how they all felt that their various slaves, particularly Cindy, would benefit from spending some time with her.

"Well, I have been known to have some success," said Miss Francesca, modestly, "like young Steven here."

At this point she looked behind her, nodded her head and moved aside to allow her latest 'success' to enter. He was naked to the waist and yet he sauntered into the room as if he owned the place. At the sight of his magnificent body, images of his erect cock swam back into my mind and I felt a twinge deep within my pussy, no wonder that my mistress was looking pleased with herself.

"Come on Steven, there's a good boy, let's join our guests for breakfast," she said; "Charlotte, go and bring more food for us at once."

"Yes, mistress," I said, hurrying past her and back to the kitchen.

What was going on - was my mistress going to invite Steven to stay with us and have the run of the house? Julia was still lapping water out of her bowl as I grabbed a bowl for Steven, but there was no sign of Ellie. She must have been off to another part of the house tidying up. I returned to the dining room with a tray of food and stood by the doorway with it. Miss Francesca was sitting at the head of the table, sipping tea and Steven was by her side.

"Ah, there you are, Charlotte," said Miss Francesca, "Now, put the food on the table."

As I obeyed her I was horrified to hear her casually announce that while final arrangements were made for the swap she would have me beaten, partly for the guests' entertainment and partly to show how well trained we were. Without even looking at me she waved me over to stand in front of a window.

"Bend over there Charlotte, where we can all get a good look at your delicious little rump while Ellie uses the crop on you."

I was well enough used to beatings but never had my submission to my mistress been so casually taken for granted, and so publicly at such an hour of the day! For the first time since I had given myself to Miss Francesca I felt the stirrings of rebellion. But if I disobeyed she would be shamed in front of her friends and I couldn't do that to her, besides my punishment would be terrible!

Slowly, and facing away from everyone at the table, I prepared myself. First I hiked my tiny skirt up over my buttocks and then spread my legs so that I could grasp my ankles when I bent over. I was acutely aware of how my pussy lips would be pushing back towards the audience as I did so and somehow it seemed so much worse in broad daylight than it had the previous night. As I bent right down I glanced back through the arch of my legs and found that I was being completely ignored by everyone except Steven, who was staring intently at my exposed bottom and sex. Immediately my pulse began to race. If I was going to get a thrashing for no good reason and my mistress chose to ignore me, at least one person looked as

75

though they were going to enjoy my suffering and that's really all a slavegirl needs to get her juices flowing. Proudly I flicked my hair back and looked up to arch my back prettily. Ellie had re-entered and been told to fetch the crop, now she came to stand behind me.

"How many strokes shall I give her Mistress?" She asked.

"Oh give her two dozen, that should give us time to talk and finish our coffee."

Twenty four! I bit my lip to stifle the whimper I couldn't help giving.

"And don't go easy on her," Miss Francesca continued, "or you'll take her place. And Charlotte?"

"Yes Mistress?"

"No screaming or any such nonsense while we're talking."

"Yes Mistress." I managed. All I could hope was that this demonstration of her power over us would earn me a good reward.

I settled myself for a serious beating and Ellie laid the crop across my cheeks before lifting it away to deliver the first stroke when Steven broke in.

"Ellie, before you start, Charlotte has such a pretty bottom lift her skirt up higher so we can see it better."

I felt Ellie obey but mainly what I felt was a jolt of excitement which nearly took the top of my head off. I saw again and tasted that wonderful cock which had filled my mouth last night. I risked a quick glance back through my legs. Yes! Steven was still watching me intently while the others chattered among themselves. I looked up again, resolved to relax into my beating and try to muffle the groans and cries of mixed pain and ecstasy I was bound to give under twenty four of the crop. And for the very first time I cared about how someone other than my mistress would react to the sight of my willing submission.

76

Ellie swung in the first lash and I got down to the serious business of not making any noise! We had both been well taught how to give and receive a beating. The lashes were laid on firmly and slowly. The whippy shaft of the crop scored bright lines of pain across my trembling buttocks, making me flinch and jerk each time, but Ellie gave me plenty of time between lashes to appreciate the pain, absorb it and let it fuel the fires which were gathering between my open legs. I knew Steven would be able to plainly see the traces of my gathering excitement - and I wanted him to. He was watching, and this one was for him.

That thought hastened my first orgasm and I had to grit my teeth hard to stifle my moans but I couldn't stop the shudders that ran through me and made my legs tremble as my pussy juiced frantically while the cruel thrashing went on and on. I longed for Ellie's fingers or tongue to play with me or Steven's cock to ram into me.

But at last the lashes stopped falling. I had no idea whether I had taken all twenty four or whether this was just a break, so I stayed down and heard Miss Francesca tell Ellie to serve more coffee. She laid the crop across the small of my back and did as she was told, leaving me panting and exposed. Again I risked a quick look back through my legs. My mistress was arranging the order in which we were to be lent out; Martin would have us first, then Olivia, then Jeremy and finally Rupert. If necessary we would be given time in between to allow for any marks to fade, and there was general laughter at this. Obviously we were in for more beatings like the one I was going through now! But why was Miss Francesca doing this to us? I couldn't think straight with my poor bottom stinging and burning and my pussy quivering and spasming with excitement. Ellie came back and I had to face the rest of my beating, but before it started Steven

77

broke in again.

"Miss Francesca, Charlotte's got another ten to go. Why don't we let Ellie play with her for a bit?"

My mistress laughed fondly and said that after last night, she could refuse him nothing. "Lick her pussy if you like Ellie, but if she makes any noise give her an extra five."

I could have blessed Steven as I felt Ellie's cool tongue begin to lap across my weals and then make its way down along the slit of my sex till it licked at my throbbing clitoris and sent tingling jolts of pleasure all through me. I was determined not to suffer an extra five lashes but it took all my self control to stay silent as time and again Ellie licked at me, pushing her tongue between my labia, up into my vagina and then trailing it across my anus. I shook and trembled as at last a massive orgasm burst through me, but somehow I stayed silent.

The last ten lashes went by in a blur of delicious pain and pleasure, and at last I was allowed to stand up, panting, sweating and dishevelled.

Miss Francesca still didn't pay me any attention, merely waving me away to fetch Julia for Olivia. I had to take careful little steps to the kitchen to allow the spasms of my last orgasm to subside.

When I got there I told Julia that it was time for her to go and helped her to stand up. She whispered her thanks and trotted off to meet her mistress in the hallway, whereupon she dropped to her knees, between Olivia's feet. "Are you going to take her home like that?" asked Miss Francesca.

"Of course," said Olivia, simply.

I was sent to get her clothes and when I returned I found Olivia's Rolls Royce outside the front door. The boot was open and Julia was being made to climb into it, I watched her clamber in and crouch down and her mistress slammed the lid down, sealing her in. I walked over and handed her Julia's dress, which she took without saying a word to me, waved to my mistress and sped off down the driveway. I turned and followed my mistress back into the house and then into the dining room. Martin and Jeremy were stood talking to each other and it seemed that they were ready to leave as well.

"Thank you, so much for your hospitality, Miss Francesca," said Martin, "and I look forward to coming back here next week to start the ball rolling."

"Yes, it has been wonderful," said Jeremy, joining in the praise, "and I can't wait for my turn either."

"Don't mention it, gentlemen," said Miss Francesca, "just don't forget to take your property back home with you; although I'll be seeing Cindy in a few, short days."

The men laughed but I could see Cindy biting her lip nervously, she was obviously thinking about Ellie last night.

Cindy was fortunate enough to travel home in Martin's BMW, still fully clothed and in the passenger seat beside her master, but Rachael was not so lucky. Jeremy put her evening dress on the back seat of his Bentley but she was destined to journey home in the boot, as Julia had done, only Rachael would have to keep her handcuffs on. With great difficulty, she climbed into the boot, lay on her side and huddled down as Jeremy banged the lid down.

We watched them drive away and then walked back into the house to find Steven, fully dressed and talking to Ellie. I was surprised because I thought that he would remain as Miss Francesca's pet, but it seemed that he had other plans.

"Ah, there you are, Miss Francesca, I'm going to get off now."

"Very well, Steven dear," said my mistress, "but

I was hoping that you could stay with us for a while."

"I'm sorry, but it is what we agreed upon," said Steven, "and I think you'll have to admit I served you well last night."

My mistress put her arms around him and gave him the most lascivious kiss I had ever seen her give anyone, pressing and rubbing herself against him, I saw her tongue flick hungrily into his mouth. He returned her passion, his hands roving over her breasts and buttocks, I felt a strange emptiness inside me at the sight of how much desire for each other they displayed. It was as if Ellie and I didn't exist for her as much as we had only a day before. My bottom burned again at the thought of how I had been displayed in the dining room, he had watched but was now ignoring me, he wanted my mistress and suddenly I was in the grip of insane jealousy. But then Steven broke the kiss and turned to leave, pausing to kiss both Ellie's and my hands and to give me a brief look, he seemed to be trying to tell me something with his eyes but I couldn't understand what. In the end he just patted one scarlet buttock, walked out of the house, jumped into his car and sped off down the drive. All three of us watched him go, lost in our own thoughts of concern and desire.

The days until our swap passed too quickly. Our mistress treated us as usual, harshly at times, lovingly at others and it seemed as though the strange party had not had any lasting effect. I relaxed and mocked my feelings of jealousy, Miss Francesca seemed quite happy with us again. And at least Ellie's and my bottoms had a chance to heal, but all too soon it was our last day before it all started.

"Now, girls, we've got things to do," said Miss Francesca, after breakfast on that day. "This afternoon we had better do a photo-shoot and get you two ready for your visit to Martin's house."

"Yes, mistress," we said, automatically and in

unison.

"Do your jobs and then meet me in the lounge at one o'clock," said Miss Francesca, firmly, "we will eat this evening and not bother with lunch."

"Yes, mistress," we chorused again.

"We need to do a 'dungeon scene' scene for that American magazine," explained Miss Francesca, "so you be the 'sub' Ellie and you be the 'Dom', Charlotte. You know the drill and what you have to wear, but with plenty of make-up this time. Now, off you go and get on!"

"Yes, mistress," we said, scampering off to set to our tasks.

With our work done, Ellie and I went off to get ourselves ready to play out the chosen scenario in front of our mistress's lenses. We had done dungeon scenarios before, but with the roles reversed. This time I put on the tight, leather basque, seamed fishnet stockings and high-heeled ankle boots, whereas Ellie donned the tiny pink baby-doll night-dress and minuscule panties, white ankle socks and high-heeled red shoes. I put my hair into an austere ponytail and put on some large glasses, with ordinary glass in the frames. Ellie put her hair in bunches, tied with pretty pink bows.

We then applied liberal amounts of makeup, although Ellie added several freckles with her eyeliner pencil, in a successful attempt to make herself appear younger. She looked so sweet and innocent and not a day over sixteen; good enough to eat and, later on, I hoped that my mistress would allow me to. I gave her a brief hug and we went off downstairs to the lounge to meet our mistress, who was ready with her cameras and her tripod mounted flash bulbs. She was busy preparing films as we entered, so I stole a glance at her as she worked.

She was wearing what she normally wore whilst she photographed us; close-fitting brown leather trousers, white blouse and high-heeled brown suede shoes. Her black hair was tied up at the back of her proud head and her face was made up to her usual, high standards. I could see her firm breasts, free and straining against her blouse, for she rarely wore a bra when she was working. I felt my knees weaken and a pulse between my legs as I watched my mistress, all the time wishing that it was me that she was manipulating with her strong fingers and not her camera equipment.

"Ah, there you are, girls," she said, noticing us for the first time, "and so beautifully attired for our session."

"Thank you, mistress," said Ellie and I, in unison again and curtseying to our mistress.

She went on to tell us in detail what she had planned. Ellie and I squirmed in excitement as she told us..

The shoot went ahead as planned, with me sitting in the lounge, reading an incredibly graphic magazine filled with pictures of a tall blonde woman flogging a diminutive brunette who was suspended by her wrists from the ceiling of a dungeon type room. It certainly didn't help me to calm down and gather myself together for the session; far from it, in fact, for I became more aroused and stimulated from the erotic pictures on the pages in front of me. Miss Francesca took a couple of snaps and then went out into the hall to capture Ellie descending the stairs, her thumb in her mouth and a light brown teddy-bear in her other hand - the spotless lamb approaching the slaughter.

The camera flashed and whirred and Ellie and I acted out our parts to the full, going well beyond the call of duty. I looked stern and cross at being interrupted and Ellie looked timid and frightened at finding herself at my mercy. I dragged her out of the room and down to the cellar, whereupon I sat on one of the chairs down there and pulled her over my knee and spanked her, lightly at first and then harder and harder as our passion grew. I knew that I was not a natural sadist, but there was something about having Ellie over my knee and slapping her bottom with my hand. Something that made me shudder with excitement and desire. Just as her firm little buttocks shuddered under each resounding smack

All the way through the session our mistress was talking to us, guiding and encouraging us, showing how pleased she was with our efforts at every opportunity. The fact that she was satisfied with us served only to inflame my passion more and I found myself moaning with pure, unrequited lust, as I administered Ellie's punishment. And, as I pulled down Ellie's panties I saw her moist lips peering out from her clipped bush and I began to detect the unique odour of her arousal. I continued to spank her for a while, as hard as I could, to ensure that the reddened cheeks would show up on the pictures.

After a while of this I made Ellie stand up and pointed to the punishment box in the corner of the cellar, telling her to get the strap and to bring it to me. When she returned, I made her bend over the punishment bar, which consisted of two poles embedded in the floor, each about a metre high and connected by a padded bar across the top. I spread her legs, tied her ankles to the posts and then bound her wrists to a small hook protruding from the wall in front of her.

I ordered her to arch her back and thrust out her bottom and, before I began to strap her, I paused to drink in the scene I had created. Ellie's long legs were stretched and taut, her muscles twitching occasionally under the strain of holding her position. Her heavy breasts swung below her, almost falling out of the short nightdress; her labia, wet and open.

I took hold of one of her bunches of hair and gently pulled her head back and round to face me, so as she could watch me raise my arm and continue her punishment. I then strapped her buttocks with as much force as I could muster, stroke after stroke bearing down on her. Ellie cried out with pain at first and then settled down to enjoy the rest of her chastisement, breathing quickly and mewing with longing. She too had come to appreciate the paradox of deriving pleasure from pain and I realised that she was not far from an orgasm herself.

Mischievously, I stopped beating her, let go of her hair and walked round to her other side, causing her to moan with disappointment at being prevented from coming. However she was soon gasping with delight as I proceeded to stroke her buttocks, which were now scarlet after all my attentions and then continued to slash away with the strap. The loud slapping sound made by the each stroke of the strap was followed by a cry from Ellie, as she lost herself to her passion and desire to be relieved.

Her cries grew as she came closer to her orgasm but, once more, I denied her the ultimate pleasure by stopping punishing her, causing her to sigh with pure frustration.

I walked over to the punishment box and swapped the strap for a large black dildo attached to three leather straps. I fastened two straps around my waist and pulled the third between my exposed lips and up between my buttocks and tied it to the others. I went to her side, pulled her face round and forced her to lick the rubber phallus in order to lubricate it. I held it there long enough to be sure my mistress's camera captured her little pink tongue passionately licking the thick dildo which was about to be plunged into her. I then sauntered back to her upturned bottom yanked her cheeks further apart and swiftly inserted the dildo into her anus, watching how the gleaming object slowly pushed into the tight passage, stretching the opening ever wider and wider.

She cried out with pain and shock because, although she was expecting this indecent invasion of her privacy, I knew very well how the initial penetration is always surprising and a girl can't help feeling as though it shouldn't really be happening. However, she soon settled down and began to enjoy herself, once the shaft was deep inside her and moving smoothly in and out. I knew any guilt about the act was expunged by the fact that she was bound and at my mercy. I was also enjoying myself as the strap between my legs was moving backwards and forwards in a highly arousing way.

I knew that she and I were approaching orgasm again and, as I realised that my mistress had stopped taking pictures and did not allow us to climax during such sessions, reluctantly I withdrew the rubber invader, watching with delight how her entrance gripped the shaft tightly as I withdrew it. I knew just how desperately Ellie's body was trying to retain the dildo, aching for it to penetrate her just once more, she wriggled her hips and moaned as it came out but I moved round to stand beside her and made her lick it once more. Her sweet little mouth opened wide and I shoved the gleaming shaft deep inside, she made little grunts of delight as she sucked on it and licked at it again when I withdrew it. She groaned with disappointment once more and her tongue reached out to try and lap at the last of her juices when I finally removed the dildo and put it back in the box. I released Ellie and sat back down on the chair. I then told her to fetch the baby oil and, having done so, to place herself across my knees again and in my lap.

Sulkily, she did as she had been told and, placing the bottle of oil in my hands, she arranged herself as I had commanded. The oil was cool as I poured it into my hands, but it soon warmed up as I applied it to her crimson cheeks and gently rubbed it in. By now, I was also lost in my own world of fantasy and lust and I deliberately brushed my arms against my solid nipples, which jutted out hard against my corset. Both Ellie and I were drifting off towards paradise; Ellie because I was massaging her lovely reddened bum and me because my breasts were responding to my brief but effective touches.

"Hey, you two, the session's over," shouted Miss Francesca, breaking into our trances. She could see what was happening and felt that she had to reassert her authority over us, by thwarting our attempts to come. "I hope you're not trying anything on without me, are you?"

"No, mistress," we said, not entirely convincingly.

"Well, I hope not," said Miss Francesca, "because I had wanted to treat you two, as a going away present and because you've worked so hard this afternoon. However, if you've already had your fun, then I won't bother."

"Oh, no mistress," I pleaded, "we did nothing, I promise you."

"Very well," said Miss Francesca, "now, Ellie, go and prepare supper for us and Charlotte, go and pack a bag for you and Ellie to take with you to Martin's."

"Yes, mistress," we said, back in unison.

"There's a list on your bed, containing the things Martin wants you to have with you."

"Yes, mistress," I said, following Ellie out of the lounge in order to set about my task.

As Ellie went off to the kitchen, I went upstairs to my room, where I found a piece of paper with Martin's handwriting scribbled across it. I quickly started to collect the things that were on the list. First came the items of restraint and discipline: steel handcuffs, two; leather manacles, two; bit gags, two; ball gags, two; strap on dildo, one; vibrator, one; chastity belts (with attached dildos),

86

two; leather hoods, two. Then came the instruments of correction and punishment: crop, one; cane, one; cat-o-nine tails, one; five-fingered tawse, one; dressage whip, one.

Finally there were a number of objects of clothing, including maids' uniforms, schoolgirl uniforms, various items of underwear and footwear. He also wanted baby-dolls and a couple of special gowns, although I had no idea where he intended to take us out to. Obviously I would need a large bag for all this gear and I suspected that my mistress had helped Martin put this list together, with a few helpful suggestions. I sighed and retrieved my duffel bag from my closet, smiling as I did so, for this was the bag I had stuffed most of my clothes in when my mistress and I had first ventured up here.

I put all the things that Martin had specified into the bag and then went back downstairs and, leaving the bag in the hall, I walked into the kitchen. My mistress was already sat in there at the table reading the post that she had not got round to as yet. Ellie was standing at the sink, washing celery in preparation for the meal. Everything else was ready and I knew that we would eat soon, which was just as well because I was famished. I went over to Ellie, to see if there was anything I could do to help her, but my mistress spotted me as I crossed the floor.

"Ah, you're back, Charlotte," she asked me, "did you get everything that Martin wanted you to take with you on your little trip?"

"I think so, mistress." I answered.

"I know that you two are very worried about the next four weeks," said Miss Francesca, this time to both of us, "but you will be alright, I assure you."

"But we will miss you, mistress!" Ellie blurted out, unable to contain herself.

"I know, I know," said Miss Francesca, overlooking the fact that Ellie had broken the house rules by speaking without permission; "I will miss you two as well, but I feel that it will do you good, to have some time in the hands of different masters and mistresses."

"Yes, mistress," said Ellie, miserably. I knew how she felt, but I was too well trained to voice my opinions. I was just as unhappy about the whole thing as Ellie was and I was very concerned about what would happen to us both.

"Would you like to know what your treat is to be?" asked Miss Francesca, sensing, correctly that words alone would not appease us.

"Yes please, mistress," we said, almost simultaneously.

"Well, after our meal and after you've washed up and cleared away the dishes," she said, teasing us by stringing out her explanation, "we will retire to my bedroom and spend the night together; all three of us, all night!"

"Oh, thank you, mistress, thank you!" we cried, our synchronisation totally gone in our shared excitement. What a thrill and what an honour - a whole night with our mistress and each other!

After that, we could not eat our meal quickly enough, wolfing down our food and sharing the task of tidying up and washing the dishes. I then served Miss Francesca her customary brandy in the lounge and Ellie and I knelt, either side of her chair, waiting for our next instructions and hoping that it would not be long before we all went upstairs, together. But Miss Francesca made me put Vivaldi's 'Four Seasons' on the stereo and kept us kneeling and waiting for an hour, relishing every drop of the brandy and savouring the rich music, which filled the room.

Eventually, she ordered us to go upstairs, strip to our heels and hold-ups and handcuff each other's hands behind our backs. We scurried upstairs and began to take our uniforms off in my room, so as not to make a mess of our mistress's chamber. I then cuffed Ellie's hands tightly behind her back and grabbed a pair of handcuffs for myself. I was used to securing myself in this way and closed one metal bracelet around my right wrist, put my hands behind me and, with my right hand, snapped the other bracelet onto my left wrist. We then went to Miss Francesca's room and discovered that our mistress was already there, so we both knelt at her feet and waited for her next command.

"Very good, girls," she commented, " and now you will remove my clothes, without the use of your hands and be careful with my garments, or else!"

"Yes, mistress, " we said, setting about our new task.

And it certainly was a difficult one, especially as I had to pull my mistress's boots off, which I did by putting the heel of each boot in my mouth, gripping the leather with my teeth and tugging them off, inch by inch. Ellie undid the fastenings of Miss Francesca's blouse with her mouth, moulding her lips around each of the buttons in an attempt to free them. As she moved down our mistress's body, loosening the buttons as she went, Miss Francesca's breasts fell free, her soft creamy white skin spilling over the crisp material of the blouse.

Soon, our mistress was standing naked before us - a rare and truly magnificent sight, her neatly cropped bush scarcely hiding her glistening lips, her nipples already hardening at the prospect of what was to come. She then proceeded to lie on her bed, put her arms behind her head and stretched her legs wide apart, allowing us access to her fully exposed and gaping quim.

"Come and lick my nipples, girls; one at each side!" she ordered and we did so, as quickly as we could, ending up bent over and working on her engorged nipples like a pair of suckling puppies.

It was not long before all three of us were emitting sighs of longing and desire. Miss Francesca was enjoying what we were doing to her and, even though Ellie and I were still bound, the fact that we were so close to our naked mistress and actually touching her was enough to send both of us slaves half way to heaven. Our mistress began to spank both of our bottoms, gently at first and then harder and the bedroom was soon reverberating with loud slapping noises. She was not annoyed with us, but she wanted to reinforce her control over us as well as to encourage us and the short, sharp stinging smacks soon had Ellie and me panting with lust.

"Go and stand at the foot of the bed," she ordered us eventually, "and lick my feet and then up my legs, towards my lips, but not them just yet - I'll tell you when I'm ready!"

"Yes, mistress," we cried, scurrying of to our new positions.

We began to kiss and lick her feet and to gradually work our way up her beautiful, long legs. Our mistress was immediately pleased with our efforts and she started to moan and sigh, louder and louder as Ellie and I toiled our way, ever upwards.

"You may now lick my pussy, one at a time, starting with Ellie!" said our mistress, almost losing control of her voice as she surrendered to her passion. Ellie instantly shuffled up to our mistress's open and glistening lips and her bush which was bedewed with her juice, pushing her tongue between her labia as soon as she had steadied herself, her breasts dangling down either side of Miss Francesca's firm thigh.

"Whilst you are waiting to lick me, Charlotte, you may rub yourself off on my leg," said Miss Francesca, generously, "and the same goes for you Ellie, when she

90

takes your place, but you must both lick your slime off my legs when we are done!"

"Yes, mistress," I cried, for Ellie was far too busy licking her mistress's pussy to give her an answer. I felt the muscles in my mistress's leg go rigid and I knew that she was close to coming. I hoped that she would not let herself go before I had a chance to taste her juices in my mouth. And, sure enough, my mistress did not let me down and soon ordered me to change places with Ellie, who, rather disappointedly, had to cede her place.

I clambered up to that part of my mistress that I desired most of all and licked between her pouting lips, savouring the distinctive taste on my tongue. I was lost in my own passion, lapping at my mistress's sex and rubbing my own, soaking quim on her lower leg, as hard as I could. I pushed the hood of Miss Francesca's clit back and discovered that her clitoris itself was hard and throbbing. I began to nibble it, which caused my mistress to shudder with excitement and I realised that she was approaching her orgasm. I wanted to claim the prize of making my mistress come and I knew I had succeeded when Miss Francesca grasped my hair, pulled me closer into her pussy and surrendered to her orgasm.

Her whole body seemed to go still for a moment as the waves of pleasure flooded from her quivering sex. And, having helped my mistress achieve samsara and leave her body for a moment on a wave of pleasure, I felt myself coming, my orgasm slamming through my body like an express train, making me feel weak and spent but also elated. I heard Ellie cry out as she realised that we had come and her frantic rubbing finally came to fruiting, causing her to come enthusiastically as well. We all lay completely motionless for a few moments and then Miss Francesca reminded us to clean her legs with our tongues, but that we should lick the leg that the other slave had worked on.

It gave me even more pleasure, to taste Ellie's pussy juices as I obeyed, for she tasted, if anything sweeter than my mistress. We were then allowed to sleep all night at either side of Miss Francesca, hands still cuffed behind us but, nevertheless, close to our mistress. It had been a perfect day, taking part in the highly erotic photo-shoot, serving Miss Francesca and then, the ultimate honour, being allowed to sleep with our mistress. I drifted off to sleep at my mistress's right side, 'spooned' against her back with my nipples brushing against her soft skin as she held onto little Ellie at her other side. All thoughts of the next day and the arrival of Martin gone because, at least for now, we could stay with our mistress until the dawn and that pleasure comforted us.

Chapter Five

The next day did come and all too soon. I woke up first and realised that we had slept until fairly late and that we were still huddled together, much the same way in which we had gone to sleep the previous night; Ellie in Miss Francesca's arms and me snuggled up to my mistress's back. I was loath to rouse the other two and lay there for a while, listening to their breathing, which was deep and completely relaxed. I knew that I could not be happier than at that moment, lying next to my mistress, our naked bodies close and, at some points, touching.

However, I also understood that Martin was coming for Ellie and myself and that, if we were not ready, Miss

Francesca would be cross with us. I did not want my last image of her, before we went, to be that of an angry and disappointed mistress. I quickly moved away from her, hoping that she would not stir. With a little difficulty I got out of bed and then walked round to Ellie's side of the bed, in order to rouse her.

"Ellie, Ellie," I whispered, nudging her shoulder with my forehead, "we must get up!"

Slowly she blinked herself awake and we crept back to our rooms, undid each other's handcuffs, quickly washed ourselves and, as we did not have much time, we simply put on our court shoes and white frilly aprons, which barely covered out breasts and the tops of our thighs. We then went down to the kitchen to prepare breakfast and to make sure that everything was ready for Martin's arrival. Ellie made a final check of the things that we were to take with us and I took the breakfast tray up to Miss Francesca's room, to find that she was still fast asleep.

Briefly, I stood and looked at my mistress, who had thrown most of her covers off in her sleep and whose naked body was exposed. I caught my breath as I gazed upon the sight of the uncovered woman who had just helped me to a special orgasm. Her firm breasts rose and fell in time with her breathing and her nipples were hard, having been exposed to the cooler air of the room. Her legs were slightly parted and I could see her dark bush failing to hide the pink lips beyond.

"Mistress, wake up please, mistress," I said, as loudly as I dared, "or you won't be ready for when Martin comes!"

"Oh, good morning, Charlotte," said Miss Francesca, opening her eyes and sitting up. "Charlotte, about Martin and the others," she said, coming wide awake at once. "What I want to say is well...I want you to look after Ellie over the next few weeks. You know that she is still young and a little impetuous and I don't want her to get into too much trouble with such as Olivia or Jeremy, for instance."

"Yes, mistress, I will try to take care of her as much as I am able." I said, proud that my mistress had confided in me and asked me to care for my fellow slave.

"Now, pass me my breakfast and get me my leather dress out and my ankle boots out," ordered Miss Francesca, "I want to look my dominant best to receive Cindy."

"Yes, mistress," I said, placing the tray on the bed.

I walked over to her wardrobe and took out the dress to which she had been referring. It was a strapless black leather garment, with a corset type bodice, tightened with laces and a long, close fitting skirt, with a wide slit, which narrowed towards the upper thigh. I laid it on the bed as she washed herself and retrieved her fishnet stockings, boots, and full-length leather gloves. She would wear her full regalia to welcome young Cindy today and I felt a twinge of jealousy that she would be spending a week with my mistress and not me.

I helped Miss Francesca dress in complete silence, feeling sorry for myself all the while. I pulled the laces of the dress as tight as I dared, causing my mistress to sigh with the tension I had created within her frame. For a moment I thought I'd gone too far, but I knew that my mistress always had her stays as tight as possible in order to accentuate her fabulous figure. I knotted the laces, securing her within her constraints and then aided her to put on the rest of her garments. Standing back I looked upon the exquisite image I had helped to create.

My mistress looked simply Elysian and I could not resist the urge to fall to my knees and kiss her shiny boots. I abased myself before her and licked the leather for all I was worth.

"Please don't send me away, mistress," I heard myself pleading, "Let me stay and serve you, I beg you, mistress!"

"Come now, Charlotte," answered Miss Francesca, kindly but firmly, "you wouldn't expect me to break a promise that I have made to my friends, would you?"

"No...mistress," I said, miserably resigned to my fate.

"Now let us go, I think I hear a car in the driveway," said Miss Francesca, turning away from my prostrate form and walking to the door.

I rose up from my knees and followed my mistress along the corridor and down the stairs to the hall. Martin had arrived, for we found Ellie answering the door and admitting him to the house; Cindy was nowhere to be seen.

They greeted each other, Martin practically gawping at the vision of beauty and power before him.

"And where is the lovely Cindy?" asked Miss Francesca, looking around.

"She is in the car," replied Martin, "and all ready for you."

"Very good, Martin," said Miss Francesca. "Now, Charlotte, go and get Cindy and bring her to the dining room. Ellie, bring Martin and myself some coffee."

"Yes, mistress," we said, setting about our duties.

"You'll have to untie her ankles if she is to walk in here!" said Martin

I went out to Martin's BMW. I was used to being outside without any clothes on and had often been bound naked to various trees by Miss Francesca as a matter of discipline or punishment. Cindy, on the other hand, was obviously not used to being unclothed and outdoors. As I opened the boot, she shrank back in a futile attempt to hide herself from me. She had been stripped and cruelly bound, with wrists and elbows tied behind her back, knees and ankles also bound with the same white rope.

With great difficulty I helped her out of the boot and undid the ropes. Then I led her into the dining room to discover that Martin and Miss Francesca were sat at the table, sipping the coffee that Ellie had brought for them. Ellie was stood by the door, legs apart, hands behind her back, head bowed.

"Bring her over to me and have her kneel down," ordered Miss Francesca.

"Yes, mistress," I said, bringing Cindy over to her and forcing her to her knees, as if symbolically handing her over to my mistress.

"Retie her ankles," said Miss Francesca, "she won't be going anywhere for a while. I have a few things to discuss with her first of all."

"Yes, mistress," I said, tying the hapless Cindy's ankles together, almost as tight as Martin had tied them originally.

Miss Francesca told Cindy that she was to spend the next week at Gilbert Manor and that she expected absolute obedience from her otherwise she would be severely punished. I noticed that Cindy's thighs were covered in whip marks of the deepest red and it seemed that Martin had beaten her in preparation for her week at the mercy of my mistress. How I wished that I could take her place instead of having to go off to Martin's house. However, we were part of the bargain and it was decided that Ellie and I would be taken to Martin's house trussed up in the same way as poor Cindy had been.

However, as I listened to Martin and my mistress talking about us as if we were pieces of luggage I could not help but feel strangely excited at the prospect of what would happen to us at this relative stranger's house. The first flutterings of arousal quivered between my legs as I thought about the prospect of being owned by a man for the first time. I closed my eyes and pictured Martin ordering me to serve him, bound and totally at his mercy, a vision that turned my insides to jelly with desire.

I was roused from my fantasies and ordered to retrieve the bag, which I had prepared earlier. Ellie was told to fetch some ropes and the two dominants proceeded to bind us, Martin tying Ellie in exactly the same way in which I was being bound; very skilfully and very tightly. At least I was being constrained by Miss Francesca, her strong fingers pulling the ropes as taut as she could. I smelled the AnaÔs AnaÔs on her body, mingled with the leather of her costume.

When Martin and our mistress had finished binding us Miss Francesca gagged us with ball gags to keep us quiet on the trip to his house. She then kissed us and Martin carried us out to his car over his shoulder, one at a time. He was obviously very strong, but also surprisingly gentle, but we were very uncomfortable in the darkness which enveloped us when Martin shut the boot lid, started the car and sped off towards his house. We did not even know where he lived and could only hope that it was not too far away.

In fact the journey only took about ten minutes, but it felt like an hour to us, bound and crumpled up in the darkness of his boot. It was hot and stuffy and I tried to move over to comfort Ellie who I knew was scared and trembling. I snuggled up to her, rested my head on her shoulder and rubbed her back with the side of my face.

When the car finally stopped it was not long before the lid opened and light flooded into the boot. Martin reached into the boot and took hold of Ellie, gently lifting her out and carrying her towards his house. As I lay alone in the boot I began to wonder what Martin would do with us over the next few days. He did not seem to be as cruel as some of the other guests that had beaten Ellie the two nights ago, but Ellie and I were still to be at his mercy and he had said that he was looking forward to beating us.

However, before I had the chance to think any further about Martin's intentions, he returned to the car, picked me up carried me to his house and into one of the downstairs rooms, where Ellie was kneeling, waiting for us to arrive. Martin placed me on the floor next to her and helped me to assume the same position.

"Welcome to my home, ladies," said Martin, "and I hope that you will enjoy your stay with me and, if you behave yourselves, I'm sure you will. Now I'm just going to get your stuff out of the car."

"Here we are," he said on his return, looking into the bag, "I wonder what we should do first? Oh, you can't talk can you? Well, perhaps we should start with a cup of tea for me."

He walked over to me, undid the ropes that cinched my ankles and knees and my wrists and elbows together and told me to stand up. Then he took some hand-cuffs from my bag, placed them on my wrists in front of me and led me to the kitchen, leaving the gag in my mouth. Once there he showed me where I could find all the things that I needed to make his tea and ordered me to bring him some on a tray as quickly as I could. He returned to the lounge to talk to Ellie, who I feared was already becoming his favourite, because he had seen her punished so severely the other night.

However, I was glad to be free and I made Martin's tea, taking the opportunity to rub my elbows and wrists that displayed the deep red lines, which the ropes had cut into my skin. When I returned to the lounge I found Ellie still bound and kneeling on the floor and Martin emptying the contents of the duffel bag onto one of the chairs. I walked over to him, curtseyed and offered him his tea.

"Ah, thank you, Charlotte," said Martin, taking his tea and sipping it, all the while looking at his two latest acquisitions with the look of man who had just been given all he ever wanted. After a moment's thought he released Ellie from her tight bonds and placed handcuffs on her wrists, as he had done with me. When he had finished he ordered us both to kneel as we had been taught by our mistress, knees slightly apart, hands resting above our pussies and heads bowed.

"Oh, what a lovely sight," said Martin, turning to look at us, "what should I do with the pair of you? I think I should start by having you in a more interesting position."

He motioned to us to go over to the wall and to position ourselves at either side of the huge fireplace, which dominated the whole room. He then bade us stand on tiptoe and padlocked our manacled hands to a couple of metal rings, which I had not noticed before. The padlocks joined the middle chain of our handcuffs to the rings, thus securing us to the wall. Martin went over to one of the chairs, sat down and continued to sip his tea, his comfort in total contrast to the awkward way in which Ellie and I had been made to stand.

Our wrists were already hurting as they pulled against the cuffs and our toes ached under the constant pressure of being stood up on. He took a long time to finish his tea, looking at each of us in turn and drinking in our accentuated curves and our exposed breasts, thrust out by the fact that our arms were stretched above us. We must have looked a pleasing sight, two helpless girls, naked and completely at his mercy. I could see something stirring in his trousers, something which I was sure Ellie and I would be introduced to at some stage.

"You two are the prettiest things that I have ever seen, after Cindy, of course," said Martin, walking over to us and proceeding to release my gag, which fell out with a wet plopping sound. Deftly, he forced my legs apart and felt between them up to my pussy, which I suspected would be moist, my bondage having begun to have its inevitable effect. Martin's probing fingers only served to enhance my aroused state and I soon found myself moaning with pleasure.

"As I suspected," said Martin, "you are wet, you little slut. I hope you don't expect to me to make you come, because it's your job to make me come!"

He proceeded to unlock the padlock, which had held me chained to the wall and drag me over to the chair where he had placed all the things that I had packed. He found the handcuff keys, unlocked one cuff and then refastened it with my hands behind my back then he forced me to my knees in front of him, undid his flies and took out his large and fully erect penis.

"There we are, my dear," he said, looking down at me and sitting in his chair, "now you suck on that whilst I watch young Ellie, suffering over there by the fireplace."

"Yes, master," I said, shuffling closer to him and his impressive tool.

Without pausing for further instructions I stuck out my tongue and began to lick the engorged head of his cock as well as up and down the rigid shaft. I heard him sigh with satisfaction and I continued with my task, putting to good use all the hours Miss Francesca had made me practise on one of her dildos, after it had been used by her, of course. I tasted his salty pre-issue and then took his penis into my mouth, inch by inch, not even gagging when it touched the back of my throat, because my mistress had taught me how to control my natural reflexes.

As I worked, I thought of him looking at poor

Ellie, still bound painfully against the opposite wall. His eyes would be roving all over her taut and helpless body, his mind full of the things that he wanted to see her wearing and the things that he wanted to do to her. I heard him groaning and felt his cock jerking in my mouth. He was becoming more excited as the minutes dragged by and, eventually, he grabbed hold of my long blonde hair, pulled my head closer to his pelvis and began to thrust himself in and out of my mouth.

It was not long before he reached his climax and shot his hot sperm into the back of my mouth and down my throat. I accepted all he had to offer, swallowing every drop with gratitude and hoping all the while that I had pleased him enough. He kept his cock in my mouth for some time, holding on to my hair and not allowing me to go free. Eventually, he seemed to recover and withdrew his now flaccid member.

"Lick him clean," Martin ordered, "and don't forget to thank him, will you?"

"Yes, master...er, thank you, sir", I said, enjoying the job of licking his member, which was still covered in semen and smelt strongly of him.

I had been really turned on by being made to suck his cock, a task made even more humiliating by the fact that I had been deprived of the use of my hands by the handcuffs. I licked every drop of sperm from his cock and was gratified to realise that he was becoming hard once more, so soon after coming into my mouth.

"Ah that's very good, Charlotte," said Martin, breathless with excitement, "but I think it's Ellie's turn to perform for me."

"Yes, master," I said, "thank you, sir."

Martin took my arm and pulled me back over to the fireplace, whereupon he transferred the handcuffs from behind me to my front and rechained me to the wall, stretched and helpless before him. Once he was satisfied that I was secure he released Ellie from the wall and told her to stand in front of him with her legs spread as wide as they would go, her chained wrists behind her head. He looked at her lewd but provocative display for a moment, her pert breasts thrust out for his attention and then he seemed to come to some decision about my fate.

"Free your gag and then strap it into Charlotte's mouth," he commanded, "and rub the ball between the lips of your pussy first - I'm sure it's just as wet as Charlotte's now."

Ellie reached round to the back of her head with her chained hands, undid the buckle of her gag and let it fall out of her mouth, with the same plopping sound as mine had made earlier. She then stood in front of me and spread her legs so that I would miss nothing of the spectacle. Her cuffed hands made their way teasingly down across her stomach, holding the strip of the leather until they rested by her bush. She then gave me a mischievous grin and bucked her hips forward as she pushed backwards with the gag. I watched helplessly as she rubbed the rubber ball backwards and forwards, her labia spreading out to let it run along the glistening pink flesh in between.

Finally, she gave a little grunt of effort and I saw the ball go up into her vagina. Waves of desire spread up from my own sex as I watched her masturbate and imagined how her sweet little pussy would be sucking and contracting around the rubber invader, its tangy moisture flooding out all over it. I could almost taste her on my tongue and writhed against my bonds. Martin laughed softly at my distress and Ellie gave one last shove into herself with the ball then sighed with pleasure as she came, took it out and offered it to me.

I opened my mouth as wide for the gag as I had for Martin's cock and relished Ellie's taste as it filled my mouth. Ellie then buckled the strap tight under my hair at the back of my head and my confinement and gagging was complete. She smiled briefly at me and then walked over to her temporary master, who was still sitting in his chair, watching intently, his cock rampant once more. Ellie knelt before Martin, as I had done earlier and waited for his next order. As I watched from my silent incarceration, Martin leant forward, took Ellie's head in his hands and kissed her tenderly on her lips. She kissed him back, arching her back in an effort to reach him and moaning with lust.

Both Ellie and I were highly aroused, but it seemed that she would be the one who would be satisfied, whereas I would have to watch her, wracked with sheer frustration. I wanted to close my eyes and escape from this torment, but I simply could not and was captivated by the scene unfolding before me. Martin pushed Ellie back, stood up and turned her round so that she was facing me. He then knelt her on all fours, spread her knees as wide as they would go and knelt down between her legs.

Without further ado he plunged his fully aroused member deep into her soaking quim, making her cry out with pleasure. She closed her eyes and surrendered to her passion, groaning louder and louder with each stroke of his cock. Our new master, on the other hand, kept his eyes open and stared at my stretched body, using me in much the same way in which he had used Ellie earlier. He had remarkable control for a man still getting used to having two beautiful girls at his beck and call, for he maintained his rhythm for at least ten minutes, sending Ellie off into floods of ecstasy, her desire rising with each flutter of excitement that Martin generated between her legs.

When Martin finally came Ellie also reached one last, huge climax, causing him to groan and her to scream joyfully. They both had their eyes closed at this point and

I looked down at the floor, sensing my frustration welling up inside me, which was worsened by the fact that I was still turned on by my encounter with Martin and by what I had seen. When I looked back up, feeling extremely sorry for myself, I saw that Martin had withdrawn his cock and was making Ellie lick it clean, as I had minutes before.

"Very good, Ellie, I am pleased with you," said Martin, fondly. "Now, go and make me some sandwiches for my lunch. You'll find the kitchen at the end of the hall."

"Yes, sir," said Ellie, rising to her feet.

"What did I tell Charlotte to call me?"

"Master, sorry, master!" cried Ellie, worrying that she had spoilt everything.

"You should have realised that the same rule applied to you", said Martin, "and now I'm going to have to punish you, so soon after arriving!"

"Yes, master. Sorry, master," said Ellie, obviously upset at incurring his wrath after having had such great sex with him.

He ordered her to kneel in front of one of the chairs, facing its back and selected a crop from out of my duffel bag. He positioned himself behind his victim and raised the whip menacingly above his head. With a whoosh he brought it down across the most tender part of her cheeks, causing Ellie to shudder and moan, her lovely buttocks quivering as the shaft sliced into them. A second, equally cruel stroke had her whimpering and the third made her scream and thrust her pelvis into the front of the chair in an effort to escape the lash.

"Please, no more, master," Ellie pleaded, "I'm so sorry - I won't do it again, I promise."

"I thought you could take a beating, Ellie," said Martin, lifting his arm in order to administer the next blow. "You will have six of the best and learn your lesson, so stick your lovely bottom out again!"

And so Ellie's punishment continued, with each of the three remaining strokes being delivered with a resounding thwack and causing Ellie to cry out pitifully and rock backwards and forwards in her pain. However, despite her contortions I could tell that the heat from the crop was creating the usual heated reaction between her legs. I could see that her lips were already glistening with arousal and her nipples were erect and pulsating. However, Martin declared himself satisfied with the chastisement and, to Ellie's disappointment, he stopped beating her and announced he wanted his lunch.

"Away you go; salmon, I think!"

"Yes, master," said Ellie, trotting off to the kitchen.

"And what shall we do with you, Charlotte?" asked Martin, putting away his still tumescent but well used penis. "As you can see, I have become quite fond of young Ellie and, although this is certainly no bad reflection on you, I intend to use her more than you."

My gag prevented me from replying, so I simply nodded my head in the hope that I would not offend him. He walked over to my helpless frame and began to caress my breasts, which were jutting out because of the way I was bound. I melted at his touch, desperate for him to release me from the torture which I was suffering. I moaned into my gag and strained to make contact with his whole body, pulling against my chains.

"Oh, you poor thing," said Martin, "you're the only one who hasn't come yet, aren't you my dear?" I nodded again, moaning even louder in an effort to plead for relief.

"Well, we'll have to do something about that, won't we?" he continued, "after all, I am not an unnecessarily cruel man."

He turned and left me on the edge once more,

heading off towards the kitchen to catch up with his little Ellie. I did not believe that he was a cruel man, even though he had refused to allow me to come and seemed to be enjoying holding me in sexual torment. Would I simply be tied and left, whilst Martin went off and had fun with Ellie?

It was not long before my new master returned and sat in his chair. Ellie followed and knelt beside him.

"Now, Ellie, what do you think that we should do with Charlotte over here?" asked Martin. "You see she is quite desperate to come and I have promised her that I will do something."

Ellie gave me her mischievous smile again and suggested she lick me while he ate his lunch. Martin was impressed with that idea but insisted she should have her hands cuffed behind her back. Ellie offered her wrists to him so he could undo them and then chain them behind her back.

Soon she was on her way over to bring me the relief that I so much desired. I was very grateful that Martin had decided to have mercy on me and I spread my legs as far as I could, which was not very far considering that I was already on tip toe. Ellie approached and sank to her knees in front of me. She leant forward, pushed her face into my clipped pussy hair and began to search for my lips with her eager tongue. As soon as she found it she started to lick between the exposed folds of skin of my excited quim.

"Oh my, you are wet, Charlotte," breathed Ellie, "let's see what we can do for you!"

She quickly found that part of me that I could never resist, pushed back the hood and nibbled the swollen clitoris for all she was worth. I felt shivers running up and down my spine as she worked away and in a moment I was gone, released from my frustration and escaping into a world of sensuality and delight. She stopped for a moment and looked up at me, her face alive with mischief, while I struggled to peer down at her from between the mounds of my breasts. She let the tip of her tongue protrude from her perfect mouth and ran it along her lips.

I was frantic for her to start again and she knew it, but she was enjoying tormenting me. It seemed as though there were going to be two people doing that throughout the week. At last she leaned forward and pushed in again with her tongue, lapping at my inner lips and I tried to open myself even more and tilted my hips towards her. At last she pushed back the hood and began to nibble and nip at my swollen clitoris once again.

My strained body shook and trembled with each surge of joy she sent through me and I moaned with desire into my gag, tasting her juices and feeling my eager lips quivering as she lapped at the entrance to my vagina. I longed for Martin to fill my aching void while all the time Ellie's clever tongue swirled and rasped my engorged bud until I came and found myself screaming almost as loud as Ellie had when she had knelt on the floor and impaled herself on Martin's member.

Ellie licked my pussy one last time, causing me to jump and then returned to Martin's feet, leaving me hanging in my chains, eyes closed and absolutely exhausted. When I opened my eyes I found that I was alone in the room. Martin had obviously gone off with his favourite without bothering to let me go. Apparently I was to spend the rest of the day chained up and waiting. I sighed and settled down as much as the handcuffs would allow, for it was going to be a long and painful afternoon.

My wrists and my feet were hurting alternately, as I played the classic trade off game of standing on my toes and then hanging off my chains. I could hear slapping sounds coming from upstairs, followed by Ellie's shrieks and giggles. It seemed that she was being 'punished', but that she was really enjoying it. I hoped that the rest of the week would not be like this, with me doing all the suffering and Ellie receiving all of Martin's sexual favours. I hoped that Martin might want to spend some time with me, apart from binding or chastising me.

However, I hoped in vain, for Martin and Ellie spent most of the week in each other's arms, pleasuring themselves and practically ignoring my plight. I made the meals each day and tidied the house, always in my maid's uniform and every day any petty detail I overlooked was punished while Ellie looked on. Martin would make me bend over his knee and I would immediately brace my hands and feet on the floor either side of him. Then his hand would crack down on my buttocks with an awful smack on each cheek in turn. The scalding pain always made me jump and my desperate gasps and whimpers would make him laugh with delight. Tears of humiliation and pain would blur my eyes each time I obediently submitted myself to him in this way.

My only comfort during these sessions was the red-hot mist of secret pleasure, which centred itself within my sex, as I pushed it up towards him and yearned for more. I was also made to serve both Ellie and Martin at table and in bed, as if I was the slave of both of them. I had to use my tongue to stimulate the pair of them and was used and then cast aside as they went off to enjoy each other, usually leaving me bound, alone and frustrated. Often I was cropped just to excite him and Ellie but always the beating stopped short of allowing me to come.

One evening was even more frustrating and yet stimulating than the others for Martin decided that he would take us out to see Carmen at the Leeds Grand Theatre. He told us to help each other to get ready, which we did with great pleasure. We stripped off the scant clothing we had been allowed to wear that day and slowly bathed one another, taking great care to soap our bodies all over, our nipples hard with excitement and our pussies unashamedly wet with much more than bath water. We dried each other, rubbing our partner's most intimate parts just long enough to keep up the high level of arousal.

When Ellie was dry I helped her to don her long red silk, strapless gown, which had a slit right up to the top of her left leg. I stroked her body through the thin fabric and it wasn't long before her nipples began to jut out below the plunging neckline. I could not resist the opportunity to kiss her full on her mouth, pushing my naked and tingling body against hers. She kissed me back all too briefly and went to retrieve my little black dress, which had thin straps and which fell only to the top of my thighs.

Slowly she pulled the dress over my head and began to smooth the sleek material down the sides of my body and over my buttocks. The dress was tight and very revealing and Ellie felt over every inch of my body in an over enthusiastic effort to brush away the creases. I closed my eyes and enjoyed the attention of her strong but sensual fingers as they wrapped themselves around me and totally possessed me. Eventually she let me go and reached for the sheer seamed hold ups that I was to wear on our night out.

Taking her time she rolled each stocking and carefully slid them up each of my long legs, lingering lovingly at the tops of my thighs and straightening the seams. By the time she had finished my sex was on fire for her and I felt incredibly turned on, encased in the sensual material of the stockings and dressed to kill in my little black number. I fumbled with my high heeled shoes and returned the favour for her, casually brushing against her sodden bush with my hands as I pulled her stockings up to the top of her legs, causing her to sigh with unbridled pleasure each time.

I paused in my efforts to prepare her for the evening to grab her shoes and kneel in front of her again. I asked her to sit in a chair and I lifted up her left foot and kissed it through the diaphanous stocking, gently licking her instep and nibbling her toes. I pulled on her high-heeled shoe and repeated the process with her right foot, placing her shoe on her foot, but this time kissing her all the way up her leg. I pulled aside the skirt part of her dress and she parted her legs, allowing me to lick between the wet lips of her pussy. She tasted divine and it wasn't long before she cried out in her orgasm.

I stood up and smiled, licking my lips and savouring her very essence one more time. Ellie looked up at me and fell to her knees, forcing up the short hem of my dress and pushing her face into my hot groin. I felt her energetic tongue darting between my legs, splitting my labia apart in an effort to repay me for the service I had just done her. I closed my eyes and surrendered to the attentions of this young scamp, who soon sent me off into a world of pleasure as waves of delight permeated every fibre of my being. I grabbed her hair and pulled her into me, thrusting my hips against her face and allowing her tongue deeper into my sex.

I cried out as I came and Ellie reached round and pinched my bottom at the point of my orgasm, making me jump but adding to the sensations which overcame me. We were exhausted and positively glowing with pleasure for each other, but our joy was interrupted by a shout from Martin who wanted to know if we were ready or not. We broke away from one another and Ellie called down that we wouldn't be long. We put on our make up on and piled our hair on top of our heads as quickly as we could and trotted off to meet our master.

As we left the bedroom I playfully slapped Ellie's

tightly clad buttocks, naked under her dress, as were mine, in revenge for her pinching me. She cried out, stuck her minx's tongue out at me and ran off downstairs giggling all the way.

Martin was waiting for us and looked very dapper, but stern in his evening suit. When we reached the bottom of the stairs, he presented us with black elbow length opera gloves to wear. We pulled them on, walked out to the car and sped off towards Leeds, excited to be out for the evening, but slightly apprehensive at having no knickers on.

The foyer of the theatre was crowded with people, all dressed up and talking in upper class accents about Carmen and other operas that they had seen. I felt very self-conscious at having no underwear on and being surrounded by so many society people. I looked at the other beautiful women in the theatre, and at the men, all in their evening suits. I was excited by being so naked and unprotected under my dress, a feeling that was exacerbated by the fact that so many of the other theatregoers were brushing up against me.

I kept thinking that they all realised that I had nothing on under my dress and that feeling made me more scared and even more excited. To add to my woes I realised that my short dress only just hung below my upper thighs, which were still covered with whip marks. It was absolute murder going upstairs for I was sure that the people following us could see up my dress and thus observe the handiwork of my new master.

Eventually though we took our seats in our private box next to the stage. Martin pulled the curtain, thus screening us off from the rest of the audience and I realised that there were only two seats. He and Ellie sat down and Martin ordered me to remove my dress. I balked at the prospect of being virtually naked in a full theatre, but I knew that I could not refuse his every command and besides it was an exciting one, as well as scary. Slowly I unfastened and stepped out of my dress, which left me in only my heels and hold ups. Martin then produced a pair of shiny handcuffs, secured my wrists behind my back and forced me to kneel before him facing him as the house lights were turned down.

When the curtain went up, Martin undid his flies, pulled out his flaccid cock and told me to lick and suck him. I obeyed and licked the end of his penis with the tip of my tongue. Soon his already large member grew in my mouth and pushed its way to the back of my throat. All my training kept me from gagging and, as Bizet's famous overture began, I tasted his salty pre-come and started to move my head backwards and forwards in time to the haunting music.

It wasn't long before Martin's body went rigid and he gripped the arms of his seat. He let out a low moan and came, shooting hot semen onto my tongue and down my throat. After a moment he pulled my head back by grabbing my hair and ordered me to perform a similar service for Ellie. I shuffled over to her on my knees and she pulled the material at either side of the slit in her dress aside, to reveal her sex. She parted her legs and I leaned forward in order to gain access to her honey pot, which was already hot for my attentions.

I smelt her arousal in the darkness and stuck out my tongue again, this time in search of her quim. I soon found what I sought and licked between her exposed lips, tasting her juices as they snaked along her slit. I parted her inner lips and found the hardened bud of her clitoris, which I lapped like a cat with cream. Eventually I pushed my head further forward and nipped her clit with my teeth, biting gently and sending Ellie off into a world of delight. She gasped and held the sides of my head in her hands, encouraging me to greater efforts on her behalf. I held her clit in my teeth and circled the part that I had captured with my eager tongue.

Ellie responded by groaning loudly and I feared that the people in the next box would hear her. Finally she gave in to my probing tongue and came, giving out a cry of pleasure, which was fortunately drowned out by a high note from the character of Carmen on stage. I released her clit and knelt up, my mouth full of the combined taste of Ellie and my master. I was pleased with myself and could see from Ellie's eyes that she was grateful. However, I was not rewarded for my work and was made to kneel by the door of the box, facing the wall and was not allowed to watch the opera.

Three hours later Martin told me to dress and he led us back through the theatre, which was full of people all jostling to go home. I was worried again about what people were thinking, especially as I firmly believed that everybody knew what I had been made to do in the box. However, we made it out of the theatre and back to the car.

When we got back to Martin's house, we went up to his bedroom and I was made to lick their feet whilst they kissed each other on the bed. Finally, when they were ready to make love, I was strung up in the corner and forced to watch them thrashing about on the bed. I soon reached the stage where I was beginning to resent Ellie and laughed to myself at the fact that Miss Francesca had asked me to look after her - who the hell was going to look after me?

I didn't think that Ellie did it on purpose; she had just been swept up by feelings of relief, that the week away wasn't so bad, at least for her, and by her feelings for Martin. She had not been with a man for a long time as well and was thoroughly enjoying her time with Martin. Martin, for his part, decided that the best way to deal with us was to treat me as some sort of house slave and to take Ellie as his lover. She slept with him every night and I was usually tied down to one of his guest beds and we spent no time alone together.

The evening after the opera things got much worse for me because Martin decided to take me down to the cellar. He made me stand on a box and strung me up by my wrists to a beam above me with a thick white rope. He took the box away and left me dangling while he retrieved an evil looking bullwhip, which he uncoiled menacingly. He began to flick the long leather lash gently against my helpless skin, causing me to shiver in anticipation. Perhaps the whipping would not be too bad after all because whenever the frayed end of the whip snapped against my skin I jumped as tiny needles of exciting pain possessed my suspended body. I was just beginning to enjoy myself when Martin decided to up the ante and beat me harder.

I heard the bullwhip slash through the air with a loud whoosh and I was suddenly wracked with pain as the cruel leather wrapped itself around me and cut into my defenceless skin. I screamed with pure pain and begged for him to stop, but he had his eye in and drew back his arm once again. He was breathing heavily, but that sound was drowned out by a terrifying crack as he brought the whip down on me again, engulfing me in a sea of agony. Red hot lines appeared all over my body as each lash struck home and I was sure that I was bleeding, but as I looked down I saw only angry red whip marks and no blood. It was small comfort to realise that I was in the hands of an expert.

More merciless strokes followed and it felt as though my whole body was on fire. The force of the blows began to spin me round and my breasts were presented as tempting targets for the whip, targets that were indeed soon flogged. The braided leather cord landed agonisingly on my nipples, causing me to suck in my breath and adding a new dimension of misery to my predicament. I was lost in a mist of agony but, despite my anguish and Martin's total lack of concern for my suffering or maybe because of it, my nipples were hard and my sex responded as it usually did when I was beaten. I was aroused by what I was subjected to and found that my juices were beginning to seep down my thighs - I could not understand myself, this was the heaviest and most frightening beating I had ever had but I was being turned on by the tortures inflicted upon me. Time after time the lash cracked across me, lacing my back, breasts, stomach and thighs with livid lines.

But I wasn't the only one enjoying my torture. As I spun and screamed I saw Martin's face alive with excitement and behind him I saw Ellie, her legs apart and one hand frantically rubbing at her pussy while she stared at my helpless body.

At long last Martin stopped, re-coiled the whip and placed it under my feet, which were dangling several inches from the cold concrete surface. He and Ellie left, turning out the light as they went and I was alone, hanging painfully in the darkness. I could not remember how many times Martin had struck me and all I knew was that my skin was red hot and hurting and that I had a dull ache in my wrists. But despite that my pussy was wet through and my nipples were rock hard with frustrated arousal. It was Ellie who came to release me some time later and it was she who helped me back up to my room and bound me to my lonely bed. She paused only to kiss me and to assure me that everything would be alright - she did not take the time to relieve me of the great need for satisfaction that was beginning to gnaw away at my very soul.

I was at the end of my tether with Ellie, right up until the penultimate night, when she redeemed herself and sneaked away from her master's bed to come and see me, tied down, spread-eagled to my small bed in the room next door. She tiptoed into the room, holding her fingers to her lips and pleading with me to keep quiet.

"Charlotte, my love, are you alright?" she asked me guiltily.

"Well, I have been better!" I said.

"Look, I'm very sorry about all this, but I'm doing it for both of us."

"I haven't seen you doing anything for me over the last few days!"

"But, Charlotte, Martin has threatened to punish you every day and I have pleaded with him not to!"

"I have been punished every day!" I said, indignantly.

"Do you remember what happened to you the other night?" she asked, referring to the episode with the bullwhip. "Well he wanted to hang you by your wrists and flog you like that every night," insisted Ellie, "but it was me that managed to prevent him from doing that!"

"Oh, I didn't realise," I said, slightly mollified by this news. "But, you've had all the fun with him and I've had all the grief!"

"I know and I'm very sorry for that, but he seems to like me and you know what it's like as a slave - there's no point in upsetting our masters or mistresses, is there?"

"Yes, but you don't have to enjoy it so much, do you?" Ellie was right, about us having no choice as slaves and running with our luck when we could, but it was so galling for me to be the one that had no luck at Martin's place.

"I'm sorry, Charlotte," repeated Ellie sincerely. "Would you like me to beg Martin to make love to you tomorrow, before we have to go home? I have been asking all week and he's ignored me, but he might listen if I try again."

116

"Yes, please," I replied, grateful to have the chance to sleep with Martin and share some of the joy that Ellie seemed to have monopolised from the first day. There was something else that I wanted, before she went back to her master's side. "Could you possibly...?"

"Make you come?" interrupted Ellie, grinning. "Of course I will, Charlotte, but we'll have to be quick about it because, if Martin notices I've gone, he'll flog the pair of us and nothing I say will stop him!"

She quickly pulled back the sheets to reveal my naked and helpless body, still whip marked and already on fire from the discussions about Martin and what he might do to me. She knelt on the bed beside me and began to kiss my nipples with her tender, moist lips. I sighed and tugged in vain at my bonds, knowing that I couldn't escape and that Ellie couldn't release me and, therefore, enjoying the feeling of being totally helpless. She gradually kissed down my concave stomach to the edge of my bush, kneading my breasts with her hands as she went and making me moan as they dug into the weals which crisscrossed them.

She certainly knew how to turn me on and the moment her tongue touched the outer lips of my quim, I closed my eyes and floated off into my own fantasy world. My pussy quivered with excitement and I felt a series of tiny explosions going off between my legs. Miss Francesca had trained her very well and she was putting all her skills to work on my behalf. When she finally exposed my clitoris and began to lap it like a little dog, I came with a fierce intensity that I had not experienced for a long while.

When I opened my eyes I found myself alone again, for Ellie had silently left to return to her master, knowing that she had fulfilled her promise to me. I lay there, tied and tired, but content and I fell asleep thinking of my friend and the things that she would beg Martin to do for me. How could I have doubted her, that little girl who had come to Gilbert Manor and worked her way into the affections of Miss Francesca and myself? She was, in her own way, being faithful to me and trying to make things all right for the pair of us.

And, sure enough, she was as good as her word and begged Martin to take me, any way that he wanted to. He relented and informed me that he would 'have his way with me' on the last night before Ellie and I were due to be delivered back home. I went weak at the knees when I heard him make his promise and spent the rest of the last day looking forward to the night I would spend with Martin and wondering where Ellie would be whilst I was with him. I set about the duties I had been given, whilst Ellie and Martin swanned off to town to do some shopping.

They eventually came back in the early evening and sat at the dining table, whereupon I served the meal that I had created for them both. I was wearing my maid's uniform, as usual, with seamed stockings and no underwear. My pussy was already wet with anticipation and I hoped that Martin could smell my arousal as I leaned over him. I wanted him to know that I was hot for him and that I would serve him as well as I could when he took me to his bed, or wherever he was going to take me later on.

The time dragged by and I knelt dutifully at Martin's feet, waiting for my next orders as he chatted to Ellie. I knew that he would make me wait, but I did not mind for I also knew that he would not break his promise and that all the pent up frustration that had grown within me all week would be released as I gave myself to him. Finally he gave the order that I was to follow him and Ellie up to his room and my heart fluttered as I realised that my moment had finally arrived. I stood up eagerly and trotted after them up the stairs and into his room, a place that I had only been to as a menial servant before and never as a lover.

"Remove your clothes down to your stockings, both of you," Martin ordered, taking his clothes off and then sitting on the bed in order to get comfortable to watch us undress.

We quickly obeyed, folding our clothing neatly on the bedside table. For once it seemed that Ellie and I were equals again, slaves dancing to the tune of our shared master. When we had finished we knelt, side by side at the bottom of the bed, knees wide apart and heads down.

"Ellie, you have had the pleasure of my company all week," continued Martin, "and now it is Charlotte's turn to enjoy me; do you understand?"

"Yes, master, I do," replied Ellie, shooting me a brief, reassuring glance.

"But it would be a shame to send you away for the night, so I will tie you up in here so you can stay with us and share our joy!"

"Yes, master; thank you, master," said Ellie.

Martin made her lie on the floor whilst he bound her wrists to the leg of the bed at its head and her ankles to the foot. He then told me to approach him and, when I obeyed, he produced a ball gag, and pushed the ball between my legs. He roughly parted my lips, already wet with anticipation and rubbed it hard along the entrance of my vagina, causing shivers of excitement to run through my whole body. Abruptly he pulled it away and gagged Ellie with it. She would taste me as Martin made love to me, just as I had tasted her when Martin had taken her on our first day.

He tied my wrists tightly together behind my back with a short piece of rope and dragged me onto the bed with him. His cock was already hard and I pressed myself against his naked body, kissing him deeply and sighing with desire. It was not long before he threw me onto my back and my bound wrists and spread my legs as wide as they would go. He then thrust his tool deep inside me, not even bothering to check whether I was wet enough; I suppose he knew it anyway.

Masterfully he began to pump away at me with long slow thrusts, pausing only to bite my nipples occasionally, sending me to ever-higher planes of ecstasy. As he slid in and out of me I cried out with every stroke, thanking him for having mercy on me. I felt the tip of his cock probing deep within me and I couldn't help remembering the bullwhipping as his shaft continually brushed against my clitoris, stimulating me even more. It wasn't long before we both reached our climax together, Martin groaning with delight and me screaming unashamedly as I succumbed to the floods of pleasure pouring through me. I had not had a cock for a long time and Martin had made it well worth the wait. We both fell asleep soon afterwards, with me still bound but in his arms, lost in my dreams and not sparing a thought for poor Ellie, who remained tied on the floor at the left hand side of the bed.

I enjoyed the last night at Martin's house, as all the pressure that had been building up within me since we arrived there had been released in one huge rush. However, something in the back of my mind reminded me that I would be glad to be back at my mistress's side and probably happier than Ellie would be. I didn't know how she would react to having to leave her new master, but I knew that, despite the fact that Martin had taken me to the stars I couldn't wait for the morning to come.

Chapter Six

I woke to find myself bound and still in Martin's arms. I was contented to be in this position, especially as I knew that Ellie and I were to return to our mistress. I peered over the side of the bed in the half-light of early morning and saw that she was still lying on the floor, tied to the legs of the bed. She was asleep, but was moaning softly, presumably because she was so uncomfortable. I decided not to wake her just yet, as she would suffer less if she were sleeping.

Martin, on the other hand, was sleeping deeply in total comfort at my side and, although I was glad to be going home, I realised that he had not treated us too badly, especially young Ellie. I was sure that we would not be as fortunate at some of the other places that we were headed for and I hoped that the good time Ellie had had with Martin would help her through some of the torrid times ahead. I was very concerned about the next three weeks, but at least we had got one of our trips out of the way.

It was at that point that Martin broke into my thoughts and fears with a large yawn - he was awake.

"Good morning, Charlotte," he said, turning to look at me. "Now, be a good girl and untie young Ellie would you?"

"Yes, master." I said.

He did not bother to undo my bonds and so, with great difficulty, I got out of bed, knelt on the floor and loosened the knots that had held Ellie in place all night. She woke up, smiled at me and was soon rubbing her wrists and ankles, which were circled by deep red rope marks. She stood up slowly and stiffly and helped me to my feet and we both approached Martin's side of the bed in order to wait for his next commands.

"Good morning, Ellie," he said, looking his

favourite up and down. "Did you sleep well last night?"

"As well as I could, master," replied Ellie, dutifully.

"Would you like to punish Charlotte for making you so uncomfortable?"

"No, thank you, master," said Ellie quickly, glancing at me.

"Are you sure?" asked Martin, slyly, "after all, she did enjoy my cock and spent the night in my bed, didn't she?"

"Yes, master," said Ellie, "but she has been a good slave all week."

"Yes, I suppose she has, but I'm going to punish her anyway, just one last time."

It seemed that suddenly everybody was now punishing me just for their own pleasure! First my own mistress had had me cropped in front of everyone before giving me away, then Martin had given me the most ferocious beating of my life, and now just when I thought I was safe, I was for the whip again. Part of me was horrified, but that other, primal part of me, the slave part of me was already wondering if I would be whipped hard enough!

I was soon knelt over the end of the bed, with my legs spread wide and my arms behind me. He told Ellie to untie my wrists and then to kneel on the bed and hold my arms so as to keep me secure and get a good view of the proceedings. I put my arms in front of me and Ellie dutifully knelt astride them, spreading her own legs wide apart so that her damp quim was resting on my wrists. She also held on to my upper arms and I realised that she was going to get a lot of pleasure out of my predicament.

I suppose that she was only following orders, but it was still galling for me to be the one being punished again, as well as being the architect of her fun. Martin produced a leather bound paddle and immediately brought it down sharply across my left cheek with a startling splat! The pain, which flashed from my bottom made me lurch forward causing my wrists to slide between Ellie's spread and flattened labia. She sighed with satisfaction, knowing that every stroke from Martin would produce a similar effect for her. Martin struck me again, this time bringing fiery pain to my right cheek and producing another stimulating jerk for Ellie's benefit.

"Ooh yes master!" she moaned. "Harder! Give her more!"

Martin was pleased to oblige her and settled down to beating out a steady rhythm on my buttocks. If I had had any doubts about whether or not I would be beaten hard enough to get pleasure from it, I soon lost them and after each Splat! and jerk forward I was pulling back to offer my bottom up for the next one.

My arms were wet from sliding backwards and forwards along Ellie's sodden slit and I noticed that she had closed her eyes in order to concentrate on her pleasure. Two more vicious strokes had me lunging between her legs again and, although the paddle hurt like hell, I couldn't help being turned on by the pain and by Ellie's obvious delight. The next blow distressed me even more, but I felt my nipples hardening and rubbing on the bed covers as I shot forward again. Martin's last smack with the paddle was enough to send Ellie and me over the edge, for I darted forward to the extent that my elbows brushed against her clitoris, causing her to cry out with joy as she came. I managed to come as well, although the little flutter of pleasure that I felt was not quite as intense as Ellie's, who put her head back and continued to moan with pleasure. Martin said I'd been punished enough for the moment and ordered me to go and fetch the breakfast. He fastened handcuffs on me before the red marks of the ropes had had a chance to fade and then I trotted off to get the breakfast tray as usual.

When I returned I found Martin was lying naked on the bed with his hands behind his head and Ellie was on her knees, between his spread legs, licking the soft skin below his testicles with her eager tongue. His penis was erect and he was watching her auburn hair, bobbing up and down between his thighs, obviously enjoying himself. I knew just how skilful Ellie was with her tongue and felt another pang of jealousy as I observed her giving pleasure to her new master. I was told to stand and watch Ellie work. He had not retied her wrists and so she began to use her hand on his rigid shaft, gripping it and slowly masturbating him.

Martin sighed and closed his eyes, relaxing and giving in to Ellie's delicate tongue and highly trained fingers. She opened her jaws as wide as she could, took his testicles into her mouth and began to suck them. At the same time she began to move her hand up and down with increasing speed and vigour, each stroke making Martin moan with pleasure. He was close to his climax and rapidly became desperate for it.

"Harder, harder," he cried, turning his head from side to side in his excitement. "I'm coming!" he shouted at last. "Swallow it, now!"

"Yes, master," said Ellie, raising herself up and lunging for the swollen tip of his cock. She was too late and Martin ejaculated into her face, his creamy white sperm splattering itself all over her beautiful features. As I watched, Ellie jumped back, surprised that she had arrived too late and a little stunned as to what to do next.

"Well, that's a bit of a mess, isn't it?" said, Martin, after he had recovered.

"Yes, master," said Ellie, ashamed of herself, "I'm very sorry, master."

"Yes, I'm sure you are and I'll have to deal with

you before you go home, but first you'd better ask Charlotte to lick that off your face and clean you up."

"Charlotte," she said, "would you please lick our master's come off my face."

"Yes of course, miss." I said, putting the tray onto the bedside table and walking round to where she was still kneeling on the bed.

Once there, I put my hands behind my back, leaned over and began to lick Martin's issue from her face. It tasted just as I remembered from the first day that we had arrived, slightly salty but quite delicious, an experience made even more sweet by the fact that I was being forced to wash Ellie clean with my tongue. I felt my nipples hardening as I ran my tongue over the face of my fellow slave and I sensed that she was becoming aroused by my efforts. She began to breathe deeply and thrust her breasts towards me as I worked.

I dared not touch her and kept my hands firmly behind my back, although I desperately wanted to reach round and squeeze her breasts and pinch her proffered, firm nipples. As I licked around her mouth, she pursed her lips and kissed me passionately, her tongue darting swiftly between my lips. I sighed deeply and kissed her back, all thoughts of the punishment that we might incur gone from my mind.

"And what do you two think you're doing?" asked Martin.

"Nothing, master," I said, hastily, pulling away.

"Nothing at all" said Ellie, suddenly worried for herself.

"Well, if you like being kissed," said Martin, "I'll introduce you to the kiss of my belt. Stand together at the foot of the bed and put your arms around each other's waist."

"Yes, master," we said, fear spurring us back into

unison. We stood together, holding each other tightly, our nipples brushing together, thoroughly excited by our close proximity.

"Now, carry on kissing one another," ordered Martin, "and I'll warm your bottoms for you both."

We obeyed, kissing each other as passionately as we could manage, tongues fencing in our mouths, bodies touching and rubbing. Martin took up position at our side, swung his arm back and brought his belt, which he had retrieved from his trousers, down onto Ellie's exposed buttocks. She jumped and cried out in pain, the impact of the stroke pressing her harder against me. I felt her hard nipples brush against the soft flesh of my breasts, making them tingle. But it was soon my turn to dance to Martin's tune as he landed his second stroke on my helpless and already burning cheeks.

This made me thrust my pelvis forward and rub against Ellie's close-cropped pubes with my damp bush. The following strokes came thick and fast, causing a crescendo of pain in our poor bottoms, but also turning the pair of us on even more and causing us to cavort together in a jig of delight and anguish. And, sure enough, it was not long before Ellie and I reached our longed for orgasms, as the pleasure overcame the pain. And this time I got the better of the bargain, as the pleasure of my previous beating added to the present one and sent me to a truly blinding climax. Martin only stopped beating us once he was sure that we had come and he began to stroke our hair.

"What a pair. You two are something else," he said, "I've learnt a lot about the way I should treat Cindy when I get her back. And, with that in mind, I think that you should collect your things and I'll take you back to your mistress."

I gathered all the things that I had brought in my duffel bag and Ellie tidied up the kitchen, once Martin had finished his breakfast. He allowed us a small cup of coffee and a piece of toast each and then we were on our way, both naked and in the boot of his car, but only with our handcuffs confining our wrists in front of us. We were much more comfortable than we had been on the journey to his house and both Ellie and I were happy to be returning to Miss Francesca, even though it was only to be for one night before we were sent away again.

Once we reached Gilbert Manor the exchange was quick and simple and as soon as Martin and Cindy had gone Ellie and I threw ourselves at our mistress's feet and began to lick her thigh-length boots, which she wore to complement the leather corset, gloves and studded collar. It seemed that she wanted to re-assert herself over us on our return to Gilbert Manor, both by what she had on and how she treated us. She gently took hold of our hair, brought us to our feet and pointed upstairs, intimating that we she should go up there in front of her. We immediately obeyed her and scurried upstairs joyfully, leading our mistress and hoping that she had exciting plans for us - and indeed she did.

For the rest of the day Ellie and I served our mistress as enthusiastically as we could, attempting to prove to her that we were ecstatic to be back at her command. We were both made to lick her pussy several times. We were glad to bring pleasure to her and we could not get enough of her, whether we were sucking and nibbling her nipples or lapping at her quim like eager children licking a very tempting ice-cream cone. Miss Francesca even allowed Ellie and me to play with each other as she watched us.

At one point she told Ellie to lie on her back and spread her legs, whilst ordering me to straddle her face and burrow my own face into Ellie's auburn bush. She then encouraged us to work on each other by flicking my buttocks and Ellie's thighs with her ever-present riding crop. We needed no encouragement and simply converted the pain that the slashing of the leather-covered switch sent through our bodies into the most exquisite pleasure. The combination of our probing tongues and the fire from the crop soon triggered our orgasms, which slammed through us and left us limp and listless.

However, there was no let up for us and we were soon set to work bathing our mistress and preparing the evening meal for her. Both Ellie and I lovingly led her to her bath and gently soaped away all the traces of our sexual excesses. Our mistress lay back in the steaming tub while I soaped her shoulders and her breasts and Ellie washed her feet, up her lovely long legs and the tops of her thighs. Eventually, as I rubbed her nipples and Ellie parted her labia and caressed the opening to her vagina, our mistress began to moan softly, enjoying our explicit attentions.

She grasped the sides of the bath and allowed herself to be pleasured by her slaves, closing her eyes to fully appreciate the sensual delight. We knew that she was close and, when she leant forward to kiss my mouth, I realised that she had come. She gave in to the ripples of pleasure surging through her and, after she had recovered, she whispered her thanks.

That night we shared the cooking of a meal and the three of us ate together in the kitchen, as we had the night before Martin came to pick us up. It was great to be back, but Ellie and I could not shake the memory that Olivia was going to turn up the next day in order to begin our week at her mercy. After the meal we went back to our mistress's bedroom but, finding ourselves exhausted by our efforts throughout a day, which had passed by in a blur of happiness, all we could do was fall asleep in a bundle of contented girl flesh.

I woke the next morning refreshed and happy to

be back at Gilbert Manor and under the control of Miss Francesca, who lay sleeping peacefully between Ellie and myself. Silently I slipped out of bed and wandered down to the kitchen to make my mistress breakfast in bed. When I returned to the bedroom I found the object of my undying loyalty and affection sitting up in bed and talking to Ellie. She was still naked and knelt on the floor at Miss Francesca's side, arms behind her back and legs spread as wide as she could.

Her head was down and her auburn hair covered her face and I could not resist stealing a glance at her pussy, which was peering out from her beautifully trimmed bush. I could see that her lips were already wet and that she was obviously excited at being in that submissive position before her mistress. I felt a twinge of jealousy again and wondered whether she would become the favourite of Gilbert Manor, thus making me the whipping girl again. I placed the tray on a table and listened to what Miss Francesca was saying to her.

It seemed that we were not to go to Olivia's straight away and that we were to have a sort of week off. I sighed with relief for this meant that we could stay with our mistress for a little while longer, giving me a chance to recover from our week at the mercy of Martin and to serve the woman I loved. And it was not long before we slipped into our old routine of Ellie and me working for Miss Francesca and desperately trying to earn the right to sleep with her. Our mistress seemed to realise that I had had a hard week and hardly punished me at all, except for a few customary swipes with her crop for minor misdemeanours. Pleasant enough but nowhere near strong enough to bring me to orgasm.

We completed a couple more photo-shoots and, on the nights that Miss Francesca chose to sleep with Ellie, I found myself alone in my room with my hands cuffed in front of me thinking about the events of the last two weeks. I thought about the way Martin had whipped me and used me and could not help becoming excited, remembering the way his cock had turned my insides to jelly and reduced me to a shivering, helpless wreck. I also thought about Steven and the way that he had whipped me while I had pleasured him. I shuddered at the thought of how addicted to the whip I seemed to be becoming, but I found myself fantasising about being naked and bound in his room and about him punishing me with various instruments of chastisement. It seemed to me that Miss Francesca was choosing to spend the nights with Ellie more and more, but what really puzzled me was my own reaction to that. I wouldn't have minded if only she'd paid me the compliment of enjoying beating me. But it seemed as though she didn't even want to do that.

As the long, lonely nights dragged on I would lie on my little bed, close my eyes and part my legs under the sheets. I pictured myself chained spread-eagled in the centre of a large, empty room, my feet barely touching the floor and my wrists aching from the strain of being held in such strict bondage. Steven would then enter the room in front of me, holding a wicked looking dog whip, with a short wooden handle and a three-foot lash fashioned from twined strips of leather. He would dangle the whip in front of me and make me kiss the handle. In my mind's eye the leather hung between my exposed and jutting breasts and the frayed end of the whip brushed against my bush and tickled my labia.

In my bed I would be lost in my fantasy and my chained hands would invariably stray to my pussy and begin to stroke my moist lips. I jerked as I imagined Steven's free hand caressing the side of my swollen breasts and I slid a finger between my labia and plunged it into my sodden pussy. The master of my dreams then pulled

130

his whip away and walked round behind me and I moaned and trembled at the thought of what he would do to my helpless body, becoming ever more excited at the thought that I could do nothing to prevent him from doing whatever he wanted to. My groaning would become louder as I descended into my wildest desires and all thoughts of being discovered playing with myself were gone from my head.

In my imagination I looked over my shoulder and pleaded with my master with imploring eyes, but I knew that he would not show me any mercy and I actually found myself hoping that he would not. He would raise his hand and the lash would hang limp for a moment before he brought it down as hard as he could across my back. I imagined being pushed forward by the force of the blow and being enveloped in a storm of pain. I would cry out in agony, both in my dreams and in my lonely bed, but I knew that it was what I wanted and, by the time I was picturing Steven preparing for the second stroke I would have three fingers deep in my vagina, thrusting up and down like a piston.

It was not long before my breathing quickened and I felt myself drifting off into a world of self-induced arousal. The tremors of delight that I was creating between my legs soon started to spread through my whole body and I was quickly wracked by floods of pleasure. To tease myself further I withdrew my fingers and brought them up to my mouth, giving me the chance to taste my own juices and to tweak my hard nipples with my other hand. I pinched the nipples viciously, causing myself to gasp and then pushed my fingers back inside myself in a frantic attempt to finish myself off. In my mind, Steven's whip cracked mercilessly down on my back and buttocks, time and time again. And I would writhe and scream in helpless, submissive frenzy.

My orgasm would then come very swiftly as I could no longer stem the tide that I had created for myself. Panting like a bitch on heat I would surrender to my carnal desires and cry out with joy as I came. This was the pattern for my nights alone at Gilbert Manor and, although the way I was tied or the instrument of correction may have been different, Steven would always be the architect of my suffering and, of course, my happiness. I would then fall asleep curled up on my side with my fingers in my mouth, still tasting my arousal and dreaming of my Steven, my master.

I spent the last night before we were to go to Olivia's house in this way, but my dreams were interrupted by Ellie's urgent voice calling to me, urging me to get up and get ready. I had been allowed to sleep late and it was nearly time for Olivia to arrive and take us away.

"Where's Miss Francesca?" I asked, sitting up.

"She's already downstairs," answered Ellie, "she let us sleep in as a treat for being so good at Martin's house, but now it really is time for us to get going."

Ellie made the bed and tidied the room whilst I washed my body as well as I could at the tiny basin. I looked round and noticed that Ellie was naked, apart from black court shoes, so I slipped mine on, then hurried, naked, downstairs to the kitchen where Ellie had already rejoined Miss Francesca, who was resplendent in her tight white jodhpurs, black riding boots and jacket.

"Good morning, Charlotte, did you sleep well?"

"Yes thank you, mistress," I said, dropping to my knees in front of my mistress and kissing her feet.

"Come now, Charlotte," said Miss Francesca, "get up and have some breakfast because Olivia is probably on her way over here as we speak. Now I want you two girls to look after each other over the next seven days, because I'm not sure what Olivia intends to do with you," there

132

was a note of anxiety in her voice. "She has been a dominatrix for a lot longer than me and her standards may be a lot higher. Just try to behave yourselves and it shouldn't be too bad."

"Yes, mistress," we said, touched by her concern for us.

Just then the doorbell rang and my mistress signalled that I should answer it. I put my cup down, scurried off towards the front door and opened it. I was not surprised at all to find Olivia stood at the door, her slender, muscular body clad in a business style suit, with a short skirt, seamed stockings and high heels. Julia was knelt at her side wearing nothing but a black leather G-string, wrists cuffed behind her back and head bowed.

In her usual brusque manner she ordered me to take her to Francesca. Olivia looked at her riding gear when I had shown her through and asked if she was indeed planning to ride that day.

"Steven is coming round later and I thought we'd take a turn around the grounds," Miss Francesca replied casually.

"What about Julia?" asked Olivia.

"Don't worry," said Miss Francesca, "I'll find something for her to do."

"I'm sure you will. Now it's time that I took these two off your hands for a while."

"Yes, I think that perhaps you should," agreed Miss Francesca, "and Julia and I can get to know each other."

"Now, which of you can drive?" Olivia asked Ellie and me.

"I can, mistress," I replied, for Ellie had not passed her test.

"Well, go out to my Rolls and get the costume bag from the back seat."

"Yes, mistress," I said and scampered off to her car to retrieve the bag.

I was very flustered at the thought of my mistress spending more time with Steven, but I could not allow myself to worry about it too much. I just had to concentrate on being obedient to my current mistress. When I came back I found Ellie and Julia kneeling together by the kitchen table, at which sat my mistress and my new mistress, Olivia. She ordered me to open the bag, which I did to reveal a grey jacket, a pair of leather gloves and a grey peaked cap. I was then instructed to put these on and I obeyed, pulling on the expensive jacket, which fitted quite snugly and fell just to the tops of my thighs. The gloves and cap completed the ensemble and I was transformed into a chauffeur, one with long, shapely and naked legs, emphasised by the short jacket and high heels. Miss Francesca kissed us both and escorted us to the door, leaving her new charge kneeling in the kitchen. We walked outside with our new mistress and Olivia told me to open the passenger door and, as I did so, she and the still naked Ellie climbed onto the luxurious back seat. I then nodded to Miss Francesca, silently mouthing a sad good-bye and proceeded to take my place in the driving seat.

"Drive us to Pickering and I'll give you directions from there," ordered Olivia.

"Yes, mistress," I said, turning the key and bringing the huge, purring engine to life.

I drove down the driveway to the open road and then towards the North Yorkshire Moors and, ultimately, Pickering. I could soon hear giggling from the back seat and it seemed that Olivia and Ellie were enjoying themselves behind the tinted glass, which separated the back passenger seats from the front and driving seats. The external windows at the back were also tinted and, therefore, Ellie and her new mistress were hidden from the outside world.

I found it difficult to concentrate on the road as I listened to them, Ellie giggling and then moaning suggestively and Olivia sighing loudly, obviously satisfied with her latest quarry. I tried to take my mind off what was happening in the back by concentrating on the road and I noticed, to my shock, that a police car was following us and that its blue lights were flashing. My heart immediately raced in panic as I thought of my scanty uniform.

I pulled over and watched in terror as the police car stopped and an officer got out and walked over to my window. I wound it down, my hands shaking and was told to get out. I obeyed sheepishly, swivelling carefully with my legs pressed together so he wouldn't see my nakedness. When I stood before him his eyes travelled appreciatively down my long legs, and then back up again to where the jacket just hid my crotch.

Of course I could not produce my driving licence, and with a leer the officer said he would have to search me. He told me to turn round and made me face the side of the Rolls Royce, whereupon he grabbed my wrists, placed my hands on the roof and kicked my legs apart as wide as they would go. Because I had been standing several feet from the car I found myself bending over slightly and jutting my barely covered bottom out for all to see. The only saving grace was that he had pulled me over on a very remote stretch of road. He told me to keep absolutely still as he checked me out and in my mind's eye I could see him rubbing his hands with glee.

I was acutely embarrassed but did as I was told, for fear of upsetting the man. Raising my hands to put them on the roof made the hem of the jacket ride up and I knew I was displaying the bottom half of my buttocks for him. He crouched down and began to run his hands up my left leg, all the way to the top, where his hands briefly

135

caressed my exposed pubes. I shivered involuntarily, finding the whole thing both disturbing and exciting. His wandering hands moved to my right ankle and began to work their way ever upward. I was trapped between being revolted and stimulated by what was happening to me and as his fingers reached my bush again, my lips were already shimmering with arousal.

I felt his breath on my neck as he slipped his hands under the jacket and ran them up and down my body, pausing far too long on my breasts and I was shocked to feel myself hoping that he would notice that my nipples were already hardening. He stood back and I thought that he had completed his search, but I realised that he had only stopped in order to remove his truncheon from his belt.

"Now we'll find out what you're really hiding missy," he said, "so spread 'em!"

He shoved the truncheon between my thighs and roughly tapped each leg to force them even further apart. I tried to obey, but he was not satisfied and he stepped over to my left-hand side, raised the baton high in the air and slashed it down onto my proffered globes in one swift move. I cried out in pain and pushed my legs as far as they would go, but not before he had struck me again and accused me of obstructing a police officer. He then stood directly behind me and began to trace the outline of my taut legs with the end of his truncheon. I shuddered as the short wooden pole travelled up the outsides of my legs and was then transferred to the more sensitive areas of my inner thighs.

I actually heard myself groaning quietly with pleasure and felt myself pushing back against the exploring probe. Eventually the officer pushed the truncheon between the tops of my thighs and I felt the hard unyielding wood brushing against my exposed labia. I closed my eyes and the stirrings between my legs began to permeate my whole body. Realising that I was responding to this treatment, the officer began to rub the truncheon backwards and forwards until it split my lips and invaded the entrance to my vagina. I moaned with pleasure and pushed against the intruder in an effort to entice the truncheon all the way into my pussy.

However, to my great disappointment he withdrew the potential dildo and announced that he would have to question me further down at the police station. He produced a pair of shiny handcuffs from his jacket, pulled my right arm behind me and closed a bracelet around my wrist with a loud click. My left wrist was next and I soon found my face pressed against the glass of the rear windows as I tried to support myself.

"Before we go, you'd better clean this, you slut," he said, pointing to the truncheon, which was covered in my juices.

I was instantly ashamed of myself, but he made me stand up, turn round and then crouch down in front of him on my haunches. It was difficult for me to balance with my hands cuffed, but he grabbed a bunch of my hair and thrust the truncheon in my face.

"Lick it clean, you whore," he ordered, "or I'll make you sit on it all the way to the station."

I was appalled to find myself thinking that I would most probably enjoy that, but I dutifully opened my mouth and took the black glistening phallus in my mouth, working on it as though it was the officer's own cock. When he was finally happy that I had cleaned it sufficiently he dragged me to my feet and was leading me away to my fate when the window of the Rolls was wound down and Olivia leant her head out.

"That will do, Brian," she said loudly, " I think we've had enough fun with her."

"Very well, Olivia," said the officer, laughing and

pushing me down onto my knees once more, "but she's cleaned my truncheon off so nicely after juicing all over it, it seems a shame not to see what else she can do with her pretty little mouth."

"True. And if the one I've got in here is anything to go by, she'll be pretty good," said Olivia, "Charlotte, while you're down there, see to the gentleman! And you, Ellie, you horny little bitch, get licking as well! I didn't tell you to stop!"

Anger at Olivia's cruel game, and relief that it had indeed been only a game, flooded through me. Relief won and my sluttish arousal once again warmed my pussy as I knelt by the road and watched as the officer undid his flies and pulled the rigid shaft of his sex free of his trousers. It reared up, thick and throbbing in front of my face and I shuddered at the size of it. But instinctively I opened my mouth, put my head forward and began to lick along its already hard length. I remembered, with a flutter of pleasure, what I had been made to do at Martin's house and was determined to prove that I could perform as well for any man. It never occurred to me that this man was a stranger. He had a cock and I wanted to serve, with every fibre of my being.

I lapped enthusiastically and I heard the by now familiar sounds of a highly aroused man, as he groaned happily at what I was doing for him. I parted my lips as wide as I could and took the tip of his throbbing member into my mouth, tasting his delicious pre-come as I did so. He was very large indeed and I experienced a moment of panic as he filled my mouth and I thought I could not take him. However, I forced myself to relax and was delighted that I did not gag, even when the tip of his cock brushed the back of my throat.

I began to suck with all my might and Brian took hold of fistfuls of my hair and pushed his penis even further down my throat. Another moment of panic gripped me and I thought that I would choke, but sense prevailed and I sucked, while breathing through my nose as both Miss Francesca and Martin had taught me.

I stopped sucking for a moment and he let out a moan of disappointment, pulling my hair in an effort to make me continue. I was temporarily elated at the sense of power I felt but, remembering that I was on my knees and cuffed, whilst he had the keys to release me I decided to relent and continued to suck his stiff and bloated cock. He came quickly after that, jerking violently in my mouth and shooting his seed down my throat. I gulped and swallowed all that he had to offer me and, with a satisfied sigh he withdrew and patted me on the head.

Reluctantly, Brian released me and allowed me to get back into the car. He thanked Olivia for letting him play with me, told her he'd see her at her next party and drove off in his car. Somehow I managed to concentrate again on driving towards her house. I was shocked at how turned on I had been by being exposed and felt by a complete stranger. And how eagerly I had then obeyed the order to suck his cock. Slowly I ran my tongue over my lips trying to recapture the taste of his come. I tried to concentrate again on the road ahead, but I could not expel the feelings Brian had roused within me and spent the rest of the journey wondering what it would be like to be frisked and chained by Steven, before being made to kneel before him. And as those thoughts ran through my mind I became aware of the soft warm leather under my naked thighs.

It was a new and sensual experience for me, normally when leather came into contact with my thighs it made a violent and thrilling contact. Now I knew that my pussy was still wet from my encounter with Brian and I imagined myself polishing the leather with my juices and my pubes as I moved around in the seat. From behind me came continuing sounds of urgent sexual endeavour, slowly I allowed my thighs to part, and keeping just one hand on the wheel I let the other wander down into the warmth between them. Probing gently with one finger I parted my outer lips and found the stub of my clitoris thrusting eagerly out from its moist hood. Smiling secretively to myself I let the huge car purr on, and my thoughts run free while I circled and probed between my legs with luxurious slowness.

It took three quarters of an hour to reach Pickering where reluctantly I had to stop playing with myself. During that time Ellie's moans had increased to cries and then shrieks of pleasure. I had no idea what Olivia had done to her, but she was enjoying it to the full and I could feel jealousy rising in me again. I decided to intervene and seek further directions.

"Mistress," I called, through the glass, "we've reached Pickering. Where should I go now?"

"Take the road out towards Whitby and turn right when you see the entrance gates to my little home - Pinton Hall," ordered Olivia brusquely.

"Yes, mistress," I said, taking the appropriate road and looking out for the gates.

After five minutes I spotted them, turned off the road, and drove along a wide driveway. I gasped as an enormous building came into view, which looked like a palace and which was set amongst extensive grounds. If this was Olivia's 'little home' then she certainly was an impressive lady. Once I had stopped the Rolls at the front door of the house, I opened the passenger door for Olivia, who gracefully exited the vehicle, smoothing her skirt back down over her long thighs and walked towards the huge doors. Ellie got out as well and gave me a brief, reassuring look.

140

"Everything's going to be alright," she whispered and turned away to follow Olivia.

"We'll see," I said, closing the door and walking after them both.

"Come along, you two," shouted Olivia, " don't dawdle, or I'll have to beat you."

"Yes, mistress," we cried, increasing our pace instantly.

We entered the massive hallway and Olivia closed the door behind us - we had arrived and were now entirely at her disposal.

"We will eat lunch together and I will explain what I expect from the pair of you," said Olivia, leading us towards her dining room. I was ordered to take off my uniform while Ellie laid the table. We did as we had been told and were soon sat at the table eating a delicious Russian Salad and listening to our new mistress, hoping all the while that she had plans for us that would entail more pleasure than pain.

"Whilst you are here, you will be dogs," began Olivia, "mere pets for me to do with as I please. I will take you for walks around the house and have you serve me all day and night," Olivia continued, "and you will eat the rest of your meals from bowls on the floor and sleep in dog baskets, as Julia does."

"Yes, mistress," we responded, all our hopes vanishing as she spoke.

"If you please me, I may allow you some pleasure or a few doggy treats," said Olivia, pleasantly, "but, if you disobey me, you will be taken outside, tied to a flogging post and whipped to within an inch of your lives."

"Yes, mistress," we said. So that was how it was going to be. Ellie's pleasant journey had not been a precursor to the rest of our week - she had just been testing out Ellie's sensitivity to her touch.

"Your time as my pets begins as soon as our meal is finished," said Olivia, "and, as it appears that it is then I think you should both wash up and prepare yourselves for the rest of the week."

As soon as the last plate was dried and put away in the cupboard we returned to the dining room to receive our next orders.

"You will now remove your shoes and each put one of these collars on," said Olivia, producing two black leather, studded collars and handing them to us. We obeyed and then knelt on the floor, as that was where Olivia was pointing, with our hands behind our backs.

"No, on all fours," said Olivia, firmly, "like little doggies."

"Yes, mistress," we responded, placing the palms of our hands on the floor.

"Now, let's go for a walk around my house," said Olivia, fastening short chain leads to our collars.

She wandered casually out of the dining room, pulling us along behind her with both leads firmly in her hands. We followed, scrambling along as best we could on all fours, finding it difficult to keep up with her. She explained to us the function of nearly every room, pausing occasionally to pat our heads or stroke our bottoms, which were constantly thrust out by the positions we were in. And she gave us the full guided tour, which took almost two hours, by the end of which our knees hurt and we were definitely tired of being pulled around. We finished the tour in Olivia's bedroom, which was large and spacious and dominated by a mahogany bed.

"This is where we all spend the night, unless one of you has been naughty and has to remain in the cellar," explained Olivia. "You haven't seen the cellar yet, but I'm sure that you will, soon enough. You see, the cellar is my very special place, where very naughty bitches have to go to be punished."

We both shuddered. Being potentially bound outside was bad enough, but the cellar sounded even worse than that and we tried as hard as we could to avoid either fate. However, unfortunately for us, we failed despite our best efforts. In fact it only took another hour before one of us was in serious trouble - sadly, it was Ellie.

"How could you be so clumsy, you naughty little bitch?" Olivia shouted at her. "I'm going to have to punish you now and Charlotte will watch as a warning to her."

Poor Ellie. After such a good start with her new mistress she was in trouble with her so soon. She had been crouched in the corner of Olivia's living room and had been summoned over to where she was sitting, talking to me. I was knelt on the floor in front of Olivia, explaining to her how Miss Francesca and I had travelled up to North Yorkshire. Olivia had wanted Ellie to join us, to tell her how she had come to be part of our set up at Gilbert Manor and I watched as she set off to crawl across the floor to us. My pleasure at watching her beautiful breasts sway beneath her as she crawled towards us turned to horror as she wiggled her buttocks too far and knocked over a small table, which stood by Olivia's chair.

Unfortunately for Ellie the table had on it an expensive vase, which broke into a million pieces the moment it hit the floor. Olivia was furious and dragged the hapless Ellie, still on all fours, by her lead down the cellar steps, telling me that I should follow them both. It was very difficult to go down the stairs on our knees, but we managed it and, as Olivia turned on the lights, we realised that she had taken us down into nothing less than a dungeon. It was complete with a rack, stocks and all manner of manacles hanging from the walls and ceiling and Olivia pulled Ellie over to a pillory, which stood in the corner of the cellar.

"This is where you will spend the night, you blundering young pup," Olivia shouted.

She forced Ellie's wrists and neck into three appropriately sized semi-circular holes in the lower half of a board attached to a sturdy wooden frame. Once she was in place, Olivia brought the upper half down, padlocked the side and Ellie was secured, bent over with her bottom sticking out vulnerably behind her. She then walked over to a large glass cabinet, which was filled with various whips and instruments of torture, and selected a particularly nasty looking riding crop.

"I am now going to teach you a lesson, Ellie," said Olivia, menacingly, "and then you will remain in this position until Charlotte comes to release you tomorrow morning, do I make myself perfectly clear?"

"Yes, mistress," whimpered Ellie, "I'm so sorry, mistress."

"You soon will be," said Olivia, taking up position behind Ellie and slowly raising her right arm high above her head.

She brought the crop whistling down across poor Ellie's defenceless buttocks with a terrifying cracking sound. Ellie cried out in anguish at the ferocity of the first blow and the firestorm of pain that it had created in her lower quarters. However, this did not deter Olivia from carrying out the punishment that she had promised Ellie and she continued to beat her with as much force in every stroke as the first one. I had been ordered to kneel by the side of the pillory so that I could see both Ellie's reactions and Olivia's remorseless wielding of the crop. I stared at Ellie's face all the way through her chastisement and she looked like a soul in torment, screaming and crying with huge tears rolling down her cheeks.

I felt so sorry for her and I could not imagine her deriving any pleasure from this treatment, but I could not help being turned on by the spectacle unfolding before me and I felt my pussy quivering with excitement as I watched. Ellie was helpless and being beaten severely by this unforgiving Mistress and I should have been horrified. Instead, I was incredibly turned on by the sight of her buttocks shuddering under each terrific blow and her hips desperately wriggling to try and ease the pain. I found myself wishing that it was me confined and suffering under Olivia's lash. I knew now that I could take the whip better than Ellie, and that when Olivia beat me, as she surely would, we would both enjoy the flogging. My nipples hardened and I experienced a twinge deep within my vagina.

I knew that my juices were flowing and, as I knelt and watched Olivia thrashing Ellie, I quickly put my left hand between my legs and rubbed a couple of fingers along my moist slit. I peeled back my lips and gently massaged my clitoris, aware that Olivia would not be happy if she caught me, but not caring about the consequences. My fingers were soon wet and I thrust them into my vagina and began to masturbate vigorously. Luckily, Olivia was too busy to notice and, just as Ellie let out a particularly noisy cry of anguish, I reached my climax and moaned loudly. I withdrew my fingers, licked them and returned my hands to the floor.

I looked up to see if Olivia had realised what I had been up to, but I got away with my outrageous behaviour. She was still raining lashes down on Ellie's striped bottom, her strong face alive with the excitement of domination. I wondered what she would do with me when she had finished with Ellie and I did not have to wait too long before I found out for, after about fifteen minutes of slashing away at poor Ellie's reddened globes, she simply turned away from her victim, grabbed my lead and proceeded to drag me back up the narrow staircase. It was only late afternoon but Ellie had to stay there for the rest of the day and through the night as well. I, on the other hand, followed my new mistress all the way up to her bedroom where I knelt at the side of her bed whilst she removed her clothes, down to her stockings and gleaming high heels. Her body was not as luscious as that of Miss Francesca, but more lithe and muscular. Her breasts were small but firm and high, the nipples jutting out hard with her enjoyment of Ellie's flogging. She picked up my lead and pulled me towards her.

"Lick my shoes!" she ordered, her voice husky with anticipation.

As ever I felt a breathtaking wave of excitement spread up from my quim as I humbly bent to lick the shiny leather and abase myself at the feet of a mistress. As I relished the pungent taste of the leather I knew she would be looking down at me, looking at the long line of my back and the swell of my buttocks, and I shuddered in delicious fear. She would be assessing me for the whip. There was no way she would allow me to spend a week serving her without beating me.

At last she tugged my lead.

"Enough." she said curtly.

She settled herself on the bed, lying full length on her back above her sheets and ordered me to climb onto the bed between her open legs and to lick her pussy. I obeyed immediately and realised that Olivia was even more aroused than I was for her lips were wet and her bush matted with the juices that she had already emitted. The musky aroma of her arousal greeted me as I moved closer to the full and pouting labia. I took a deep breath and began to work, my tongue lapping away for all I was worth, my arms around her thighs pulling my head closer to her gaping quim. She had a strong and distinctive taste, which I certainly did not find abhorrent and it only served to make me more aroused by what I was being made to do. She held my lead tightly so that I couldn't forget that I was in her control, the collar rubbed under my chin as I licked and that too fuelled the fires between my legs. I was a slave licking her mistress to orgasm. I ran my hands up under her strong, smooth thighs and clasped her buttocks as my excitement grew, my fingers found the cleft of her cheeks and as she moaned and writhed I spread them, groping until I found the closed bud of her anus, then I teased it and rubbed it just as my tongue was teasing the stiffly erect little pleasure bud at her front entrance.

Olivia soon gave in to my frantic lapping at her clit, my tongue aching as I pressed hard and my face soaking in her pungent juices and she climaxed with a contented groan, pulling my lead in order to spur me on to a greater final effort. It was deeply satisfying for me to have made Olivia come but I felt as though I had been left high and dry for, when she had recovered, Olivia got up, put on a robe and announced that we would be going back down for some supper, which I would have to prepare. Despite my earlier masturbation I was desperate to come again and there was an aching need deep in my vagina. But she tugged my lead and I had to follow her downstairs to the kitchen. She sat silently and watched me prepare a meal for her, which she ate at the table whilst I knelt at her side. Occasionally she would give me scraps of food to eat from her hand but there was no food of any kind for poor Ellie down in the dungeon.

After the meal Olivia went to watch television in her lounge, whilst I was left kneeling in the hallway, so that I could answer the door or telephone should anyone call. As I waited I thought about Ellie, bent over in the cold and dark of the cellar, with no idea of the time and the whole night stretching ahead of her. I desperately wanted to sneak down and comfort her, especially considering that Miss Francesca had asked me to look after her. I wanted to hold her and kiss her, but I dared not and I suspected that I had been left out in the hall, near the cellar door, as a test of my discipline and resolve - I did not want to fail my mistress.

Eventually, after what seemed like hours, Olivia emerged from the living room, took hold of my lead and pulled me back upstairs to her bedroom again. Once there, she pulled a large dog basket from under the foot of her bed, placed handcuffs on my wrists behind my back and looped the lead around a leg of the bed. She informed me that I would be sleeping in the basket for the night and then removed her robe, stockings and shoes, clambered into her bed and proceeded to fall asleep without another word.

I was very uncomfortable in my little bed and it took me considerably longer to slip into the arms of Morpheus. And, when I finally drifted off, it only felt like seconds before I heard my mistress breaking into my much-needed slumber.

"Charlotte, wake up, you lazy bitch!" she shouted.

"Yes, mistress," I said, struggle to raise myself up with my cuffed hands.

"Go and release that little slut from the pillory," she ordered, "and then both of you make me breakfast."

"Yes, mistress," I said, attempting to undo my lead and free myself from the bed leg.

"Come on, Charlotte. You don't want to be punished for being slovenly, do you?"

"No, mistress," I replied, "but I can't get loose."

"Ah, I see," said Olivia, getting out of bed and coming round to unlock the handcuffs. "I'm used to Julia being able to deal with this sort of thing with her cuffs on. Francesca has not trained you properly yet. But don't worry, I'll soon have you doing all sorts of things with these babies on."

"Yes, mistress, thank you, mistress," I said, standing up as soon as she had released me from the cuffs.

"Now, off you go."

"Yes, mistress," I said, trotting out of the bedroom and down the staircase to the cellar door, wondering all the time what kind of a state she would be in.

I opened the door, turned on the light and descended the stairs, peering over to where she had been confined for the night. Not surprisingly she was still there, only on her knees, her wrists and neck straining at right angles to her arms and body. Even in the dim light I could see how ravaged her backside was. Her head was bowed and she was whimpering quietly and she did not even notice me as I approached her.

"Ellie, are you alright?" I asked softly.

"What...who's there?" she whispered.

"It's me, don't worry," I said, as reassuringly as I could. "I've come to release you."

I found the key and unlocked the padlock, swinging open the top half of the pillory's board. I helped her to stand up and to walk towards to the cellar steps.

"Oh, thank you, Charlotte," said Ellie, looking up at me with eyes full of grateful tears. "It was awful, just awful..."

"I know, baby, I know," I said, stroking her hair in an effort to comfort her.

We walked up to the kitchen and Ellie sat at the table slowly sipping a glass of water whilst I prepared Olivia's breakfast. She looked terrible, but at least the colour was returning to her face and I gave her a piece of bread as she had not eaten since the previous lunchtime. I then took Olivia's tray and the recovering Ellie up to the bedroom and presented them both to our mistress.

"Good morning, Ellie," said Olivia, jovially, "have you had a pleasant night?"

"No, mistress," said Ellie, "but thank you for asking."

"You don't surprise me," said Olivia, "Julia has told me how uncomfortable a night in the pillory is. Sometimes, she tells me, the discomfort is so extreme that she comes. But at least you have learnt you lesson. Yes?"

"Yes, thank you, mistress," replied Ellie, "I won't be as clumsy again."

"No, I'm sure you won't. But that doesn't mean I won't flog you again."

"If you wish to give me another beating mistress, I shall accept it gladly." Ellie said bravely.

"We'll see." Olivia said tersely, but I thought there was a slight smile of approval, just for a moment.

Olivia ate her breakfast and explained how the rest of the day would enfold. We were to help her bathe and dress and then we were to be taken for a walk around the house for exercise. We would then carry out various housekeeping duties, cook meals and generally be at Olivia's beck and call, all the while remaining on our knees where the various jobs permitted. Every infringement of any of Olivia's petty rules and regulations would be ruthlessly punished, as Ellie had found out during the previous night.

This turned out to be the pattern for the whole week with Ellie and me serving Olivia as well as we could, but, inevitably, falling foul of her vicious brand of justice. We tried our best, but we just could not keep up to her high standards. The usual punishment, for small offences such as failing to dust properly or not keeping still enough when she used one of us as a footstool, was cleverly devised. Ellie or I would have to cross our forearms on the floor and lay our heads on them, leaving our bottoms stuck up in the air. The one who wasn't being punished would have to straddle the victim's head and lean over her back to hold her down. This meant that each time the dog whip or crop was cracked over the buttocks of the one being punished, her head would inevitably jerk up as each lash sliced into the soft, wriggling flesh, and this meant the one doing the holding down had her open pussy rubbed and pummelled by the victim's head, at the same time as being able to watch the beating and savour the full spectacle.

But Olivia was very clever, she never beat us long enough or hard enough to drive us to a slave's orgasm, consequently the one holding the victim never got enough rubbing either. After several lashes she would dig her hand into our quivering sexes and laugh at the juices she found there, but then declare the punishment over. So after each punishment we were excited and terribly frustrated. And as these punishments were meted out four or five times a day, Ellie and I became increasingly desperate.

Our jobs became more and more difficult and it became quite plain that we had been set up to fail in them. In fact I had become so desperate that I found myself wishing that Olivia would just get on with flogging us properly rather than tormenting us with her minor punishments. But that torment was obviously part of her pleasure. Eventually I dropped a pan of vegetables whilst trying to cook with my hands cuffed behind me. Olivia was plainly delighted that at last I had failed badly and while Ellie cleared up the mess she led me outside into the grounds to the dreaded flogging post, which turned out to be a pole sunk into the ground and about eight feet high.

Near the top of the pole was a wooden ledge, which stuck out at right angles and which had a sturdy ring attached to its underside. It was to this ring that I was secured, by means of a rope passed through it and then tied to my handcuffs, which Olivia had refastened in front of me. By the time she was finished I was forced to stand on my tiptoes about a metre away from the pole itself, with my arms stretched above me. The steel of the cuffs was already cutting into my wrists, but I realised that I would probably be here for sometime, that is, after Olivia had punished me.

She began by running her cool, strong hands up and down my body as though testing it to see how it would stand up to punishment. She hefted and stroked my buttocks and breasts, slid her fingers between my legs and pulled and pinched my nipples until they stood out hard and red. I couldn't restrain a moan of pure pleasure at being so helpless in the face of this appraisal, and just before what was bound to be a thorough whipping - at last.

"Ellie's a willing little soul," Olivia whispered, "but she has a lot to learn about herself. But you Charlotte, you know what you are and what you need. Don't you?"

"Yes mistress." I replied, aware that the whipping was only moments away, my juices were flowing and that I couldn't wait for it to start.

Olivia unhooked the dog-whip, which she always carried around with her, from her belt and proceeded to uncoil its wicked looking lash. She waited for Ellie to return and, when she had and knelt by her side, Olivia raised her whip and began to beat me over my buttocks, thighs and back. The pain of the very first lash, as it cracked across my naked flesh left me gasping for breath. It landed full across both cheeks and the noise of the whip was so loud that some birds flew up from a nearby tree. I tried to draw in some air to scream, but the second lash caught me unawares. It nearly knocked me off my feet and left me swinging from the rope.

I screamed alright then and I realised that Olivia had a

much heavier hand than Miss Francesca. It felt as though red-hot wires were burning their way into my soft skin. The third stroke curled wickedly around my legs with the frayed end of the whip biting the fronts of my thighs. I tried to twist away in a futile attempt to shield myself and caught the fourth one full across my belly. It knocked the wind out of me and I hung there helplessly while Olivia calmly continued with a remorseless rhythm, her arm swinging way backwards and then forwards with all her strength.

She was very good. Each hard lash was delivered after an interval which allowed me to experience its full pain and absorb it before the next one fell. I found myself watching, mesmerised as Olivia's arm swung again and again until the pain at last reached that crescendo where it began to blur with the fires that had begun to rage between my legs, fires ignited by my helplessness in the face of such cruel domination. I yelled lustily until I was hoarse and could not support my weight any longer. I begged Olivia to stop, but she did not relent and continued the punishment until I was covered with angry red marks. My body was in turmoil and, despite my protestations, I knew that she had judged me correctly, this was what I wanted. I was a slave after all and what more fitting for a slave than a good thrashing. This thought burned through my mind as I orgasmed helplessly, tide after tide of piercing pleasure washing over me with each smack of the whip on my vulnerable body.

At last I hung limp and exhausted in my bonds.

Olivia came to stand in front of me and kissed me with surprising tenderness.

"That was good wasn't it Charlotte?"

"Yes mistress. Thank you." I whispered.

"But a really good orgasm like that one has to be paid for." She put her hand between my legs and felt up into my vagina which was still quivering and flooding. She chuckled and withdrew it, making me groan in longing for her to keep on.

Then they left me to my agony, Olivia pulling Ellie along by her lead on her hands and knees across the grass. As she crawled along Ellie looked over her shoulder at me, giving me a sympathetic look as she knew just how much I was suffering. Not only was I still experiencing the pain from the flogging as the pleasure receded, but my hands were already going numb from the pressure on my wrists and my toes were aching from trying to reduce the stress on my upper arms. It was a long day for me, constantly in pain and left out in the heat of a Yorkshire summer afternoon.

The grounds were truly lovely, set as they were in the midst of the moors and I found myself wondering about the paradox of this house of pain existing amongst such delightful surroundings. I could see the rolling moors away to the north with purple heather coating the tops of the hills. The wooded valleys stretched down to the flat and fertile Vale of York to the south and I could just make out the regular patterns of the distant fields. And there I was, exposed, a naked and soundly whipped slavegirl bound in such an unnatural way staring at the beauty of nature all around me. At least the thought of how naked I was and how obviously a slave excited me enough to help with the pain of the bondage.

I also wondered whether Ellie was being made to serve Olivia as I had on the first night and I felt the jealousy welling up inside me again. However, despite my efforts to take my mind off my predicament, I could not escape the discomfort and, after many endless hours of torture, I was extremely pleased to see Ellie crawling across the lawn to set me free.

"Let's get you back inside," said Ellie, releasing

my bonds, "because I think Olivia has another job for us to do."

"Well, I hope I'll be able to use my hands this time," I said, rubbing my wrists, "or I'll be back out here again."

However, I was not allowed the use of my hands because we were taken up to Olivia's bedroom and I was tied down to the bed, arms and legs spread wide in a taut 'X' shape by our temporary mistress. She ignored my groans as my sore back rubbed on the bedding. She cuffed Ellie's wrists behind her back and removed her own clothes. Apparently, Ellie had not been made to pleasure Olivia whilst I was strung up outside and we were supposed to provide that service for her together. Olivia and Ellie climbed onto the bed with Olivia straddling my face and Ellie putting her legs on either side of my stretched thighs.

Olivia lowered her already sodden pussy down onto my mouth and I began to lick at her gaping lips, her juices filling my mouth with every stroke of my tongue. As I worked, I could feel Ellie moving around in an attempt to lean forward, presumably in order that she could lick and suck Olivia's exposed nipples. Olivia's thighs clamped my ears but I could soon hear her groaning loudly with delight at what we were doing to her. I felt strong fingers kneading my breasts and pinching my nipples and it seemed that Olivia was encouraging me to lick harder and deeper, which I gladly did.

She began to moan even louder as Ellie and I pleasured her and she did not realise that her two little bitches were pleasuring themselves as well. Ellie's bush was positioned just above mine and, as she leant forward to work on Olivia's breasts, her mound rubbed against mine, sending shivers of excitement shuddering through both of us. I thought about the way I had been treated that afternoon and that made me even more aroused. Unbeknownst to Olivia we began to rub against each other and, as Olivia reached yet another climax, Ellie and I came, our cries of joy being drowned out by Olivia's.

We carried on working for a little while longer, to disguise the fact we had come and, eventually, Olivia bade us stop. All three of us were exhausted after the session and, even though it was only early evening, Olivia untied me, cuffed my hands behind my back and secured both of us in our baskets for the night. I had no trouble getting off to sleep that night because of my ordeal in the gardens and my efforts underneath my mistress. We had experienced our most enjoyable evening with Olivia; it would only get worse after that.

One afternoon Olivia decided that she wanted to display us in her garden for a couple of guests that she had invited round for tea. She made us serve the pair out in the back garden and they turned out to be two middle-aged women, both dressed in austere but tight fitting clothing, with extremely high-heeled ankle boots. Apparently they were both dominatrixes and it was their usual practise to come round and take tea with whichever of them had fresh meat to offer on display. We were both nude, apart from high-heeled court shoes and had our wrists cuffed in front of us, so it was quite difficult to carry the trays of teas, cups and cakes. The women seemed totally unconcerned at being served by two bound and naked girls and I assumed that they had been similarly served by Julia in the past.

When they had all that they needed Olivia told Ellie to fetch several lengths of rope from the house and led me over to a nearby tree. She undid my cuffs and, when Ellie had returned, she began to bind me to the tree with my back to the trunk and my wrists tied tightly together around it. She then bound my elbows together, causing me excruciating pain and my breasts to stick out proudly in the afternoon sun.

A rope around my waist and around the tree secured me even more firmly, but the piece de resistance was the way Olivia grabbed my ankles, pulled them up either side of the trunk and bound them to my wrists with yet more rope. With my feet off the floor all my weight seemed to bear down on the rope around my waist, which seemed to work its way up to my rib cage, but that did not concern Olivia as she stood back and admired her handiwork. She then moved onto Ellie, whom she bound in a similar way to a tree next to mine and we were both soon moaning at this newly imposed discomfort.

Olivia told us to be quiet, or she'd punish us and took out some clamps from her handbag. With a look of sadistic pleasure on her face she proceeded to attach them to our nipples, which hurt outrageously the moment she let go of them. But she had not finished just yet and, pausing only to wink at her friends she produced some more clamps of a similar design. I dreaded to think what she was going to do with them, but I soon found out as Olivia took hold of one of my pussy lips, cruelly exposed by the way I had been bound. Without pausing to think of the pain and discomfort I was already enduring she attached one of the clamps to the sensitive yet captive flesh. She quickly repeated the process and went off to do the same to poor Ellie, leaving me to my torture. I winced as the pressure from the clamps built on my poor labia and nipples, but was completely helpless to do anything about the increasing pain as the ropes held me firm against the tree.

I could see that Ellie was suffering and wondered how long it would be before one of us cried out in our torment. Olivia and her friends actually placed bets as to which of us would break the silence rule first and Ellie and I held out as long as we could. The bondage was so severe that the excitement such cold, casual cruelty would normally have aroused in us was swamped by the pain. Poor Ellie could not take it for very long and she screamed for mercy and begged for the clamps to be taken from her. One of the guests cheered and took a small number of coins from her companions while Olivia came over to Ellie and glibly informed her that she would have to stay like that for the rest of the day, whilst I could be released for not complaining.

I heard Ellie whimpering as Olivia untied me and I was led back to the house with the two guests, where I could still plainly hear Ellie sobbing to herself in her pain and discomfort. I was ordered to make dinner for everyone. The kitchen overlooked the place where Ellie was bound and I could not help but stare at my friend occasionally as I prepared the food, her head bowed and her auburn hair covering her face, which was no doubt contorted in agony. Her pretty breasts heaved as she panted and moaned, and I could see the heavy clamps biting into her soft pussy lips.

It took all my self control to concentrate on my work but when I had finished I smiled and waved encouragingly at the stricken Ellie and went through to the lounge, whereupon I curtseyed and announced to the women that I had done as I had been told to.

"About time too, you lazy slut," said Olivia, bitchily, "now come over to me, we have something else that we want you to do!"

"Yes, mistress," I said, scampering over to her and kneeling at her feet at which point She produced a pair of handcuffs and snapped them on my wrists behind my back.

"Now my friends and I have become very excited at the turn of events this afternoon," Olivia continued, "so you can crawl around and satisfy us. I think you know what to do and you can start with me!"

"Yes, mistress," I said, turning round and bending forward between her knees, which she had spread as wide as she could. She had no panties on and I could see and smell her arousal so I snuggled between her hard thighs and began to lick her protruding lips. She sighed and I knew that I had hit the right spot. Gently, I pushed my tongue between the folds of her labia and searched urgently for the bud of her clitoris. It was hard and wet and I lashed it with my tongue. My mistress grabbed my hair to indicate that I was doing the right thing and shoved my head closer to her.

As I lapped at her most secret of places she began to pant and I dared to nibble her clit lightly with my teeth. She cried out with pleasure and I knew that, as she pulled my hair so tightly, she had come. She went rigid as the orgasm spasmed through her very being and let out a great moan of delight. She pushed me away eventually and, without a word of thanks, ordered me to go over and perform the same service for one of her friends. I was already tired from my efforts, especially as I had to lean over without the support of my hands but, fearing further punishment, I crawled over to one of the women, who like Olivia had raised her skirts, spread her legs and revealed her naked pussy.

She was also turned on, but she smelt and tasted different to Olivia and somehow sweeter. I licked her, as I had licked Olivia and I suddenly understood why she tasted sweet for she reached over me to a table at her side, stuck her finger in a pot and smeared some of the contents between her quivering lips. It was honey and designed, I think to make me work harder and it did. I could not remember the last time I had been allowed something sweet, and so I lapped at the honey-laden labia like a happy puppy. The woman was amply rewarded for her ingenuity for she came enthusiastically after only a few applications of the honey!

Licking my lips gratefully I crawled over to the owner of the third quim that I had to satisfy, but she announced that she wanted something called the 'head dildo'. Olivia laughed and produced a very strange device, telling her she had made a good choice. The 'head dildo' turned out to be two rubber phalluses, one larger than the other both attached to three leather straps. Olivia made me crawl back to her and fastened the device around my head, first forcing the smaller dildo into my mouth. It tasted of rubber and made me gag at first but, as I crawled over to the intended recipient I worked out what was expected of me.

I struggled between her spread legs and slowly, but surely inserted the larger phallus into the woman's soaking vagina. She groaned and arched her back as I pushed upwards and inwards and, when my nose reached her pubes I knew that the dildo was fully inside her. I began to pull the dildo out and push it back in, desperately trying to keep a good rhythm going, but this was quite difficult without the use of my hands. However, the woman did not seem to mind and, after only a few strokes she cried out with pleasure as her orgasms flooded through her.

She grabbed my head pulled me towards her one last time and the strong aroma of her arousal filled my nostrils. When she had finally finished coming she shoved me away and I was made to stand in the corner, legs spread and hands on head whilst Olivia discussed my performance and then their latest adventures with their slaves. I found myself frustrated again, having become very aroused at what I had been made to do for them, without being allowed to come myself.

It was dusk before I was allowed to go out and

free Ellie. I had thought I might be able to use my fingers or tongue to bring her to a climax she must be desperate for, but Olivia accompanied me, to make sure I didn't.

She was stern, constantly demanding and very careful to ensure that we never got any pleasure from pleasuring her.

On our last night with her, for no apparent reason, she took us out into the grounds and hung us by our wrists from the branches of two different trees some fifty yards apart. She stuffed 'penis' gags into our mouths so we couldn't speak and made sure that we couldn't see each other. Then she left us, straining up onto tip toes, each isolated in our discomfort. She came back every hour or so throughout the long, cold night and beat us both in turn with a cat-o-nine tails. But never long enough or hard enough to make us come. And because I couldn't see Ellie, I couldn't even derive any pleasure from seeing her pretty little body under the whip, I could just hear the lashes landing and tried hard to picture her jerking and twisting at the end of her rope, just as I did when it was my turn.

We spent an agonising night and Olivia enjoyed every moment of it. By the early hours she was openly masturbating with a dildo in one hand while she flogged us with the other.

I began to wonder, in the brief moments of painful peace, what I was doing there at all. Yes I was bound and helpless, but there had been many times when either Ellie or I had been free and one of us could have freed the other, overpowered Olivia and escaped. But escaped to where and from what? We were out in the middle of nowhere, with nowhere to go. And then there was the bondage and the punishments, which caused great pain and discomfort but which seemed to be exactly what I wanted and even needed. I knew that, were I to be freed, I would only crawl back to my mistress or even master now and beg to be bound and beaten.

I resigned myself to my ironic fate and, when morning finally came and a fully clothed Olivia came over to my tree and released my wrists, I fell to my knees, and kissed and licked her boots in gratitude.

"Untie that little bitch over there and I'll drive you both back to Francesca, " she said coldly.

I could only nod my head, as the gag remained in my mouth. Olivia turned on her high heels and left me to complete the task of freeing Ellie, which I soon did, causing her to fall to the floor in the same way as I had. I left the gags in place, as I had not been told to remove them and we both helped each other to stumble back to the house.

There we found Olivia, who confined our hands behind our backs with handcuffs, attached leads to our collars and led us out to her Rolls Royce. She bundled us into the back, got into the driver's seat herself and drove us away from Pinton Hall. It wasn't just the gags that kept Ellie and me quiet on the way home, for we were both thinking about what our mistress would do to us when we got there. Olivia's coldness to us made us both feel as though we had let her down and we realised that we would be made to pay.

Chapter Seven

Miss Francesca was actually very pleased to see us when we finally reached Gilbert Manor, even though she had obviously had a wonderful time with Julia and, more importantly for me, Steven in our absence. As we were released from Olivia's car our mistress came out to greet us, dressed only in her robe and high-heeled mules, her eyes lit with joy. She hugged us both and then nodded to Olivia, who watched the touching reunion with a face as stern as ever.

She proceeded to tell Miss Francesca of every infringement of her strict rules that she could remember and one or two that she made up on the spot. Ellie and I could not complain about the trumped up charges for we were still gagged. And, even if we could argue we knew that Miss Francesca would have to take her word against ours and that, as liars, we would be punished even more severely. Instead, we stood bound and mute, heads bowed to accentuate the shame that we felt at letting Miss Francesca down.

Our mistress listened to Olivia's tale of woe and assured her that she would do something about her two unruly slaves as soon as the morning's exchange was complete. She then went back into the house and retrieved Julia, who was wearing her G-string and her handcuffs behind her back, as she had seven days before. She followed Miss Francesca and had no hesitation in kneeling on the gravel driveway in front of Olivia. I winced for her and feared that she would have a heavy price to pay for the week away.

Olivia dragged Julia to her feet by her hair and pulled her over to the boot of her Rolls Royce. She bundled Julia in, closed the lid, then, with a curt nod to Miss Francesca, she climbed into the car, and drove off.

163

Our mistress led us down to her cellar, and bound our wrists in front of us. She took another long rope and tied our wrists together, facing one another and threw the end over a hook in the ceiling. Then, having pulled the rope as hard as she could and tied it off, she had Ellie and me standing on tiptoe, face to face and completely at her mercy. The next moment she produced a long, thin leather switch and, however unwillingly, began to slash away at our buttocks.

Every forehand stroke caught me out and brought a line of fire to my helpless cheeks, whereas it was my mistress's backhand that made Ellie jump and cry out with pain. We were soon both in agony, However, despite our growing distress the fact that we were being forced to rub up against one another's naked bodies was highly stimulating. I soon forgot the pain and concentrated on the delicious feeling of brushing up against Ellie's hardening nipples.

We were both shrieking at each lash, but also beginning to moan with lust, our lips moistening with every stroke and the heat rising within us. We realised that Miss Francesca had bound us in this way so that we would derive some pleasure from what she was being forced to do to us, but could not help but enjoy the delightful mix of pain and pleasure, which Ellie and I were sharing. It was not long before my juices began to flow from my vagina and seep down the tops of my thighs. It took only two more thwacks on my defenceless cheeks before I came, yelling out loud in my excitement.

Ellie soon followed suit, screaming with pain and pleasure and Miss Francesca decided to halt the beating, knowing that we had come. She released us and let us kneel at her feet.

"Well, how are you both?" she asked, looking at the whip marks that covered our bodies.

"Oh, we're fine," I said as bravely as I could, "and very glad to be back here, mistress."

"It looks as though she was hard on you both," observed Miss Francesca, "but I'm sure that you deserved it."

"We tried our best, mistress," said Ellie, pitifully, "but we just couldn't reach her high standards, whatever we did."

"I know," said Miss Francesca, turning us round to get a closer look at the marks on our backs. "She certainly went to town, didn't she?"

"It was awful, mistress," I said, "and we did miss you so."

"Yes, but I'm sure that it did you good." said Miss Francesca.

"But she made us act like dogs all week," cried Ellie, outraged.

"Well she has a thing about making people into animals, a bit like Rupert does," said Miss Francesca, "and you will have to behave yourselves there because it might be just as bad as Olivia's, but I can't go back on my agreement now. But I have missed you, so let's see what you can do for me now that you're back."

And our mistress certainly did make use of us for we spent the rest of the day and the night making love to each other up in her bedroom. Ellie and I were so pleased to be back that we both managed to put the idea of a week with Jeremy well out of our minds. We enjoyed one another's bodies far into the early hours, with short breaks only being taken to eat and for our mistress to tell us all her exciting tales of her week with Julia. It seemed that she had had a wonderful time with Olivia's young slave girl, whose subservience to Olivia was only surpassed by her sexual prowess and skill with her tongue

Miss Francesca smiled dreamily as she also recounted all the things that she had done with Steven, who had turned up a few times during the previous week. Apparently he had great stamina and superb technique and what he could not do with his tongue was not worth doing. She had also enjoyed riding on his fantastic cock, while Julia had been forced to watch, bound in the corner of her room as I had been the first time I met Steven. In short, Miss Francesca informed us, he was absolutely sensational and, as she talked both Ellie and I felt intensely jealous and I found myself thinking about Steven - if only I could have spent a week with him, I would have had nothing to complain about.

When Miss Francesca decided that she had told us enough she surrendered to the exhaustion that had been caused by our sexual excesses and, although she bound us tightly to the foot of the bed as a matter of discipline, we were uncomfortable but completely satisfied after the pleasure drought that we had both experienced during the week with Olivia, and very happy to be back with our mistress once more.

However, the night passed all too quickly and the dawn brought with it a beautiful morning and the much feared arrival of Jeremy, whom Ellie and I hoped would not be as monstrous as he had been on the night of the party. We got up first and prepared breakfast for our mistress and tried to ready ourselves for our week with him.

However Miss Francesca surprised us once more and announced, to our joy that Jeremy would not be coming over for us and that the plan to be handed over to him for a week had been changed. Our mistress had seen the vivid red marks covering our bodies and had relented. Perhaps she feared that Jeremy would treat us even more harshly and that we might be returned from a whole week at his house in a very bad state indeed.

Instead it turned out that we were only to spend

the weekend there and our mistress would deliver us herself. She informed us that all we would need was our highheeled ankle boots and we scampered off to retrieve them from our rooms, almost giddy with the relief of being spared a whole week in the tender care of the feared Jeremy. We put our boots on and came back downstairs to find Miss Francesca waiting for us with two pairs of handcuffs, two black collars and a couple of black leather hoods.

We were instructed to put the hoods over our heads and Miss Francesca fastened the laces and the buckles tightly at the back of our necks, thus taking our sight away and greatly reducing our ability to hear her orders. We were both encased in oppressive darkness and yet the seductive smell of the leather filled my nostrils making me shiver with the thrill of being once more at my mistress's command. I was even more excited by the fact that she quickly cuffed our wrists behind our backs, locked the collars round our necks and began to push us towards the main door. We were chained and naked, save our boots, collars and hoods and being forced outside, not knowing where we were heading and with no way of finding out for ourselves.

As we shuffled tentatively and carefully outside the fresh air of the morning hit our exposed bodies and I shuddered as I imagined the gooseflesh spreading across my skin. Miss Francesca pushed us again and we stumbled over the gravel of the driveway, the crunching of the tiny stones just a distant, muffled sound in our ears. After a few steps I bumped into Miss Francesca's car and halted. The door was opened for us and I heard our mistress ordering us onto the back seat, which turned out be a difficult manoeuvre with our cuffs and hoods on. We struggled across the leather seats, constantly knocking into each other until we finally settled down as best we could.

At first I tried to work out which way we were

going, but I soon lost count of the left and right turns and my mind turned to thoughts of where we were bound and of what would happen to us when we got there. I assumed that we were on our way to Jeremy's and I could not get the memory of his severe treatment of Ellie at Miss Francesca's party all those weeks ago, out of my mind. Images of the way he had flogged her filled my mind and I began to panic and I felt the pace of my breathing increase and the soft leather clung to my face as I sucked in gulps of air. I knew that I had to calm down and I snuggled up to Ellie for comfort.

She responded by resting her confined head on my shoulder in an effort to soothe my fears, although I was sure she that she was as frightened as I was. Thus we travelled the rest of the in the relative silence of our hoods and jostled by the occasional bump in the road. The journey seemed to go on forever, but it at least felt good to be next to Ellie and to know that we had each other, whatever happened to us. Despite the discomfort of resting on my cuffed hands I drifted off to sleep, lulled by the movement of the car and the proximity of the girl who had shared so much of the pain and agony I had experienced over the last few weeks.

As I snoozed I dreamt of Steven. He had been in my dreams a lot recently and this time it was he who had put me in cuffs and had me at his mercy. He was naked and in my mind's eye I was staring at his large erect penis, licking my lips in anticipation of him possessing me and entering me. He pushed me back onto a bed and I moaned with pleasure as he spread my legs and climbed on top of me. I shuddered as I felt the tip of his cock brushing against my pubic hairs and my pouting, already wet labia. I arched my back against his firm body and was about to accommodate him deep within me when I was jolted awake from my dreams by the screeching of brakes.

The car stopped and Ellie and I lurched forward, almost finding ourselves on the floor. As we tried to settle back onto the seat the passenger door flew open and I heard Miss Francesca ordering us out of the car. Again we struggled along the seat, clambered out of the car and stood next to each other, our bodies caressed once more by a gentle breeze in the cool air. Although I couldn't see anything I knew my nipples were hard, partly because of the contrast from the warm car but also because of my experiences with Steven in my head.

Suddenly I felt my mistress tugging at the straps at the back of my neck and the hood was loosened and dragged over my head. I winced and closed my eyes as bright light hit them and it took me a little while and considerable blinking before I could open them and take in my new surroundings. We were standing at the side of the road in the middle of a wood.

I turned and looked at Ellie as Miss Francesca removed her hood. She looked cold and very nervous, but neither of us said a word for we were too well trained to voice our fears in front of our mistress.

When Miss Francesca had finished she made us kneel on the hard asphalt of the road and walked off to the other side of the car. To my great surprise she returned pulling Rachael along behind her by a lead attached to a collar around her slender neck. She was blindfolded and was wearing a tight fitting white corset, cream stockings and red high-heel court shoes. Her chestnut hair was bound into a French plait with a red ribbon and her wrists and elbows were cruelly bound behind her back with clean white rope. Her discomfort was completed by a huge rubber ball gag, which filled her mouth and prevented her from speaking.

As we watched Miss Francesca dragged Rachael to the back door of the car and was about to push her in when she noticed something on the seat and turned back to us.

"My, my Charlotte my dear," she said with a grin, "you have enjoyed your trip haven't you?"

"Mistress?" I said, puzzled at her comment.

"The seat is all wet!" she said, "Have you been playing with yourself somehow?"

"No mistress," I said, desperate to convince her that I had not been naughty again. I must have been more excited than I thought by my dream.

"Well, you'd better clean this up before I go, hadn't you?"

"Yes, mistress," I said, getting to my feet with great difficulty and running over to the car.

Miss Francesca pulled Rachael to one side and I knelt down again and began the humiliating task of licking my own juices from the leather seat where I had been sitting. As I licked and tasted the slightly salty leather I thought about what my mistress had said ñ 'before I go'. What could she have meant by that? Should she have said 'we'? I did not have to wait long for an answer. When she was satisfied that I had done my job she pushed Rachael onto the back seat, slammed the door shut and made Ellie and I stand next to one another.

"This is your destination, my dears, or at least as far as the car is going," she said, smiling mysteriously as she spoke. "I am going to take Rachael back to Gilbert Manor now and you two will have to make your way to Jeremy's from here on foot."

"But, mistress," I spluttered, unable to hold my tongue any longer, "Which way do we go?"

"Head through the woods that way," she said, pointing vaguely behind her, "and you'll find his house after about ten miles. There are no paths and it may take you 'till tomorrow morning, so look after yourselves."

170

"But, mistress," I pleaded, as she turned and walked round to the driver's seat, got in and closed the door, "You can't leave us like this!"

"No, of course, you're right," she said. "Come here!"

I gasped with relief and we trotted round to her. She wound down the window and threw a small key into the ditch by the road and ordered me to remove my hand-cuffs. Miss Francesca watched as I scrabbled around in the mud to retrieve the keys. There was a dribble of cold, filthy water in the ditch and by the time I found then I was splattered with mud from ankle to buttocks. I began to try and release my cuffs, which was quite hard to do and took a lot of twisting round and looking over my shoulder. But I finally managed it and was then ordered to remove Ellie's and give both pairs and the keys back to Miss Francesca.

"There," she said when I had completed my task, "we can't have you going for a walk in the woods totally helpless, can we?"

"But, I thoughtÖ" I blurted out, disappointed that my hopes of redemption had been dashed.

"Well, you thought wrong," said my mistress, reading my thoughts. "You are still going to walk to Jeremy's, but you will at least have your hands to look after each other. So, I'll see you in a couple of days. Have fun!"

With that she started the engine, turned the car round and sped off back the way we had come with her new prize bound and helpless in the back seat. As she tooted the horn merrily, Ellie broke down and ran after her, begging her to stop and take her back.

But Miss Francesca did not come back and we stood and watched the car disappear into the distance. We had been abandoned and our only hope of returning to relative civilisation was for us to hike through the woods to whatever fate Jeremy had in store for us. I took the shivering Ellie in my arms and gave her a hug, our naked breasts touching. She was already crying so I kissed her forehead and stroked her hair.

"It's okay, Ellie," I said not altogether convincingly, looking over her shoulder at the dark foreboding woods which surrounded us, "everything is going to be alright."

"Why did she leave us?" she asked, "How could she do this to us?"

"I don't know, but we'll have to get a move on," I said, pulling myself from our embrace and guiding her towards the section of woods which Miss Francesca had directed us to, "let's go!"

With that we set off into the woods, which seemed to be made up mainly of tall conifers in ordered lines for as far as the eye could see. I led the way hoping all the time that I had chosen the right direction and praying that no-one, other than Jeremy would find us. It was ironic that we would soon become desperate to find Jeremy, the one person who neither of us wanted to spend any time with at all. The going was very tough, because of the lack of path and we were constantly tripping over hidden roots and ducking just too late to avoid being whipped across the face by wildly flailing branches.

To a casual observer, we could have been two hardy hikers simply lost in the forest, all very innocent of course, were it not for the lack of clothes and the humiliating slave collars, which had been locked around our necks and which were not removable, at least not by us. Were it not for our naked, lost and helpless state a walk in the woods would have been very pleasurable for us. To be free in the open air and unimpeded by chains and fetters would have been a pure joy, were it not for the fact that we faced the prospect of spending the night out in the wilds, with no food or protection and at the mercy of the elements and of whoever or whatever came our way.

We walked for hours along the seemingly endless lines of trees, all standing to attention and pointing our way into the distance. We were cold, hungry and already tired from our exertions, but we knew that we had to keep going. Eventually we came to the end of the regimented conifers and they were replaced by more natural deciduous woodland. Oaks and sycamores replaced pine and fir and we found ourselves scrambling down a slope towards a distant stream. The undergrowth became thicker and less managed and our way was strewn with fallen trees and branches.

Ellie and I stayed close together for mutual support, stopping occasionally for breath and to agree on the course we were taking. It was at one of these pauses that our predicament became much worse, as I turned to Ellie to speak to her, lost my footing and began to fall. As I slipped backwards I grabbed Ellie and we both plunged into a steep sided hole, which had been made by the unearthed roots of a huge fallen tree. We slid down the muddy walls of the crater and landed in a heap in the bottom. We shook ourselves and stood up and, when we realised that we were both alright we hugged each other and laughed out loud for the first time since this nightmare had begun.

The hole was about fifteen feet deep and the sides were caked with slippery mud and as I tried to scramble up towards freedom I slid back down and landed on the floor of the hole again, covered in mud from my fall. Ellie tried and experienced the same thing as I had and was also splattered with mud. It soon became apparent that we would have to help each other if we were to get out of the hole. I knelt down at the base of the wall and told Ellie to climb over me. She understood what I was getting at and placed her foot on my knee, pushed up and put her other foot on my shoulder. As she did so her pubic bush was pressed into my face and I smelled the distinctive odour of her arousal. Her labia brushed against my nose and I realised that she had been turned on by our embrace, despite the seriousness of our predicament.

She lingered a little too long in that position and then pushed off my shoulder in order to reach a branch. However, she missed it, slipped off my shoulder and fell past me back to the base of the hole. We laughed again at the comic nature of our situation and I told her to try again at a different part of the wall. She did so, this time deliberately pushing her pussy into my face as she climbed up me and I could not resist the temptation to stick my tongue out and lick between her pouting and sodden lips. She shrieked with surprise and fell back once more, this time taking me with her and landing on top of me. I found myself on my back and her legs were astride my lower torso, her breasts squashing mine and her face just above me.

"So, you think that's funny do you?" she said, smiling all over her pretty face, "Well I'll show you!"

With that she grabbed my arms and pinned them to the ground above my head. I struggled beneath her, but she had a strength belied by her slight frame and I was soon completely at her mercy. In one fluid movement she bent down, kissed me full on the mouth and then moved her head down to my helplessly jutting breasts. She closed her teeth one of my nipples and gently bit it. I gasped in shock and opened my mouth to protest but she let go of my nipple and kissed my open mouth again, her tongue darting between my parted lips. I tried to move my head to one side, but she was too strong and I soon lost the will to fight as her tongue entered my mouth and began a passionate dance with mine.

I lifted my head up as far as I could and kissed her back, pushing my tongue into her mouth. Without freeing my arms she raised her right leg, lifted it over mine and forced my legs apart so that her upper thigh was resting on my pussy and her own wet sex straddled my thigh. And she was wet for I could feel her juices on my leg, juices which spread across the taut skin as she began to slide herself up and down my thigh, moaning all the while as she continued to kiss me. I started to thrust myself against her leg in an effort to match her arousal, but she had already gone off into a world of her own. She threw her head back and cried out as her first orgasm rocked through her thoroughly excited body.

As she came she gripped my wrists even tighter and I winced as she nudged her leg harshly between my legs to enhance her passion. I was still excited myself, but I sensed that Ellie was getting the better of the situation. Her whole being went rigid as she orgasmed yet again and then she flung herself off me, not even allowing me to derive the full measure of satisfaction from the encounter. We lay still for a while and I wondered whether her fierce passion had been driven and fuelled by her fear at being naked in the woods. However, I could not ponder this thought long as she crawled back over to me and the object of her affection this time was to be my own, unfulfilled sex.

Once more she straddled me, this time with her legs either side of my head and her breasts dangling above my stomach. She lowered herself onto me and pushed her face into my neatly cropped pubic hair. In a flash her tongue was out, gently licking my labia and pushing the lips of my sex apart. She used her hands to spread my legs wide apart to afford her better access to my pussy and her probing tongue was soon deep within my vagina. As she worked between my legs, she forced her sex down onto my face. So, not wanting to disappoint, I opened my mouth and stuck my tongue out, seeking her most intimate of places to work on.

I reached up and parted her cheeks with my fingers and lifted my head again as I linked along the length of her quim, as my mistress had taught me and then deftly dissected her inner lips and searched for her clitoris. When I located her bud I found that it was erect and practically quivering, so I lapped at it with my tongue with rapid strokes. She began to moan immediately and I knew that I had hit the right spot. Despite the fact that waves of pleasure were flooding through me, thanks to what Ellie was doing, I concentrated on my task and separated her inner labia even further with my lips and tenderly nibbled at her clit. That excited her even more and, after a few spasm that seemed to wrack her whole body, she came again, crying out with delight and burying her head in my bush.

She stopped licking my pussy and lay still for a while, not caring that she had, once again failed to send me off to heaven, simply revelling in her own pleasure. I did not blame her, for I knew that she had tried her best for me and that, in the past I would have experienced orgasmic fireworks with that kind of treatment. It's just that I craved more these days, something long and hard and unarguably male. Even if Ellie had had a dildo I would not have come properly. It was cock that I wanted, preferably Steven's, but it was getting to the stage where even Jeremy's would do!

When her breathing had slowed down once more Ellie climbed off me, turned round and lay down by my side, taking me in her arms as she did so. She sighed deeply and closed her eyes, drifting off into a deep sleep almost straightaway. Even though I was frustrated I kissed her forehead and lay back, staring up into the sky and, as I did I realised with a shudder that it was already getting dark. Also, we had been warmed by our sharing of passion but, as we had stopped I discovered that I was quite cold and that I would get colder as the night progressed. I huddled closer to Ellie in order to keep us both warm and she groaned in her sleep and snuggled up to me.

I listened to the sounds of the forest and, beyond Ellie's heavy breathing I could hear the rustle of the evening breeze through the leaves and the occasional call of a bird flying home to roost. I wished that we could fly home, but we were stuck in this hole and every sound in the creeping and expanding darkness made me jump. The snap of a twig made me think that prowlers, or perhaps Jeremy himself were close by and on the verge of discovering this trapped catch of naked slave flesh. Even the hoot of an owl scared me half to death.

I must have drifted off to sleep myself eventually, but I was soon awakened by droplets of water on my face. On top of everything else it was raining and now pitch black! Ellie had turned round and rolled away from me a little, so I shuffled over to her, put one arm under her head and the other around her waist and drew her tightly towards me. I was shivering, both from cold and fear and being closer to Ellie at least took some of the fear away. I tried to think pleasant thoughts and inevitably found myself thinking of Steven and more especially his penis, large and erect and there, just for me.

I closed my eyes and imagined him caressing every inch of my naked body before thrusting his lovely cock deep within me. Oh, how I wanted cock until my very soul ached for it! My hand strayed between Ellie's legs and I fondled her bush, still damp from her excited state earlier. Again she moaned with pleasure in her sleep and pushed back against me. It seemed that Ellie was happy with female company, but I wanted more! I gently stroked Ellie's lips again and discovered that her pussy was actually sodden, She must have been having very sweet dreams, like mine in the car that afternoon. I took one of her labia

177

and squeezed it between finger and thumb, causing her to jump slightly, but also to groan even louder.

Ellie loved any sexual contact with women, even in her sleep and I continued to oblige her, whilst imagining that I was with Steven and that it was his foreskin that I was playing with. I ignored the rain and reached down the front of her body with my other hand and grasped one of her breasts. I located her nipple and pinched it, gently at first and then with more force. She was panting now and almost awake, so I rubbed my nipples up and down her back, creating enough friction to make then erect and hyper-sensitive. As Ellie came for the third time I managed to achieve an orgasm of sorts myself, although I slipped into a fitful sleep still desperate for cock and lamenting the lack of it.

It was early dawn when the snap of a twig woke me and I sat up in alarm, listening carefully for more evidence of intruders. Ellie stirred as well and looked up at me with fear in her eyes. The rain had washed some of the mud from us and she looked as pretty as ever, if a little dishevelled after a night in the wilds. However, I resisted the temptation to ravish her again there and then and decided that it was time to get out of the hole and search for Jeremy's house. I stood up, helped Ellie to her feet and began another assault on the slopes that had imprisoned us. The rain had made them even more slippery and I fell back a few times, replacing most of the mud that the rain had washed from me.

However, I eventually managed to grab a root and, with the help of Ellie pushing at my bottom I crawled out of the hole. I looked around me quickly but saw only low lying mist at the base of the endless trees and none of the imagined dangers. I turned, reached down into the hole and gave Ellie a pull up out of the hole, although a few slips on her part meant that she was similarly coated with mud again. We smiled at each other, happy to be out of the hole and glad to have shared each other's bodies the night before. I quickly checked the direction we had been going in and we set off together hoping to finally reach our destination, but not believing we would ever make it.

In the event it only took us a couple of minutes to find a house, in a wide clearing in the trees. We had not been able to see it the previous evening because of the leaves but, had we not fallen into the hole we would probably have stumbled across it last night. We looked at each other, laughed at the irony of it and headed off towards it. It never occurred to us what we would do if it were not Jeremy's house, we just wanted to be out of the forest: naked and filthy we might have been, but of pride we had none. We entered the garden and I tentatively knocked on the door, fearing the worst but almost fainting with relief when it was Jeremy who answered it.

"Well, well, where on earth have you two been?" he asked, grinning all over his face, "You look as though you've been dragged through a hedge backwards!"

"Oh, master it was terrible!" I whimpered and proceeded to tell him all about our nocturnal adventures, except for the lovemaking.

After all, I did not want to incur punishment for illicit lovemaking. Jeremy laughed and said that we should take a shower, together, and availed himself of the opportunity to watch us clean away all the mud we had accumulated over the last twelve hours or so. He observed as Ellie and I removed our boots, climbed into the shower and soaped and scrubbed each other. He made us rub between each other's legs for his entertainment. I was too tired to get excited again, but I knew that Ellie was enjoying herself, even with our spectator.

I took a loofah and rubbed it enthusiastically between her legs, making sure that her labia were parted and receiving the full attention of the hard sponge. She grabbed me and kissed my opened mouth again, searching for my tongue with hers and thrusting her body against her. It seemed that she was intoxicated with the cleansing, warming water and allowed herself to succumb once again to my efforts on her behalf. All the time I kept stealing glances at Jeremy's crotch in the hope that I would somehow earn the right to impale myself on his cock. I wanted an orgasm badly but I wanted a man to give it to me, even if that man had to be Jeremy.

Once we had showered, Jeremy made us dry one another with large towels and, once dry, we were kept naked and shepherded up to the kitchen for coffee, which he ordered Ellie to make. Jeremy simply sat, drank his coffee and looked at me, apparently pleased with what he saw. It did not take him long to drag us up to his bedroom, strip off his clothes and to lie on his large four-poster bed and stare at us, his manhood growing at a rapid rate at what he could see and what he temporarily owned.

"Now, you sluts, let's see what you can do for me," he said lewdly, "Ellie, kneel on my left side and lick my balls, whilst you, Charlotte, come round to my right side and suck my cock."

"Yes, master," we said, rushing to obey him.

It was quite difficult to bend over with our hands tied behind our backs, but our training, with Miss Francesca and Olivia stood us in good stead and we promptly set about our task. Jeremy seemed to like what we were doing because he began to moan and sigh, occasionally smacking our bottoms to encourage us. I sucked Jeremy's swollen member with all the skill I could muster, in the hope that I would endear myself to him before he started handing out punishments. As I worked on his stiffened cock I ached to have it inside me, thrusting in and out of me fulfilling my every desire. I licked his hard stem, smelt his arousal and became intoxicated by the musky aroma. I realised then and there that my need was driving me to distraction and I wanted him, desperately.

"Alright, you can swap over now," he ordered, "and we'll see if Ellie's as good as you are at giving head." "Yes, master," we chorused, our foreheads touching as we transferred the object of our attention.

"That's a good girl," said Jeremy, as Ellie began to worship his straining penis with her fervent tongue. "You've both been instructed very well by your mistress, although how on earth she managed to teach you how to suck cock.... She hasn't got one herself, has she?"

"Of course not, master," said Ellie, disturbed by his outrageous suggestion.

"Alright, don't be so touchy, I don't want to have to punish you for sticking up for your mistress, do I?"

"No, master," said Ellie quietly, "sorry, master."

"Now get on with your work," said Jeremy, "and don't speak with your mouth full!"

Ellie continued to serve him in silence, not wanting to incur his wrath or his particular brand of punishment, which she had already experienced. Jeremy was a dangerous man and needed only a minor infringement of his rules and codes to be roused into action with his ropes and whips. However careful we were Jeremy would find some reason to chastise or discipline us and so our quiet dedication could only reduce our suffering and not prevent it.

"Ah, that's good, carry on, carry on!" cried Jeremy, won over by Ellie's efforts. "I'm coming! Now, swallow every drop, or I'll flog you raw!"

Ellie obeyed her master, gulping down everything that he had to offer her. I continued to lick his balls as they emptied their load into Ellie's mouth and, when his cock had ceased to jerk between Ellie's lips, we both raised ourselves up to kneel with straight backs and knees spread. We were too frightened to have enjoyed the session, but Jeremy clearly had. He lay still for a while with his eyes closed, recovering from his orgasm, which seemed to have temporally exhausted him. After a while, he opened his eyes and looked at the girls that he would have at his mercy for the rest of the weekend.

"Very good," he said, "very good indeed; your mistress has taught you well. But how did she teach you?"

"She made us practice on a large dildo," I said.

"No doubt the same dildo that she uses on herself, the randy lesbian."

"Yes, master," I said, refusing to be riled by his taunting.

"Does she taste good? Is her slit as sweet as honey, like all lesbians claim theirs are or do you have to be forced to suck the dildo when she's finished with it?"

"We like to serve our mistress, in any we can," I said, realising that he was trying to trick us into defending our mistress and, thus, forcing him to punish us.

"I bet you do," he sneered, "you lesbians are all the same; licking each other's pussy and hating men because they have cocks and you don't."

"We do as we are told, master," I said simply, "or else we are beaten."

"Yes, I can see that she's really gone to town this time, hasn't she?" asked Jeremy, looking at the fading whip marks on our bodies.

"It was not Miss Francesca who did this to us," I explained patiently, "it was Olivia."

"Well, she's as bad as Francesca," continued Jeremy, "she beats her slave to show her power over her, when what she needs is a real man. Olivia and Francesca are a pair of feminist bullies who both need someone like me to cure them."

182

"My mistress is not a bully!" shouted Ellie, unable to ignore the jibes and rising to the bait.

"And you just can't resist earning yourself more punishment, can you?" said Jeremy triumphantly, for he had tricked Ellie into answering him back and she had fallen into his trap beautifully - now he had the excuse he wanted to beat her.

He ordered us to stand and then dragged Ellie by her hair out of the bedroom and downstairs, telling me to follow them as he went. Having reached the hallway he produced a long piece of rope from a cupboard and secured one end to Ellie's bound wrists and then proceeded to take the other end of the rope up the stairs and to thread it through one of the banisters on the overhanging balustrade. He then pulled the rope back down the stairs with him and began to heave Ellie's wrists up behind her back by means of pulling the rope down.

Eventually poor Ellie was standing on tiptoe, bent cruelly forward at the waist, the great strain of her tortured position showing in her pretty face, her taut little bottom thrust back for whipping. Jeremy fully intended her to pay for her indiscretion and to that end he retrieved a vicious looking single thong whip from the cupboard and began to slash away mercilessly at Ellie's cruelly exposed buttocks. She screamed loudly from the first stroke and hopped from foot to foot in a vain effort to avoid the seemingly endless blows, tears streaming down her face.

Helplessly I watched Jeremy flogging Ellie, powerless to reduce his ferocity and not daring to intervene on her behalf, for fear of angering him further.

However, I could not take it for very long and I soon heard myself begging him to stop and to beat me instead. How could I have been so stupid? I knew that he couldn't resist taking me up on my offer, but my promise to Miss Francesca was still in my mind and I realised that

Ellie could not have taken much more of that treatment. Jeremy stopped, looked at me as though I was mad and immediately decided that I should replace Ellie in that tormented pose.

It was the work of a moment to release Ellie and to string me up in exactly the same way as she had been. He then picked up his whip once more and began to beat me with the same force that he had used on Ellie. The dull ache from my wrists and upper arms constantly nagged at me, but it was nothing compared to the pain, which was quite awful and just as bad as I had expected it to be, every stroke sending a blast of pain ripping through my defenceless body. After only three lashes I started to scream myself.

I looked at Ellie through my own tears and saw that she was kneeling on the floor, facing away from me, obviously unable to watch the scourging of the friend who had taken her place. I desperately tried to search for the pleasure amongst all that pain and, were it Steven beating me I could have found it. I closed my eyes and imagined that it was him holding the whip and beating me. I pictured his muscles rippling as he drew back the switch and slashed it down onto my helpless cheeks and began to turn the incessant agony into pleasure. My nipples hardened and I could feel the stirrings of an orgasm growing in my loins and the pain seemed to fade away.

I sighed as I slipped away into my fantasy world but, to my intense irritation Jeremy chose that moment to stop. He put down the scourge and stood back to admire his handiwork. He seemed to like what he saw, namely two helpless slave girls, one still strung up on her tip toes and both covered in swathes of vicious scarlet marks that he had put there. After he had drunk in the scene before him he ordered Ellie to stand up and go with him down into the cellar. She quickly obeyed and I was left on my

184

own with my wrists hurting from the biting ropes and my buttocks and back aflame with the searing heat of the whip marks, reflecting on my reaction to the flogging.

It was strange to be at the mercy of a man once more and, even though it was the dreaded Jeremy I felt a pulse of excitement emanating from between my legs and running through my tortured body. Despite the fact that he had hurt me so, I could not help but feel excited at his dominance of me and thrilled at the prospect of what he might do to me when he returned. I still wanted cock and was determined to beg for it during the short time he would have possession of me. If I was lucky I might not have to beg; he might take me, if I wanted him or not! I closed my eyes and moaned openly at the thought of having his cock thrusting in and out of me, the very same cock that I had been forced to lick earlier.

I was jolted back to reality from my daydreams as Jeremy burst into the hall from the cellar stairs and strode over to me.

"Now, it's time I saw to you, my girl," he said, "and besides, you look like you're gagging for it!"

I was and I gasped with pleasure as he walked behind me, grabbed my waist and kicked my legs apart with his feet. I could hear him unzipping his flies and I sighed as he took out his sizeable cock and shoved it between my buttocks. He was already hard and when he told me to push my bottom back I did so eagerly, more desperate to have a man inside me than ever before. He reached round and roughly separated my labia with his fingers and rammed his penis between them and up into my vagina.

It met very little resistance as I was very turned on and thoroughly lubricated, but I still cried out as his member finally filled my aching void. Immediately he began to pound away at me and I pushed back to meet him stroke for stroke. His balls bounced against my bush and his hips slapped my whip marked buttocks, irritating and re-igniting the pain from my previous floggings, but this only served to enhance the total pleasure I felt. Jeremy reached up and cupped my breasts with his hands, squeezing and manipulating them like a child with playdough but I did not care.

Even when he pinched my nipples so hard that I screamed, it was a cry of pleasure and not pain. I was in heaven and I savoured the feel of his swollen manhood inside me, sliding in and out and pushing me to the very limit of pleasure. I had never experienced sex like this and, although there was very little skill involved on Jeremy's part, his brute force and the helplessness of my position drove me into a frenzy of excitement. I surrendered completely to him as he took total possession of me and I came and came until I was spent and passed out under the weight of passion.

When I regained my senses I realised that I was alone again, still bound and totally exhausted by what Jeremy had done to me. I hung in my bonds, weak from all the exertion and the punishment but utterly satisfied with my lot. I had experienced the cock I had craved and now I was content just to stand on my toes and revel in the joy of being taken by a man, oblivious to the build up of pain from various parts of my body. However Jeremy returned carrying a white apron and proceeded to cut me down and instructed me to don the apron and to trot off and prepare a meal for him.

And so it was that I cooked his lunch, wearing my boots, collar and a Mrs. Beeton apron, which was tied with a bow above my bottom and which barely covered my breasts and my pussy and left my back totally exposed. Jeremy also made me wear a small white frilly cap to complete the image and I was back in my familiar role of serving as a maid, only this time I was serving a man. And that man sat and watched me and nodded admiringly as I bent over the oven, no doubt planning what he would do with me next.

He decided that he wanted to eat his food from a tray and that I would kneel in front of him and hold the tray. He sat in his lounge and I got to my knees before him, carefully holding the tray whilst he ate. He seemed determined to get the best out of us whilst we were at his mercy and as soon as lunch was over for him he left some scraps of food on the plate, placed it on the floor and made me eat what he had left with my hands behind my back.

When he was satisfied that I had been humiliated enough he told me to follow him upstairs to his bedroom. Once there he made bend over the end of his bed and made me spread my legs as far as they would go, tying my ankles to the legs of the bed with short pieces of rope. A moment later he had bound my wrists together with more rope, the loose end of which he proceeded to secure to the bed head. This caused me to be stretched taut like a violin string, quivering and helpless.

"Rachael doesn't like it when I do this to her, but I'm sure you'll love it!"

"Yes, master," I whimpered.

Whatever did he mean? He had taken me from behind before lunch, and it certainly wasn't so terrible. In fact I had loved it. But I had the feeling that what was to happen to me was not going to be that simple and I was right. Jeremy walked round to the side of the bed and removed his trousers as I watched in nervous trepidation.

"Now be a good girl and lick this," he said, "After all, it would be better for you if it was nice and wet, wouldn't it?"

I didn't have the chance to reply as he knelt on the bed and forced his cock into my face. I stuck out my tongue and began to bring his member back to full attention, wondering all the while why extra lubrication was needed when my pussy was already wet through. I put my head on one side and took his member into my mouth, sucking it back to full life. I heard him moaning with pleasure again, hoping that he would not come in my mouth and spoil my potential fun. I was sure the he was just about to come when he grabbed my hair, pulled my head back and withdrew his cook from my mouth.

I smiled with satisfaction, hoping that he would now penetrate me once more and screw me into a state of total abandonment. He walked round behind me and, standing between my obscenely spread legs he began to explore my most intimate of places. I felt fingers rubbing my mound, slipping in between my labia and into my pussy. I moaned and arched my back to meet his probing fingers, which already had me walking on the tightrope of delight. I closed my eyes in readiness to surrender to his touch when, to my intense disappointment he removed his fingers and left me on the edge again.

He then took the juices from deep within me and began to smear them between my buttocks and around my anus, at one point actually sliding his finger up my rectum. I shuddered at the outrage of this interference, but this was nothing compared to what was to come. As he stood upright directly behind me the full realisation of what he intended dawned upon me and I looked over my shoulder at him and whimpered, begging him with my eyes not to carry out his plan for my defenceless bottom.

However, he ignored my silent plea and he roughly parted my cheeks as wide as they would go, whilst pushing his cock, which I had lovingly prepared a moment before, between my buttocks and towards its intended target. I felt the tip of his penis brushing against my anus and I groaned in terror at what was going to happen to me. He ordered me to keep still and, once he was happy that all was in order he grabbed the front of my thighs and thrust his hips forward, thus ramming his cock deep into my rectum with all the force he could.

The pain was excruciating and I screamed out loud as he began to screw me, his powerful strokes penetrating me deeply and bringing me more pain that I had ever experienced before. I cried and begged for him to stop, imploring him to have mercy upon me, but he was enjoying himself too much to pay any attention to my entreaties. I closed my eyes again and tried to bite back the gasps of pain, tears streaming down my face in a never ending river of suffering. However, as the onslaught continued I had no choice but to settle down and accept this violation.

Every time he thrust himself into me his balls bounced against my clit and the rhythm re-lit the fires of passion that his fingers had started a few agonising minutes ago. As he leaned forward and grabbed my hair to yank my head back, I knew that I had reached the depths of my depravity and the pit of my submission. I actually felt myself coming, despite my undignified position and the fiery pain from deep inside me and I sensed my breathing quickening as he upped the pace of his thrusts.

I knew that he was going to come and I did not want to lose out, so I pictured Steven again in my head and imagined that it was he and not Jeremy who was treating me in this vile and yet highly stimulating way. And so, as Jeremy cried out and shot his load deep into my rectum I came as well, unashamedly shouting out my pleasure for the world to hear. What a wanton creature I had become. Now, it seemed that, however I was treated, I could find myself turned on and at the mercy of my own sex drive.

And yet there was still something missing, or someone. I was bound and helpless in the hands of a man, which was perhaps what I had always secretly craved but it was the wrong man. I wanted Steven and I wanted him to want me, possess me and take me as his own. However, it seemed that things would not happen the way I wanted them to, after all, I was a slave with no rights and say in her own destiny. Still, a girl could dream and my dreams were always about Steven and thoughts of him made the tortures and humiliations slightly more bearable.

I looked round to see what Jeremy wanted from me next and was shocked to realise that he had gone. My anus was still on fire and I had not felt him withdraw and now I was alone but still bound and still as helpless as ever. My ankles and wrists were throbbing from the pain of the rope cutting into them and my stomach hurt from being cruelly bent over the board at the end of the bed. However, I had just experienced the most intense orgasms of my life and I could not help but feel happy, despite the awkwardness of my position.

I waited for what seemed like a long time, thinking of my Steven and wondering what Jeremy would do to me next. Eventually he returned, released me and ordered me to go downstairs and prepare more food for him. I was sure that this would be my lot if ever to fall not his hands for ever, forced to have sex with him and then cook, but I supposed that it wouldn't be all that bad ñ at least I would have pretty much unrestricted access to his cock, whenever he felt like taking me.

And this did become the pattern for the rest of my brief time in the service of Jeremy. The sex was fantastic and we even got to the stage where he forgot to bind me again after ravishing me. He allowed me to sleep naked with him in his bed, with my hands simply cuffed behind me and towards the end of the weekend he gave me permission to eat at his table, rather than licking up crumbs from a plate on the floor beside his chair. I felt that I could get to like Jeremy, given time but he could never replace Steven.

However, my new found respect for Jeremy was shattered on the last morning at his house. We woke early and began to kiss me tenderly all over my body, lingering almost lovingly over my nipples and my glistening lips. My breath quickened and I found myself extremely aroused and begging for to ram his cock deep inside me. He did not need a second invitation and he threw me onto my back, forced my legs apart and pushed his hard penis between my pouting labia and into my vagina. I cried out with pleasure as he started to thrust his member in and out of me with the strength and energy of a steam piston. I came with an explosion of colour in my head and my orgasm blasted through my entire body and rendered me exhausted but totally satisfied.

I lay back and looked up at him through a haze as I slowly regained my senses, but he was already up and off the bed, obviously with the intention of getting dressed and leaving. He ordered me to get ready and, after I had done so, he took me, with cuffs still on, down to his cellar. It was dark, as the light of the single naked bulb did not reach the dim corners of the basement. I was confused as to why we were there at first and then I noticed a small wooden box at the far end of the room. A dark question invaded my thoughts: where on earth was Ellie?

As if to answer my silent question Jeremy walked over to the box, which had edges no longer than a metre and began to open some bolts at the side. I watched, eyes open wide with terror for, as the lid swung aside I could see the tiny interior of the box and crammed inside was Ellie. She was crumpled into a foetal position, arms and wrists bound behind her, legs bound together with black straps and folded up to her chest and secured by another strap that went all the way round her tortured frame.

Her sweet breasts were squashed up out of sight

behind her thighs and her head was encased in a black leather hood. Only her beautiful auburn hair could be seen, protruding out of the top of the hood in a pony tail and her cute nose, through which she gasped for fresh air. I watched as Jeremy pulled her out of her dreadful prison and she fell over on to one side, moaning into what I could only presume was a gag under the hood. A tear came to my eye as Jeremy untied Ellie and I heard her scream as the blood began to flow through her severely restricted limbs.

"How long has she been like this?" I stammered, not bothering to ask for permission to speak.

"Most of the weekend," replied Jeremy, pleased with himself, "but I have taken her out to exercise her a few times."

So that was why he kept going; to give poor Ellie some relief. I felt angry, but also guilty because I had completely forgotten Ellie as I had lost myself in all the passion and pleasure at the hands of Jeremy. I had believed that he had been cured of his sadistic streak, but now I saw that I was sadly mistaken. Ellie had been suffering indescribable torture down here in her box as I had selfishly explored the sensuality of my master's cock. As Ellie's hood was removed she stared at me with eyes full of relief, but also tinged with hate and I looked down at the floor in shame.

When Ellie was free, Jeremy cuffed her hands behind her and led us both back up to the hall and told us to follow him out to his car. Neither of us spoke and we climbed onto the back seat when ordered and sat in enforced silence as Jeremy drove us back to Gilbert Manor. I stole a glance at Ellie once or twice, but she simply glared straight ahead and totally ignored me. Something told me that our precious friendship had come to an end and that, even though I had not forced her into her cruel confinement, I was somehow to blame.

Chapter Eight

Miss Francesca was pleased to see us again and gave us our customary hugs of welcome. Rachael was at the door when we arrived and was attired as she had been at the beginning of the weekend, with her cream corset and stockings and red shoes. She was bound and gagged and I noticed that her buttocks were covered with vivid red whip marks, an indication that she had been beaten this morning. We were exchanged with the minimum of fuss, Rachael was soon on her way and we entered Gilbert Manor, although I did envy her because she would be back in the hands of a man.

Ellie and I fell at the feet of our mistress as the car pulled away and she asked how the weekend had been. Before I could answer Ellie had blurted out her sorry tale of her experience of Jeremy's cruelty. I found myself horrified to hear how Jeremy had not only kept her in the dreadful box most of the time but that he had made her eat her food off the cellar floor and that, whilst making her jog round the room for exercise he had taunted her with stories of what he had been doing to me. I felt embarrassed as well as guilty that I had enjoyed myself at the hands of Jeremy whilst Ellie had suffered so much.

"Well, it seems that you have been having a good time, you naughty little girl," said Miss Francesca to me, "and, by the sound of it, at poor Ellie's expense!"

"Yes, Mistress; sorry, mistress," I offered pathetically from my position on the floor."

"We shall just have to make you pay."

We were informed that we would have to do another photo-shoot before we were sent off to Rupert's house and we soon found ourselves in the cellar all ready for the next session before our mistress's lens.

Miss Francesca sent Ellie off to get ready, but kept

me naked and made me lie on the tabletop while she used thick leather cuffs to bind each of my wrists to each ankle. She then took two ropes, tied them to the metal link between the cuffs, one after another and threw the loose ends of the ropes over one of the low beams of the cellar. A moment later she secured the cords separated by about three metres, forcing my legs apart and exposing my already excited pussy. I had the feeling that, whatever my mistress wanted Ellie to do to me, I would enjoy it and I detected a flutter of excitement between my legs as Miss Francesca tied the last knot. She pulled the table away from under me and left me dangling helplessly from my bonds.

As my head hung below my body, allowing my long blonde hair to fall to the floor, I noticed Ellie walking back down the cellar steps towards my defenceless form. My heart skipped a beat because, even upside down she looked fantastic. She was wearing a pair of shiny black leather thigh length boots, a leather thong and a spiked dog collar. She also had her long leather gloves on and a black opera mask completed her costume, hiding most of her pretty face, but not her beautiful green eyes. She was to die for and, if it were not for the wicked looking whip in her hands I might have been able to come at the very sight of her.

However I knew that Ellie probably had revenge on her mind and that she would use this session to get back at me. Ellie would beat me with the extended lash and I knew that there would be tears before bedtime for me. Ellie approached me and, as the camera began to flash and whirr again, she stroked the outside of my legs with the cruel scourge. I shuddered involuntarily as the leather snaked its way across my smooth skin, already sullied with goose pimples from the combination of fear and anticipation. As she reached the top of one leg, she moved the switch across to the other leg and traced the taut muscles with the hard leather. I started to moan and lifted my head to watch the progress of the whip from between the firm mounds of my breasts.

My nipples were hard and I longed for Ellie to touch them with her instrument of correction, but she did not. Instead she transferred her attentions to the insides of my legs and I was soon totally frustrated and desperate for her to put the whip down and to use her lips on me. However, she did not and continued to taunt me with the whip, sliding all the way down both legs to the very edge of my bush and then taking it away at the last moment as I struggled to move my wet mound towards her teasing lash. I cried out in my bafflement but Ellie ignored me and started to stroke my bottom, as if to prepare herself for the beating she was to give me.

Miss Francesca followed Ellie's every move with her camera and she was soon ordered to commence the whipping for the delight of the magazine readers. Ellie moved round to my right hand side, raised her arm and brought the whip down onto my defenceless buttocks with a terrifying crack! The pain blasted through me and I yelled out loud as the whip left a burning crimson line across my cheeks. I wanted to plead for mercy, but I knew that it would not do me any good, for we had to please the punters at all costs. The next stroke crossed the first one, causing me much more pain than I thought I could bear, but I had to and I stiffened my resolve to receive the third.

However, the all to familiar whistle and thwack soon had me screaming out loud and begging for mercy, head hanging down again, tears in my eyes and golden hair cascading to the floor. I pulled at my bonds to no avail and the fourth stroke slashed down on my already flaming bottom, causing me to jolt away and cry out once more in misery. The last two strokes blended into one and it was a while before I realised that the shoot was over. I lifted my head and I saw Ellie helping Miss Francesca out of her clothes and walking back over to me with her whip. She stood between my legs and rested the hard lash on my belly with the handle touching my pubes.

She then pulled the whip towards her between my wet lips so I could feel the braid of the leather rubbing against the ultra-sensitive skin of my labia and brushing against the bud of my clit, causing me to shiver uncontrollably. My mistress came over to me, wearing nothing but her high heels, faced away from my helpless body and straddled my head, which she pulled up by my hair and told me to lick her moist quim, which I did gladly and enthusiastically. She tasted divine and, as Ellie was still rubbing her whip between my lips I soon drifted off into my own world of delight.

I lapped at the very essence of my mistress and surrendered to Ellie's cruel but kind whip, as waves of sensual pleasure swept over me. I groaned as I licked, hoping that Miss Francesca would come as well and it wasn't long before she reached her climax with my tongue deep inside her and cried out with her passion. She then walked off with Ellie, leaving me hanging and I did not see them again for what seemed like hours.

When they finally came back for me, it was late and Miss Francesca gave me some scraps of food then tied me alone into my little bed, wrists and ankles secured to each of the corners with thin white rope. She returned to her favourite for the rest of the night and left me to my thoughts. I was very jealous of Ellie and angry with her. It wasn't my fault that Jeremy had favoured me and treated her the way that he did. After all, I had suffered at Martin's house for a whole week, whilst she had been pleasured by him. I tried to console myself with images of Steven in my head. It was he and not Ellie and Miss Francesca who

196

had beaten me as I hung from wrist and ankle cuffs.

In my mind's eye I watched him present me with his proudly erect member to suck and lick and I sighed as he plunged his cock into my helpless and sodden pussy. I was in a frenzy in my bed and strained against the ropes but could do nothing to relieve my frustration. I pushed my bush against my sheets and tried to rub my moist lips against the linen, but all to no avail for I could not physically stimulate my clit. Eventually I gave up trying and went off to sleep, thoroughly frustrated in my efforts to make myself come.

An unrepentant Ellie came to release me next morning. She looked so pretty, with her auburn hair framing her defiant face and I wanted to forgive her, but she seemed to want to continue our feud. In addition to this I wasn't happy about the way my mistress seemed to want to abandon me. And, with the ringing of the doorbell I realised that the time had come for me to be abandoned again, this time into the clutches of Rupert. Ellie and I had only been allowed to wear our high heels and I answered the door, thus attired. Rupert stood there by himself wearing a tweed jacket and chinos and I wondered where his offering was.

However, I looked behind him and saw the hapless Hortia and Portia confined between the shafts of a single seat, two-wheeled cart. He had obviously borrowed them for the week and they were dressed as they had been on the night of the party. Their wrists and elbows were bound tightly behind their backs and their heads were encased in bridles, complete with thick bits and plumes of feathers. Rupert pushed past me and I shuddered for I knew that he would have Ellie and me looking like them soon.

And, sure enough, Rupert produced some tack and clothes from a bag in his hand and told us that we were to wear them. We pulled the long leather boots and gloves on and, under Rupert's instructions, we put each other's bits and bridles on. There were leather straps to go round our foreheads, which were attached by more straps to the bits. The bits were thrust into our mouths, forcing our jaws apart and buckled tightly behind our heads. More feathers were fixed to our bridles and Rupert bound our elbows and wrists behind our backs with broad leather belts.

We were then taken outside and, as Miss Francesca had unhooked Hortia and Portia from the cart, we were able to replace them between the shafts. Rupert fastened wide cincher belts around our waists, which had small rings on either side and he attached them to the shafts with short pieces of rope and attached us to each other with ropes through the empty rings. When he was satisfied he climbed into the cart and picked up a wicked looking carriage whip from the back of the cart. He nodded to our mistress, who had already taken possession of her two fillies and cracked the long lash of the carriage whip high above our heads.

We pulled as hard as we could, but the cart would not budge and Rupert began to shout at us, calling us lazy trollops and accused us of not putting enough effort in. He slashed the whip down onto Ellie's back, causing her to cry out and then on to mine between my shoulder blades with a loud crack! I felt the fiery, sharp stinging on my back and redoubled my efforts and, slowly but surely, we started to make progress. Once we got the cart going it seemed to get easier but it was still hard work and I found myself gasping for breath.

Because our elbows had been bound together our breasts were thrust out in front of us and bounced up and down as we ran along pulling Rupert behind us. He sat back and shouted encouragement at us, occasionally flicking our helpless flesh with his whip to remind us of the consequences of slowing down. The wind blew in our faces and we trotted along the narrow track that linked Gilbert Manor and Bleaf Castle, Rupert's home, which was about three miles away. And, after what seemed like an eternity of panting and sweating, we finally reached his house, which turned out to be a vast Victorian mansion set amongst rolling fields and woodland.

Rupert drove us round to the back of the huge building to a set of smaller outbuildings, which turned out to be stables and which also served as our home for the next seven days. We were not to see the inside of the castle until the great party that Rupert planned at the end of the week and spent most of our time either in our stalls or outside. After we arrived Rupert introduced us to his stable hand Jack, who turned out to be a dark middle aged man with a short temper and a penchant for using his whip on Ellie and me. Rupert told him to hose us down and to show us our quarters.

Jack released us from the cart and undid the cords that held our arms behind us, which brought us instant relief. He ordered us to remove our boots and gloves and he unbuckled the bits and bridles. We were used to being at the mercy of masters and mistresses, but there was something very unusual about being naked before this man, who was simply a hired hand. However, he was not at all embarrassed and seemed used to 'looking after' girls out in the stables. He led us over to one corner of the stable, which had tiled walls and a small drainage grill in the floor.

There was a beam running across under the roof of the stable and Jack tied our wrists together in front of us, threw the ropes over the beam and pulled them down on the other side. When Ellie and I were standing on our tiptoes he secured the ropes and retrieved a black hosepipe and attached it to a tap on the wall. With no warning he turned on the tap and began to spray us with ice cold water, directing the jet up and down our taut and unprotected bodies. We screamed and tried to dance away from the freezing water as it slammed into our nipples and jetted between our legs but the rope fixed us to the spot however desperately we spun.

At first we did not see much of our new master. For the rest of the first day Jack took us out to a field in front of the stables for what he described as exercise. In the field was an unusual device, which consisted of a large metal box with a stout pole sticking up out of the centre and four more poles jutting out of the top like helicopter blades. Hanging down from the ends of the blades were chains, which were about a metre long and which had rings on the end.

Jack had made us put our boots back on, placed our bits and bridles over our heads and put our arms into long single gloves behind our backs, which he laced up tight so as to force our elbows back together. He placed our ankles in leg cuffs, which had about a metre of chain between them and fastened our bridles to the chains hanging from opposite blades. Once he was satisfied that we were secure he turned on the machine and the blades began to revolve and we had to follow where the chains led us. Round and round we paraded while Jack brought a chair out, sat down and watched us walking by him, time after time.

Every time we passed him he told us to keep our knees up and slashed at our buttocks with a long dressage whip that he seemed to have with him all the time. He was training us to prance correctly and our breasts bobbed up and down prettily with every step we took. The circular path was well worn and it was obvious that many other girls had trodden the same way, many times. The whip hurt and we tried so hard to please Jack with our prancing, but he could not resist beating yet more helpless girls in his charge.

Eventually he walked over to the machine and switched up the speed, thus making us break into a jog to keep up with the rotating blades. Jack returned to his seat and reminded us to raise our knees as we ran with some less than gentle strokes of his crop. Our jog turned into a trot and our breasts matched our knees as they bounced up and down, our bodies glistening with the effort. Our buttocks were on fire and criss crossed with crimson lines from the whip and, try as we might, we could not please Jack enough to prevent him from having his fun with us.

After what felt like hours Jack walked over and turned off the machine, allowing us to come to a panting halt. He unhooked us from the machine and led us back to the barn where he released us from our gloves and stripped us of our boots and bridles. He took us through the exact same hosing routine and soon had us dancing on the end of his ropes, desperately trying to avoid the blast of ice water. Once we were clean again Jack left us hanging to dry, like washing on a line, our wrists and toes hurting from the constant strain.

"I can't cope with this for a whole week," I whispered as Jack left.

"Well, I'm sure he'll take a fancy to you and make me suffer more!" Ellie replied petulantly.

"Look Ellie, I'm sorry about that, but I had no choice," I said, but Ellie had turned away from me and ignored my apology.

I looked at her back, saddened that, because of what had happened we did not even have each other for company. We stood in silence and waited for Jack to return, but it was actually Rupert who turned up eventually. He informed us that we were to be trained as pony girls during the week and that, on our last afternoon we were to be raced against some teams owned by his friends at his mysterious club. He said he had placed a lot of money on us winning and that, if we did not, we would be flogged raw by him.

He explained that we would have to obey Jack's every command during the course of the week and that he would effectively be our master. He could use and abuse us however he wanted to and every infringement of stable rules would be reported to Rupert and would be severely punished. Jack would be allowed to sleep with either of us, as a reward for his good service to Rupert and after the exertions of the day, we would be bound and bedded down in the hay in the stalls. When he had finished explaining the regime to us he walked over to us and felt up our bodies and legs, in an effort to assess whether we would be good at pulling his trap round the racetrack.

Once he was satisfied that we would meet the required standard he left us at the mercy of the smiling Jack. He was looking at us, appraising us for his own purposes and choosing which of us would serve him that evening. We hung helplessly, each hoping that it would not be us, but knowing that we were not likely to be able to escape his attentions for the whole week. He walked round us, sizing us up, touching our breasts and pinching our nipples, slapping our bottoms and stroking our cropped pubic hair. We both tried to pull away from him, but the rope prevented this and I felt myself responding to his enquiring fingers.

Although I certainly did not like him, I found myself wanting him and moaning softly as he explored my highly aroused body. I moved towards him, as far as the ropes would allow and was very disappointed when he deserted my side and went over to Ellie to check her body out. Eventually, after what seemed like an age, he made his choice and it was to be me - perhaps stable hands prefer blondes. He released Ellie, took her over to a stall and bedded her down for the night, which entailed tying her wrists behind her with rope and fastening a rope halter around her neck. This was tied to a ring on the back wall, thus securing her for the night and Jack left her to return to my side. I shivered with excitement at the thought of being taken by him and he released me and led me to the stall next to Ellie's. He tied my arms behind me, pushed me down into the hay and spread my legs as wide as they would go. He ripped his clothes off, knelt between my legs and began to lick my labia with his long probing tongue, which made my stomach turn over with excitement. He pushed my lips apart and lapped the entrance to my vagina and I cried out with pleasure.

I did not want to be there, but it seemed that I was in the hands of an expert and he really knew how to deal with a bound slut like me. He licked all the way along my slit and located my erect clitoris, which he began to nibble. I was in ecstasy and I felt myself drifting away, especially as he reached forward and began to knead my breasts with his skilful fingers. I forgot all about Ellie in the next stall and surrendered to the attentions of this man who now possessed me completely. He suddenly knelt up, placed my legs over his shoulders and thrust his rampant cock deep into my pussy.

I cried out with joy and it was not long before we both came, Jack groaning as he planted his seed within me. When he had finished, he did not stay long and left me bound in the same way as Ellie, only pausing to push ball gags into our mouths before he went off home. I went to sleep thinking of Jack's cock and dreaming of what Steven would have done to me in my helpless position.

In the morning Jack came back, released us and took us out to the dreaded machine. For hours we walked and trotted, round and round, knees lifting, breasts bouncing and always flicked at with the whip, until finally we were allowed to kneel at a trough and eat some kind of gruel and lap up some water.

When we had finished we were trotted back to the stable and tethered while Jack fetched a lightweight racing trap and harnessed us into it. He selected another carriage whip, took his seat and cracked it over our backs thus ordering us to pull him out of the stable, which we did, straining all the time at the belts he had fastened around our waists. He drove us away from the house towards a large field about five hundred yards away and which had a wide oval track around its edges. Jack halted us at the side of the track and explained to us that this was referred to as the Hippodrome because it was where the pony girls raced while pulling their drivers in traps such as the one that we were tied to. Jack drove us round the track, increasing our speed all the time by slashing away at us with his whip, which stung and burned but forced us to try to go faster all the time.

We were exhausted and panted for breath with every stride, but we had to keep going and Jack's whip made sure that we did so. And he kept us at it all afternoon, only pausing for brief breaks so as we could get our breath back and then on, back round the track as fast as our trotting legs would take us. When dusk fell we were totally worn out and we were driven back to the stable, fed and hosed down before Jack went through a similar choosing procedure to the pervious night's. I thought he would chose Ellie and he did, leaving me bound and totally frustrated in my stall while he had Ellie in hers.

I listened to her cries of pleasure as she must have listened to mine on the first night, mad with desire and jealousy, but unable to do anything about it. I thought of Steven and of how he would take me, bound and helpless, but that only made me more unhappy this time, so I just listened and hoped that it would all be over soon. When he had finished using her he placed the gags in our mouths and left us again, but I could still hear Ellie moaning softly into her gag as she mulled over what had just been done to her. She had obviously enjoyed herself and I could only pray that I would be selected the next night.

The daily routine settled down to exercise, feeding and hosing down, interspersed with brief respites for sleep and sex with Jack. The cycle was only broken by the arrival of Rupert himself one evening, who was dressed in his evening suit and black tie and who had the most beautiful blonde on his arm. She wore a cocktail dress of the deepest blue and looked at us as though we were attractions at some weird zoo.

She was obviously not disturbed to see two naked girls bound in Rupert's stables and actually asked whether he could make us do something to entertain them both. He said he could, undid our halters and brought Ellie into my stall. She had been the one taken by Jake that night and his semen was still dribbling down her thighs, so Rupert undid my gag and told me to lick it off and out of her pussy. As if to emphasise his point he selected a crop from a rack on the wall nearby.

I did not want to go anywhere near Ellie, not only because of the spectators but because our relationship seemed to be deteriorating. However, Rupert had the whip hand and I crawled on my knees over to where Ellie lay. She flinched away from me, as if despising my presence, but I asked her to spread her legs for me. She took one look at cruel whip, which Rupert flexed in his hands and, albeit reluctantly, she parted her knees, and I began my task. Rupert began to flick the crop across my proffered buttocks while his girlfriend simply laughed at me.

As Rupert slashed away at my bruised cheeks I began to lick up Ellie's left leg from her knee to the top of her thigh, tasting the salty remains of Jack's seed and the sweet flavour of Ellie's juices. Ellie moaned into her gag as I worked my way ever upward, moans that increased in intensity as I transferred my attentions to her right leg. I was also becoming more aroused as I licked my way toward her inviting honey pot, which was already wet again. I noticed her lips poking out from her short auburn bush. They were glistening with her juices and I shuffled closer to her pussy and began to lap at her exposed labia.

I pushed her lips apart with my tongue, located her clitoris and bit the hard bud with my teeth, causing Ellie to cry out in her excitement. I longed for somebody to perform the same service for me, but I doubted whether Rupert or his girlfriend would oblige. Instead, I was forced to send Ellie off to heaven for the second time that evening and her whole body went rigid and she came violently. I felt frustrated and left out so I desperately tried to rub my breasts in the straw between her legs to relieve myself. The straw stuck up in places and brushed against my firm nipples as I jerked my self backwards and forwards in time with the rhythm of Rupert's strokes with his crop.

I began to feel a tingling in my nipples and I closed my eyes and tried to induce an orgasm within my breasts. However, Rupert seemed to be satisfied that I had completed my task and he told me to stop, replaced the gag in my mouth and dragged Ellie back to her stall for the night. He turned and walked out of the stable with his blonde bimbo on his arm, leaving me flustered and perplexed, with no way to satisfy myself.

For the rest of the week the training became steadily more intense as the race approached and on the last couple of days he worked Ellie and me to the limit of our endurance. Our bottoms were permanently covered with angry red whip marks, which constantly ached and made it impossible for us to sit down and rest. However, this did not stop Jack using his dressage whip on us every time he thought that we were slacking in our efforts. Our food was regulated and our food never seemed to afford us enough nourishment to take away the nagging hunger pains.

By the time we reached the eve of the race Ellie and I were much fitter, but exhausted and we both prayed that we would have the energy to win the race. I was sick of the whole swapping business and I was becoming more determined to have it out with Miss Francesca when we were allowed to return to her again. Either I was to be her slave or I would be no slave at all, unless Steven would have me. I would go anywhere on the end of his lead and would be happy to do anything that he ordered me to. It was only the thought of him owning me that sustained me throughout the week of rigorous training and I longed to see him again.

However, I did not know when that would be and my fears about the race took over my thoughts completely, especially when the morning of race day came and the other teams began to arrive. They were all delivered in horseboxes and were placed in stalls to be prepared for the race. There was tack of all descriptions and many different whips and crops that made me shiver with fright. The stable hands were all men and were all as efficient as Jack was in dealing with submissive pony girls.

Jack came and got us ready for the race by making us put on our boots and gloves and by fastening the waist clinchers around us. He bound our wrists and elbows together behind us and buckled on the bits and bridles. He completed the preparations by attaching the feather plumes to the top of the bridles and by binding our hair into pony tales, which flowed from the tops of our heads. As Jack worked on me I noticed that all the other girls were being prepared in exactly the same way and that they all looked very fit, but frightened by the prospect of what was to come.

Finally most of us seemed to be ready and we were simply waiting to be taken out to the track for the big event. However, when all the pony girls were ready the stable hands left, having secured our bridles to the sides of the stalls and the anticipation became almost unbearable. Some girls stamped their feet or moaned into their bits as they waited and Ellie and I shared the sense of frustration. None of us wanted to race, but we knew that we had to and we wanted to get it over with. Eventually the large stable doors opened and a horsebox was pushed in behind a RangeRover.

We were surprised to see Jack jumping out of the vehicle and walking round to open the horsebox. Even more alarming was the fact that the pony girls that he led out of the horsebox were no less than Hortia and Portia, who were both attired as they had been when they turned up at Gilbert Manor. Jack tethered them and drove the horsebox away, leaving Ellie and I to think about who would be driving Hortia and Portia's trap.

We did not long have to wonder for the stable hands began to return, bringing with them the traps. Jack secured Hortia and Portia to the trap that he brought and went off to bring ours for us. By the time he returned, the other stable hands had already fastened their pony girls into their traps and were driving them out towards the racetrack. When he came back he was pulling our trap and had Rupert with him. It was Rupert who bound Ellie and me between the shafts of our trap and to each other while Jack mounted Hortia and Portia's trap and drove them away, cracking his wicked whip.

Once Rupert was satisfied that we were secure he climbed aboard, picked up his carriage whip and ordered us to pull him out of the stable. As we trotted along he reminded us that if we didn't win he would beat us severely and to encourage us he slashed his whip down onto our buttocks. The strokes really hurt and made us even more determined to win. However, as we approached the track we saw a sight that appalled us both and left us aghast and confused because, stood by the side of Hortia and Portia's trap was none other than Miss Francesca.

It seemed that she was going to race against us and try her best to make us lose and earn the punishment that we had been threatened with every day of the last week. She did not even acknowledge us and only spoke to Rupert as we arrived. I heard her suggest that all the pony girls be 'plugged' for the race and I wondered what she meant by that. Again, I did not have to wait long to find out because Rupert agreed and the stable hands all produced strange looking devices from bags hanging from the back of the traps.

They looked like chastity belts, only these had two black objects sticking out from them, a couple of inches apart and I realised, to my horror what 'plugging' entailed. The objects were dildos and they were to be inserted into the pony girls before the beginning of the race. Rupert brought our 'plugs' over to us. He smiled evilly at me and, without pausing to lubricate the rubber invaders he spread my legs, parted my labia and shoved one of the dildos up into my vagina.

I winced and grunted with the pain of the rude intrusion, but Rupert just smiled and made sure that the object was thrust deep within me. When he was satisfied he withdrew it and walked behind me. He made me bend forward as much as my bonds would allow and inserted the dildo into my anus and far up into my rectum. I howled into my gag with the pain of this further invasion, but there was nothing that I could do about it. When he had shoved it as far as it would go he thrust the other dildo back into my pussy, which was already wet from all this unwarranted attention.

Rupert secured the dildos by buckling the strap to which they were attached to our waist cincher belts. He followed the same procedure with Ellie, causing her to yell into her bit with alarm and, with a final pull on the various buckles, she and I were ready for the race. The dildos felt so uncomfortable within me, especially when we pulled our trap over to the starting point, but they were also turning me on and I knew that they would jerk around within us when we began to run. We were very nervous and the other pony girls, including Hortia and Portia, suddenly all looked fitter and stronger than we did. How could we win this race, which was to be ten full laps?

I could not see Miss Francesca for Jack had fixed blinkers to our bridles to make us concentrate on the track ahead. As far as I could make out there were five teams in all and it appeared that Ellie and I had been drawn in the middle of the pack. If we were to win we would have to force our way onto the inside line somehow. Rupert and the other drivers climbed aboard and took hold of their whips and we were ready for the off. I heard Jack asking if all was well and then, with a fearful bang, he fired the starting gun and we were away, with Rupert cracking his long carriage whip high above our heads.

Ellie and I pulled as hard as we could, but we found that, even before we reached the first bend, we were behind the other teams and Rupert screamed at us to get a move on. He emphasised his order by slashing at our heaving buttocks with his whip, which stung us into even more effort between the unyielding shafts of the trap. We were gasping for breath and our breasts bounced up and down painfully but we kept going, realising that the punishment for not winning would be much worse than a few flicks of the carriage whip.

The breeze blew in our faces and the week of training began to pay off as we approached the other teams, who were all straining to win just as we were. Rupert slashed at our bottoms again and I cried out and, as he steered us skilfully round the curves, we started to pass the last two teams. We were heartened by this and ran even faster, the cheers of the watching stable hands ringing in our ears. After a couple of laps we began to tire, but were gaining on the two teams in front, one of which consisted of Hortia and Portia and Miss Francesca as their driver.

I wondered how much money our mistress had on the race and how much she would enjoy whatever punishment Rupert had in store for us if we did not win. I felt real anger and was spurred on to run faster still. We passed another trap, which was being pulled by two beautiful but sweating blondes, whose large breasts were bouncing even more than mine were. Only Miss Francesca's team to pass and we might be saved, but she was slashing away at Hortia and Portia with her whip like a demon and their buttocks were glowing red with the dozens of marks Miss Francesca had blazed there.

However, we managed to ease past them at the beginning of the last lap and Rupert cheered, believing that he might win. We ran and ran, filled with joy at the prospect of having avoided the dreaded but unknown punishment. Rupert relaxed his use of his whip and we almost became complacent, giving Miss Francesca and her team the chance to go back in the lead. They overtook us, Hortia and Portia's legs flashing by in a blur of speed, their faces pink with effort and our mistress smiling with obvious glee at our misfortune.

Rupert yelled and barked orders at us, beating us with his whip and bringing a blizzard of pain to our helpless cheeks. We tried our best, but we had put our last effort into passing them before and we could not catch up with them again. We charged round the last bend and we realised that they were actually pulling away from us and, despite Rupert's enthusiastic use of his whip we knew that we had lost the race. Miss Francesca's team crossed the finish line about ten yards ahead of us, with our mistress laughing her head off. Rupert on the other hand was absolutely furious and drove us straight back to the stable telling Jack to follow us.

"You two slovenly bitches have lost me a packet!" he shouted, as Jack started to undo our tack and release us from the trap. "You're going to pay very dearly for what you've done. I'm going to punish you in front of the guests at my dinner party this evening and it'll be a punishment that you won't forget for a very long time."

He turned on his heels and left, telling Jack to hose us down and to hang us up until he was ready to punish us. Jack happily obliged and stripped us and removed our dildos with a series of wet plopping sounds. I was relieved to be free of the unwanted stimulation for, although the rubber phalluses had excited me, they had been very painful, especially when we had been made to run. Within minutes Ellie and I had been strung up in the corner of the stable and Jack was plying his hose across our defenceless bodies, causing us to gasp with shock and perform our usual dance macabre in a vain attempt to escape the icy spray.

When he had had his fun he cut us down and led us over to another part of the stable, where he made us stand on small boxes, wrapped towels around our wrists, retied them with thick white rope, which he also secured to yet another overhead beam. Once secure he kicked the boxes away and left us dangling about a foot from the floor with our toes vainly searching for support. Our wrists hurt instantly and we both cried out and begged Jack to set us free but he ignored us and we were to wait for whatever punishment Rupert had in store for us, naked and hanging helplessly.

Jack had forced the hated ball gags into our mouths after our latest shower scene and so Ellie and I could not communicate with each other even if we had wanted to although I could hear here softly sobbing into her gag in her torment. As I hung there I wondered again how Miss Francesca could let this happen to us after all that we had been through over the last weeks. Perhaps she did not care about us any more. She had farmed us out to her friends and enjoyed the benefits of their slaves in return and we had suffered on her behalf wherever we had been sent.

Losing the race and being prepared for our punishment was the last straw and the pain in my wrists only served to reinforce the growing feeling I had that our mistress had abandoned us. This feeling was confirmed when the time for our punishment finally came. Jack came for us, placed the boxes under our feet and released us. We were so grateful and fell to our knees before him but he simply told us to stand, bound our wrists tightly behind our backs and told us to follow him to the great house for the first time. He led us through the tradesman's entrance at the back of the massive building and through seemingly endless corridors until we reached a large door.

He opened it for us and ushered us into a large room, which appeared to be almost empty apart from chairs placed in darkness around the edges and two mysterious wooden objects in the centre. There were people sat on the chairs, but Ellie and I only had eyes for the wooden contraptions, both of which had four legs that supported elongated triangular blocks with the ridge of the triangle facing upwards. The legs on either side of the blocks where linked by a wooden bar and both devices were bathed in light from naked bulbs suspended above them. I shivered as I looked at them for I knew that they could only spell misery for Ellie and me.

"There you are, you lazy bitches," said Rupert, "now let me introduce to part of your punishment."

"Yes, my dears, I don't think you will enjoy this at all," said a familiar voice, "you see you have been acting as pony girls all week and now it is your turn to go for a ride on our horses." It was Miss Francesca, and she went on gleefully,"These devices are called 'horses' and you will sit on them while I punish you for the amusement of the guests. You won't have to think too hard to work out exactly what you will sit on as our friends here beat you."

"So come over here so Jack can prepare you for what you have so richly deserved," said Rupert, indicating that Jack should begin his task immediately.

Jack pushed us into the centre of the room and lifted each of us onto the wooden frames. He lifted us so that we were sitting side by side and I felt an instant pain between my legs. Jack checked that our lips were parted and pulled them briefly, ensuring that they were protruding down either side of the cruelly thin ridge. The spines of the horses were only about an inch wide and, because our feet were already off the floor, the full weight of our bodies were resting on our soft and defenceless pussies.

I tried to push down on the horse with my bound hands to relieve the pressure but Jack soon foxed that idea. He produced several pieces of rope and put one of them round the back of neck, under my arms and through to the small of my back. He raised my wrists up my back and fixed them in the centre of my back by tying the rope to the existing bonds, thus hanging my arms from the back of my neck and preventing me from supporting myself. Two more ropes bound my legs to the cross pieces of wood between the legs of the horses, ensuring that I could not move my legs or find a way of raising myself up from my painful seat.

He did exactly the same thing with Ellie and we

were both secure and suffering equivalent agonies between our lips. We were not heavy, by any standards, but our full weight rested on the already sore and gaping entrances to our vaginas. We both moaned pitifully for we were hurting and we knew that we would not receive any mercy. Rupert and his guests would want to have their fun with us. Begging for mercy was pointless, but to make sure that we couldn't Jack brought two large penis gags over to us.

I noticed that the phalluses were made of plastic this time and that the thick leather straps that held the gags in place had a large metal D-ring over where our mouths would be. He forced the gag between my teeth and buckled the device cruelly tight at the back of my head silencing me and making me feel sick as the hard plastic touched the back of my throat. Ellie was similarly gagged and Jack completed his work by reaching into his pockets and pulling out two sets of vicious looking nipple pegs. Short chains linked both pairs and Jack fed one of the pegs through the D-ring and let the spring loaded clips dangle just above my jutting breasts.

Jack pinched my left nipple and pulled it towards him, making me wince and lean forward to reduce the new pain that blasted through my tortured body. However, this created more pressure on my throbbing clitoris, so I jerked back making my nipple hurt even more. Jack attached one of the pegs to my nipple and turned his attention to my other one. Constant pain flowed from the nipple gripped by the peg, but Jack pulled the other nipple and set me rocking forwards and backwards in search of the least painful position as he attached the other peg, which had the immediate effect of pulling my nipples up because the chain was too short to allow my breasts to hang free. I bent my head down and reduced the pressure on my nipples, but this made me lose my balance and brought

215

more pain to my poor clit. I was racked with pain in my breasts and from my sex and I groaned into my gag. This was a severe punishment for two slave girls who had both tried their best for their master. Ellie too was groaning and whimpering in her pain.

"Very good, Jack," said Rupert, clapping his hands in delight, "they are now prepared for their punishment."

Prepared for their punishment? Surely we had been punished enough, but obviously Rupert did not think so.

"Every one here will have the chance to give you six strokes each with this crop," he said, flexing a long black riding crop in his hands.

"That's right, my dears," said Miss Francesca, smiling all over her beautiful face, "and you will be blindfolded so you will not know who is beating you."

She was really enjoying our discomfort and was looking forward to our punishment, which she would no doubt take part in. I quickly looked around the room before Jack took the light away with his blindfolds and I noticed, to my surprise that Jeremy, Martin and Olivia were sat on the chairs but I could not see their slaves anywhere. The other three trap drivers were not there and there was also no sign of their pony girls, but I suspected that they would not be far away. I wondered where Hortia and Portia were and then my heart skipped a beat for I realised that Steven might be there. I looked around in desperation, hoping that I had just missed him in the dark, but he was not there. I felt desolate and, when Jack secured the blindfold around my head I lost all hope and surrendered to my deepest fears.

My sex hurt and my nipples pounded with the incessant attentions of the pegs, but even more pain was coming my way and I attempted to brace myself for the whipping. Everything went silent and the anticipation started to get to me. If I hadn't had the gag in place I might have been tempted to beg them to get on with it. However, when I heard footsteps behind me I began to panic and moaned repeatedly into my gag. I heard the familiar whistle followed by a terrifying crack and a new level of pain was introduced to the upper part of my protruding buttocks.

I screamed as I tried to cope with the agony that burst forth from my cheeks. I involuntarily jerked my head back and this pulled on the pegs on my nipples, thus causing the pain from my bottom to be drowned out by the spasms in my breasts. I knew that I could not handle all the stokes that had been promised to me, but I had to somehow. The second stroke, from my unknown assailant caught me off guard and had me dragging my nipples upwards again as the pain surged through me. I tried to think of Steven as the beating continued, in an attempt to turn my world of pain and suffering into pleasure.

I saw his handsome face smiling at me through he red mist of anguish that filled my mind and it helped me to focus myself. I began to drift away from the scene of torture and depravity, in which Ellie and I were playing the central roles and I went on a search for pleasure. I realised that, as the blows rained down on my buttocks, my pussy was becoming wet and actually lubricating at the little jumps I was making in response to the brutal beating I was receiving. I had no thoughts for Ellie, even though she was sharing the same fate as I was and lost myself in a world where Steven was the one who had bound me and was whipping me mercilessly.

My nipples ached, but I knew that they were hard under the vicious bite of the pegs and the more I thought of Steven the less of a grip I had on reality. Even though my clitoris was numb from the pressure and the pain of the horse I could still feel a flutter of pleasure every time the crop forced me to move forward. The strokes merged into a total blizzard of agony but they began to mean nothing as I slipped into state of bliss with Steven's firm hand guiding me to a shattering orgasm. I screamed into my gag and the audience must have thought that it was for pain that I cried out but I knew better and even smiled as the lashes continued to rain down on me.

Eventually, after what felt like an eternity, the beating stopped and the room returned to a scary silence. I heard footsteps and the blindfold was ripped from my eyes and I blinked in the glaring light. Rupert was standing with my mistress in front of us and they were discussing how Ellie and I had taken our beatings. I looked across at my friend and saw that she was slumped forward with her eyes closed, her face stained with the tears caused by her brutal flogging. I felt a pang of sympathy for her because it seemed that she had not had an angel in her head to help her through her ordeal.

"I think that they took it very well," Rupert was saying, "I'm very impressed with the pair of them, despite the fact they lost me a fortune."

"Yes, and it's such a shame that we won't be seeing the other pony girls punished, isn't it?"

"I suppose it is, my dear," conceded Rupert, "but they had to send the girls back to the club for other members to use."

"I see," said Miss Francesca, "but I suppose we have plenty of slaves here to play with, don't we."

"We sure do," said an enthusiastic Jeremy, coming over and joining Rupert and Miss Francesca, "in fact I wouldn't mind a crack at Hortia and Portia myself."

It seemed that the slaves that had gathered were to be used by the guests in some kind of final swap to mark the end of the month of swaps. The masters and mistresses went out of the room and left us on our painful seats while they decided who would have which slave for the night. When they returned the slave girls were all naked, apart from black high heels and had their wrists bound behind their backs. Olivia had control of Rachael, Jeremy had Hortia and Portia in tow, Miss Francesca had decided to take on Cindy once more and Martin came back alone. He declared that he wanted to have Ellie for the night and Jack was duly summoned to release her from her perch.

Nobody, it seemed wanted me and I was told that I would be left on my horse for the night while the others went off to have fun. Ellie looked at me with eyes full of pity and as they had not removed her gag or her nipple pegs she could not say anything on my behalf. Had she forgiven me at last? I could not tell and they all turned and walked away from me, Jack only pausing to replace the blindfold before he too departed and I was all alone. I felt worse than I had at any point over the last four weeks. My whole body ached and I was numb from the continual pain in my breasts and my sex.

As I thought about the long night ahead tears came to my eyes and trickled down my face. I began to sob into my gag and, as my shoulders heaved with the crying I brought more agony to my tormented pussy and nipples. I was sure that not even my vision of Steven could help through this night and I started to moan piteously as I cried. I did not hear the door open or the footfalls of someone approaching me. The first I knew of the presence of another person was a hand stroking my hair, which made me jump and bring more pain to my bruised sex.

"It's alright, it's only me," said a strangely familiar male voice. "I've come to release you."

Release me? Incredible - it didn't matter who it was, just so long as they set me free. They could do what they wanted to me; I only wanted to get off that damned horse. I felt the rope that bound my ankles to the horse being untied. Strong hands lifted me easily and set me gently on the ground and I went giddy with relief as the pressure was taken off my aching lips. Those same hands removed the pegs and I winced as the blood began to flow into my nipples once more. I was so grateful to this knight who had saved me and I fell to my knees before him.

The stranger walked round me and unbuckled the restricting gag, which slid out of my mouth and fell to the floor with a clatter. I felt those hands on my still bound arms and I was assisted to my feet again. I smelt my hero and a faint trace of Polo filled my nostrils. I became dizzy with the intoxicating fragrance and leaned back against his tall, muscular form. A distant hope entered my mind, but I could not allow that hope to build too high. The man came back round to face me and he removed my blindfold. For the second time that night I found myself blinking in the harsh light of the naked bulb.

"It is you!" I said, looking directly into the eyes of the angel who had helped me through so many nights of torture and actually saved me from this latest one.

"Yes, it is," said Steven, smiling back at me and taking me in his powerful arms.

"You saved me," I said excitedly, "I dreamed that you would and you did...you came for me!"

"Yes, my little one, I suppose I did," he laughed.

"But what about my mistress?" I asked, "Won't she be angry?"

"I'm afraid that she doesn't want you any more," said Steven gently. "She has been talking with Ellie and she wants to get rid of you."

"But I gave her my life!" I exclaimed, furious and humiliated beyond imagining. "What's going to happen to me now?"

"Well, I did suggest that I take you off her hands," said Steven casually.

"And what did she say?" I asked, hardly daring to hope.

"She seemed to think it was a good idea," replied Steven, "but that there would be a price to pay for you."

"Do you mean you've had to buy me?" I asked, astonished at this piece of news and wondering how much I was worth.

"Yes, I'm afraid so. After all you are only a slave, but I have arranged to sort out the price with Miss Francesca in the morning," said Steven, "but whatever the price I will pay."

"Oh, thank you Steven," I said, overwhelmed with gratitude for my saviour.

"Ah, I think that you should call me master," said Steven firmly, "after all, you are mine now!"

"Yes, Master," I said joyfully.

With that Steven picked me up and carried me out of the room and up a wide staircase in the main hall-way. He found an empty bedroom and placed me gently onto a large mahogany bed. He did not bother to untie me but began to strip his clothes off before my very eyes and I watched as he removed his shirt and uncovered his wonderful rippling body. I held my breath as he pulled his jeans down to reveal his wonderful cock, already rampant and ready to enter my powerless but more than willing body. He walked over to where I lay, helpless and ready and climbed onto the bed beside me.

All thoughts of my aches and pains were gone in an instant and my nipples and my pussy were soon throbbing for a totally different reason. Steven took me in his arms again and I pushed myself against his naked body, desperate to get closer to him. I was at his mercy and exactly where I wanted to be. I felt giddy with happiness and relief, having been transported from the depths of despair to the heights of ecstasy by the man of my dreams.

I was prepared to go to the stake for Steven and I wanted to give myself to him completely, but there was one thing that I required to make my fantasy complete.

"Master," I said slyly, "there is one thing I beg of you before you take me."

"And what might that be, Charlotte?" asked Steven, somewhat surprised that I had dared to speak.

"Well, Master, I know that I have been severely punished this evening, but none of the strokes came from you."

"And now you would like me to beat you!" said Steven, his eyes lighting up at the prospect of confirming his ownership of me by whipping me.

"Oh, yes please, Master," I said breathless at my daring and readiness to submit myself to his discipline.

Steven, looked round in search of a suitable instrument of correction.

"I know where there is one, Master," I said, struggling across the bed and getting to my feet.

I curtsied briefly to my new master and trotted off back downstairs to the scene of my previous torture. As I suspected. Miss Francesca and the others had not bothered to pick up the whips with which they had punished Ellie and me, so I fell to my knees, bent forward and picked up one of the crops from the floor with my teeth. With difficulty I got back to my feet and sped back upstairs to find Steven waiting for me impatiently.

"Ah, - good girl," he said when he saw me carrying the crop in my mouth, "very good, bring it to me."

I walked over to him, fell to my knees before him and looked up into his handsome face, urging him to carry out his threatened punishment with pleading in my eyes. He took the whip from me and began to flex it in his hands, making the braided leather creak menacingly in my ears. My face was next to his penis and I could almost touch it

222

with my lips, but I did not. Instead I smelled his musky aroma and the faint hint of his salty pre-come and my head began to spin. I stole a glance at his rampant shaft, with its soft hardness, purple head and pulsating veins and I knew that I wanted it, deep within me to give me the satisfaction only a stiff cock could provide.

However, there was the beating to endure first and I looked up into his eyes, to confirm to him that a thrashing was not only what I wanted, but what I desperately needed. He looked down at my kneeling form, flashed me his beautiful smile and ordered me to kiss the crop. I did so, kissing and licking the leather and wishing dearly that it was his manhood that I was caressing with my tongue. Eventually he pulled the whip out of reach of my mouth and I knew that the beating would soon begin. I did not have to say a word for he took hold of my shoulders, lifted me to my feet and guided me once more to the bed.

He ordered me to lie face up, which I did immediately, spreading my legs as wide as I could and raising my hips to offer him an inviting target. and for a moment he stroked the soft skin of my inner thighs. Within seconds I was moaning with pleasure at his touch and wished that I had not asked to be beaten, wanting instead to be impaled on his superb member straightaway.

However, a whipping at his hand was what I really craved and not wanting to disappoint me Steven strode over to the window, grabbed two of the curtain ties and returned to my side. At first I wondered why I needed to be bound more than I already was, then I understood his intentions when he gently took hold of my left leg, tied one of the cords around my slender ankle and drew it up over my head. He looped the cord round a post at the head of the bed and pulled it tight before knotting it, causing me to gasp at the new tension within my body.

Once he was satisfied with his handiwork he

walked to the foot of the bed and placed the crop between my splayed legs, with the leather flap pointing tellingly at my exposed sex. I watched with fearful eyes as he repeated the process with my right ankle. He stood back and observed my racked frame, bent double and completely at his mercy, with my pussy raised up and utterly exposed between my taut and whip-reddened buttocks. He drank in the scene before him and I saw his eyes stray from my breasts, now squashed between my thighs, down to my labia, sticking out from my cropped pubic mound and begging for attention.

I strained my head up and looked down at my pussy, noticing that my lips were already wide open and glistening in my excitement, betraying my feelings for my new master. Beyond my sex I saw the whip again and glanced back up at Steven, who was also staring at the evil instrument of correction. I realised then that he was going to flog me in that most sensitive of places. I shuddered and opened my mouth to speak but Steven, sensing I was about to protest, simply put his fingers to his lips, looked me straight in the eye and picked up the whip.

I fought for control of myself, fearing that I would lose the battle with my emotions. However one reassuring smile from Steven and I knew I could cope. What he was going to do to me would hurt, but what better way for a slavegirl to be whipped by a new master? And I knew I would come through it and love him all the more. Suddenly he swished the lash through the air with a loud swoosh and I jumped, knowing that there was no escape and that my final test would soon begin.

However the crop came down gently, its hard leather-coated shaft nestling against my pouting lips. I sighed, thrilling at the touch of the leather on my sex. He began to rub the shaft between my labia, causing the leather braiding to brush at my clitoris. I moaned with pleasure, losing myself in the pleasurable feelings my master was arousing in the very core of my being. He pushed down harder and the crop split my sex in two, as he continued to saw away at my defenceless pussy. I closed my eyes and found myself crying out as I surrendered to Steven completely, my body overpowered by my first orgasm.

When I had recovered slightly I opened my eyes and saw that Steven was smiling down at me. I smiled back until I noticed that he had the crop raised high above his head. I did not even have time to take a breath before he brought it down on my sex with terrifying speed and deadly accuracy, splitting my sex again and burying itself deep within the crease of my pussy. Pain exploded from between my legs, stabbing through my pinioned frame and I wanted to scream but when I looked again into Steven's eyes I felt a strange calm sweep through me, absorbing the agony he was inflicting.

Again the crop fell with terrifying force, but I gritted my teeth and rode the pain as it carried me along and pushed me over the border from anguish to ecstasy. Steven's handsome face swam before me and as the switch completed its awful journey a third time I felt the last vestiges of pain melt into pleasure and I came for a second time, screaming for joy again and again. I heard myself begging for more as I shook my head from side to side in an effort to cope with the conflicting emotions and sensations running through my trembling body. I could still hear the crop as it whistled down onto my sex, but I could no longer feel any pain for pleasure had won the battle and I revelled in it.

But as suddenly as it had started the beating ended. I looked up and saw Steven throw the crop aside and climb onto the bed. He positioned himself between my bound legs and I saw his cock, proud and erect and more than ready. He leaned over me and cupped the back of my head with one hand, lacing his fingers in my hair. He lifted my head up and began to kiss me, his lips parted and his tongue darted out, exploring the inside of my mouth. I kissed him back and sighed as I felt his other hand stroking my thighs and straying down to my sex.

I winced slightly as his fingers reached my pussy but he gently eased my lips apart and nudged his penis towards the entrance to my vagina. His cock felt so hard after my whipping and it pressed against my labia as Steven bore down on me. He stopped kissing me for a moment and moved down to lick my jutting breasts and tenderly bite my hardened nipples. I arched my body against him and begged him to enter me for I so wanted him inside me. I wanted him to complete his mastery of me, claim his prize and take me, bound and helpless under him. And as if in response to my desperation, my master, with one convulsive thrust, rammed his sex deep into my dripping vagina, filling my aching void and giving me all I had ever really wanted.

My master now possessed me, body and soul, and I knew that I would go with him anywhere, do whatever he desired and serve him in any way he pleased.

And now for the opening of next months title "Caged !"
by Dr Gerald Rochelle

CHAPTER 1

Deborah had only been working at Theron Exports, a company trading in phosphates from North Africa, for a fortnight and still she had not found very much to do. It was run by Arabs and there were always strangely dressed and unusual looking people coming and going.

There was only one other woman who worked there, Chrissie. Deborah had met her in a club when she had first come to London, alone after the death of her parents and with no other relatives to turn to, hoping to start a new life. It was Chrissie who had got her the job.

Chrissie, like Deborah, was very attractive. They were both slightly built but Chrissie was a little taller than Deborah. Both had long, dark hair but Chrissie's was an intense black and fell around her face in heavy tangles whereas Deborah's was more brown, straighter and was cut slightly shorter. Chrissie had a large mouth with full lips and, when she laughed, her white teeth flashed. When they went out together in the evenings they helped each other with their make up and sometimes Chrissie lent Deborah a skimpy dress which clung to her smooth skin when she danced. They joked about the dress being loose as Deborah's breasts were smaller than Chrissie's. Deborah liked Chrissie, she was the only friend she had, and she looked forward to seeing her each day in the office.

Apart from her boss, Mr Kamil, Deborah had not got to know any of the other staff and when Chrissie had rung to say that she would not be in today Deborah felt lonely and disappointed.

As she scribbled aimlessly on her note pad, she heard some men in the adjoining office talking in heavily accented voices and she pushed herself back on her chair so that she could listen.

"Then they lowered this cage down. A woman was crouching inside it, she was beautiful: long, black hair, small breasts and firm buttocks. She was tied by the wrists, really tight, and the rope was attached to the bars at the top of the cage. She looked desperate and she pleaded for them to ... "

Deborah leaned back further, craning her neck and letting her long hair fall down loosely onto her shoulders.

"In the end, they undid the cage door but she wouldn't come out. A man prodded her with a short whip but she refused to move. She clung onto the rope around her wrists trying to get it loose then she leapt forward and grabbed the bars of the cage like an animal ... "

Deborah felt herself beginning to sweat as she turned her head and moved it closer to the door.

"'Get out bitch!', the man with the whip shouted but still she crouched in the cage. He reached in and she went to bite him and, when he grabbed her white panties, she yanked herself back and they ripped at the waist. You should have seen them hanging down in tatters from her hips. Her cunt was shaved and the material of her panties was caught in her naked crack."

"What happened next?"

"The man with the whip went around the back of the cage and prodded her in the back and finally he drove her out. Then he stood in front of her and forced her onto her knees. 'Suck this bitch!', he shouted as he forced his cock into her gaping mouth.

Deborah felt the veins in her temples throbbing and her heart pounding in her chest as she craned her neck back to listen.

"Then they couldn't stop her from sucking. A couple of others dragged her away and tied her up really tight, then they dragged her around the room shouting at her, 'On your knees bitch! On your knees!', but every time she tried to get up she was knocked down again and they dragged her around more."

Deborah pushed her hands down towards her knees and felt how wet and clammy they were. She squeezed her palms against the insides of her knees and pressed her legs tightly together.

"Then they bent her over this bench, ripped her panties off completely and stuffed them into her mouth. She tried to scream but they wouldn't let her. Every time she opened her mouth they stuffed the white panties in further. Her face went really red as she gulped and fought for breath then Saab came in. Oh yes, she looked amazing, yes, she was dressed in red as usual and she went straight over to the woman and gave her such a beating. Sweat poured from Saab's forehead as she whipped the cane down on the woman's buttocks then she said ... "

As Deborah strained back, her legs tensed and her knees opened enough for her hands to move upwards. She felt her sweaty palms against the insides of her thighs and, as they moved up to the tops of her smooth, white stockings, she felt the warm softness of her thin, white panties against the backs of her thumbs.

"Then Saab straddled the woman. 'Lick it bitch before your next punishment', she said. The woman reached her face up and they pulled the panties from her mouth. She didn't hesitate, she just stuck her tongue straight in. As she licked Saab between the legs, Saab brought the cane down on the woman's back. The woman screamed like an animal but Saab wouldn't stop until she was satisfied. Then Saab said, 'Bring them in now', and they opened the door and ... "

Deborah pressed her thumbs back and squeezed them against the furrow that ran along the gusset of her white panties. She lifted them away slightly and allowed the soft flesh to part along its crease. As she felt the warmth between her legs, she hung her head back further, straining the muscles of her stomach and causing the furrow of flesh to open even more.

She felt a flush spreading across her face as she thought of the woman in the cage. She pictured her being prodded and whipped and forced to suck then she thought of her licking the mysterious woman who commanded her obedience and demanded her service. Deborah pulled her thumbs higher as she imagined the mysterious woman barking her commands and her heart started pounding wildly as she wondered what it would be like to be enslaved and what other ordeals the caged woman had been forced to suffer.

Deborah wanted to hear more and strained back to listen but all she could hear was her own name being shouted repeatedly. It was as if the men were now talking about her, as if she was the woman in the cage, clinging to the bars and shrinking back as she was prodded and whipped.

"Deborah! Deborah!"

She could see herself reaching her face up between the woman's thighs and extending her tongue towards the beckoning channel of flesh.

"Deborah! Deborah!"

She pulled the gusset of her panties aside and plunged her fingers into the wet crease of her cunt. She felt its moisture running down onto her knuckles as she imagined licking her tongue out and probing it between the fleshy slit that was splayed out before her.

"Deborah! Deborah!"

She felt her tongue reaching out and she tasted the tang of moisture as its tip finally touched the swollen edges of the waiting cunt.

"Deborah! Deborah! Come in here!"

Deborah's eyes rolled back as she felt the insides of her thighs pressing against the backs of her hands then suddenly, she shook herself and looked around wide-eyed and startled.

"Deborah! Deborah!"

It was her boss, Mr Kamil, calling from his office.

"Deborah! Get in here and be quick about it!"

Startled, Deborah pulled her hands from between her thighs. Her white panties were pulled down exposing some of her pubic hair and one of the suspender clips that hung from her white suspender belt had come undone. With shaking hands, she pulled her panties back up and clipped the top of her stocking back into the metal clasp. She licked her dry lips, jumped up off her chair and smoothed her dress down at the front. Her face was red and flushed and her hair was in a mess. She tried to tidy it as she entered the office but when Mr Kamil looked at her she knew she still looked flustered and dishevelled.

Mr Kamil brushed back a length of black, greasy hair that hung across his forehead.

"Deborah, at last. What have you been doing? You look a mess. Sit down, sit down and tidy yourself up."

Deborah pulled the hem of her dress down over the fronts of her thighs and sat on the hard chair across from Mr Kamil. She felt him looking at her knees and she squeezed them together tightly so that he could not see between them. She did not like the way Mr Kamil looked at her and sometimes, when he had helped her on with her coat, he had run his hands across her breasts and squeezed them before she had moved away.

A tall woman in dark glasses and a long, red overcoat sat beside him. Her long-fingered hands rested casually on the arms of the chair, her fingers dangling like claws over the edges and a thin, gold bangle falling loosely around one of her of her slender wrists. Her black hair was cut short and her lips were neatly outlined with bright red lipstick. Mr Kamil did not introduce her but when she turned to him and whispered something he responded immediately.

"You've been listening to the men in the office again have you?"

Deborah felt embarrassed at his question and disconcerted by the presence of the silent woman.

"I couldn't help hearing. The door was open and they were talking loudly."

"That is very naughty of you, listening in to other people's conversations."

Deborah rested the palms of her hands on her knees then started to pick at her fingernails distractedly. She was thinking about the woman in the cage again and was not really taking in what he said.

Mr Kamil stood up and leant his arm on the back of Deborah's chair. She smelled his aftershave and felt the heat from his hips as he pressed them against the back of her neck.

"Perhaps you would like to tell us what they were saying?"

He pressed the front of his hips harder and she felt sweat breaking out on her skin. She squirmed forward to try and move away and, as she did, she felt her hair sticking to the material of his trousers and she eased back.

"No, it's alright really, I didn't hear much anyway."

He pressed harder against her.

"Perhaps you could tell us what you did hear then."

This was no longer a question, it was more an order and she felt frightened by the sudden change in his tone. She fidgeted on the chair, still feeling hot and flustered and still unable to stop thinking about what she had heard the men in the adjoining office talking about.

"Yes, I'm sure we would both like to know what you heard and what it made you think." He turned to the woman in dark glasses and she slowly nodded her head. "Yes, we would definitely like to know."

Deborah felt her face going red and she bit her thumb nail nervously.

"Please, Mr Kamil, I don't think - "

He leant harder against her and rested his hands on her shoulders, gripping his fingers into her shoulder blades and tightening them. She tried to pull herself away but her pressed his fingers even harder.

"Please, you're hurting me, please - "

"'You're hurting me'," he mimicked. "Tell us what you heard and stop snivelling."

Deborah's eyes widened as she felt his fingers digging deeply into her shoulders and she felt afraid as his tone of voice became even more angry and impatient.

"Come on! Tell us!"

She began to think again of the men's conversation about the woman in the cage. Had it been a film or a story of some kind or, and she went cold as she thought of it, had it been real? As she pictured the scene she felt the flush of heat returning and, in an effort to distract herself, she bit down harder onto her thumb nail.

"And take your hand away from your face bitch!"

Mr Kamil grabbed her wrist and pulled her thumb out of her mouth. The tall woman sniggered and peered over the top of her dark glasses to get a better look.

Deborah turned to Mr Kamil, flustered and confused and increasingly frightened.

"Please, can I go - "

"No, you can't go. Now, tell us what you heard!"

He loosened his grip on her shoulders and ran his hands down her arms. Before she knew what he was doing he had taken hold of her wrists and lifted her arms wide. She felt her breasts tightening inside her bra as her arms were stretched, and she struggled against him and tried to get up, but he clasped her wrists together above her head and held them tight.

"Now, go on."

She could not believe what was happening. Her mind was racing with the images of the woman in the story and she was trembling uncontrollably as she realised that she was being held captive.

"They were talking about a woman in a cage, that's all. Now please can I go - "

"That's not all," he pulled her arms higher and the material of her thin dress pulled tightly against her breasts. "Now what else?"

She could do nothing but tell him.

"They said how she was crouching inside with a rope tied around her wrists. This man prodded her with a whip to try and get her out. She was too frightened to come out though and the man had to prod her from behind to get her to move."

"Go on, and then?"

"Please, please let me go. I'll tell you but please let me go."

He slackened his grip slightly.

"And then?"

"The man ripped her white panties."

Mr Kamil held her wrists with one hand and ran the other down across her breasts and onto the tops of her thighs.

"Why did he do that?"

"Because when he tried to grab her she went to bite him."

"She was a bitch then wasn't she? She should have been punished then shouldn't she?"

Deborah did not reply.

"Shouldn't she!"

"Yes, yes, I suppose so - "

"Show me how she went to bite him."

Deborah turned to the side, opened her mouth and bared her teeth.

"Go on, show me."

She leant forward then suddenly tried to bite his arm.

"Bitch! How dare you! You need teaching a lesson like the woman in the cage."

He thrust his hand down between her thighs and grasped the hem of her short dress. He lifted it and rolled it back exposing the tops of her stockings. She pulled her knees together as he pulled it higher and revealed her white panties.

"Try again bitch and I'll show you what you get."

She did not know what to do, she felt confused and helpless. She must do what he said then perhaps he would release her and she could go. She went to bite his arm again, more ferociously this time and he thrust his hand between her legs and grabbed the gusset of her panties. She tried to bite him again and he pulled at the panties until they tore and exposed her dark pubic hair and the smooth flesh that lay beneath it.

"What then bitch?"

"He dragged her out and said, 'suck this'."

"Yes, and what did the bitch do? Was she obedient?"

"Yes, she took it in to her mouth."

"What? What did she take into her mouth?"

"His, his - "

"Go on bitch, his, his what?"

"His cock. She took his cock into her mouth and sucked it."

He let go of her wrists, twisted around and stood in front of her.

"Get it out bitch and show me."

Deborah hesitated and looked down at her stocking tops and bare thighs, her torn panties and her exposed pubic hair.

"Show me I said!"

She reached forward and pulled down the zip of his trousers.

"Get it out and show me!"

She ran her trembling fingers inside the zip and felt his throbbing cock pressed hard against the material of his trousers. She wrapped her fingers around it and felt the veins pulsating along its still thickening length. With her other hand, she opened the zip wide and eased his cock out. She squeezed it hard and pointed the engorged glans at her face.

Suddenly, she realised what she was doing and could not believe it. She let go of his cock, jumped up and ran to the door.

"I can't, I can't, please, please let me go ... "

As she grabbed the handle of the door, it opened and two of the men from the office came in.

Mr Kamil shouted angrily.

"Get back here bitch! On your knees! On your knees and suck this!"

The image of the woman in the cage flooded back into her mind again. How she had fallen to her knees and sucked the man's cock and how they had forced her to crawl around and suck them all until there was no more to suck. Deborah shrunk back against the door terrified.

"On your knees bitch!"

It was as though the story was coming alive and,

236

like the woman in the cage, she did not dare disobey. As she realised what she must do, she felt a hot flush spreading within her stomach and a wetness running across the fleshy folds of her cunt. She turned, went to the middle of the room and stood before Mr Kamil.

"On your knees bitch and suck this!"

Obediently, she knelt down in front of him and reached her face forward. As she got closer to the stiff cock, she felt its heat and she opened her mouth. She slid her lips around the engorged glans and tightened them at its back before running them down the shaft until she felt its throbbing end pressing against the back of her throat.

She opened her eyes and stared at the mat of hairs that curled around its base before slipping herself back and watching the shaft come from her mouth, shining with spit and beating hard from the pressure of her sucking lips. She ran her mouth down again then began rhythmically pulling her mouth up and down it. She felt his cock hardening even more and the throbbing glans swelling in her mouth as the pressure of his spunk built up inside. She felt it running up its length and sucked it as deeply as she could as the hot semen exploded from its end and shot down her eager, gulping throat.

She released it from her lips and licked its end until there was nothing left to come.

"Now suck this one bitch!"

One of the men from the office was standing in front of her with his hard cock thrust towards her.

"And this one."

The other man who had come in pulled his trousers down and stood beside the first man.

"Suck them both bitch!"

Still with spunk dripping from her lips, Deborah reached her hands forward and took the two cocks in her hands. She pulled them together and drew them slowly

237

into her mouth. They were both thick and hard and her lips were forced wide as they entered. She ran her tongue between them and licked their veiny skin before sucking them in and taking them as far back as she could.

Deborah sucked at the cocks frantically, pulling them back into her mouth and pressing them harder against the back of her throat every time. She gagged as they went too far but she welcomed the heaving tightness in her throat that forced her tongue upwards and increased the pressure against their throbbing weight. She pressed her tongue against the swelling ribs that pulsated along the base of each of their stiff cocks. She felt the pulsating increase as their spunk began to flow and, when she tasted it against the back of her tongue, she squeezed them hard in her hands and sucked frantically as their hot spunk burst out in strong, pulsating torrents. She tightened her mouth around them as much as she could and swallowed it all in heavy, ravenous gulps.

She fell back, wide-eyed and trembling but now eager for more.

"Stay on your knees bitch! You're not finished yet!"

Some of the other men from the office had come in and one by one she was made to suck them all. Each one finished fully in her mouth and every time she swallowed it all down, letting the creamy hot liquid run slowly along the sides of her throat and not being satisfied until she had taken every drop.

Suddenly, she was grabbed, hauled over to a desk and thrust down face-forward onto its cold, leather-covered surface. Two of the men held her by the wrists and stretched her arms out wide so that she could not get free. Mr Kamil grabbed hold of her torn panties and pulled them down. They tangled in her pubic hair as he ripped them off and she shrieked out in pain. He ignored her cries and held her bottom still with one hand while he pulled the panties down over her feet with the other.

The woman in the red coat got up and walked over. Everyone went silent and Deborah's screams got louder as she was overwhelmed with fear by her sudden captivity.

"Stuff them in her mouth and keep the bitch quiet."

Mr Kamil grabbed Deborah's hair and pulled her head back. She looked at him appealingly as he stuffed the white panties deeply into her mouth then clamped his hand across her face to stop her spitting them out.

The woman in the dark glasses held out her hand and one of the men stepped forward and placed a short, leather whip into it. She flexed it back and ran her hands lovingly along its length. She prodded its end against Deborah's back, poking it into the material of her thin dress and lifting it up in puckers.

"Strip her!"

One of the men reached forward, grabbed Deborah's dress by the neck and ripped it down to just above her suspender belt. Except for her white bra strap, her back was exposed and her naked buttocks squirmed as she fought for breath and tried hopelessly to wriggle free.

The tall woman poked the end of the whip underneath the clip of Deborah's bra strap.

"Undo that thing."

A man reached forward, undid the bra strap and it fell free at the sides.

The woman paced around Deborah, staring inquisitively at her frightened face as she rubbed her hands across Deborah's smooth back.

"You are a pretty one aren't you? Yes, a very pretty one. And you seem to like having your mouth filled. Don't you?"....................

TITLES IN PRINT

Silver Moon

ISBN 1-897809-27-1	White Slavers *Jack Norman*
ISBN 1-897809-31-X	Slave to the State *Rosetta Stone*
ISBN 1-897809-36-0	Island of Slavegirls *Mark Slade*
ISBN 1-897809-37-9	Bush Slave *Lia Anderssen*
ISBN 1-897809-38-7	Desert Discipline *Mark Stewart*
ISBN 1-897809-40-9	Voyage of Shame *Nicole Dere*
ISBN 1-897809-41-7	Plantation Punishment *Rick Adams*
ISBN 1-897809-42-5	Naked Plunder *J.T. Pearce*
ISBN 1-897809-43-3	Selling Stephanie *Rosetta Stone*
ISBN 1-897809-44-1	SM Double value (Olivia/Lucy) *Graham/Slade**
ISBN 1-897809-46-8	Eliska *von Metchingen*
ISBN 1-897809-47-6	Hacienda, *Allan Aldiss*
ISBN 1-897809-48-4	Angel of Lust, *Lia Anderssen**
ISBN 1-897809-50-6	Naked Truth, *Nicole Dere**
ISBN 1-897809-51-4	I Confess!, *Dr Gerald Rochelle**
ISBN 1-897809-52-2	Barbary Slavedriver, *Allan Aldiss**
ISBN 1-897809-53-0	A Toy for Jay, *J.T. Pearce**
ISBN 1-897809-54-9	The Confessions of Amy Mansfield, *R. Hurst**
ISBN 1-897809-55-7	Gentleman's Club, *John Angus**
ISBN 1-897809-57-3	Sinfinder General *Johnathan Tate**
ISBN 1-897809-59-X	Slaves for the Sheik *Allan Aldiss**
ISBN 1-897809-60-3	Church of Chains *Sean O'Kane**
ISBN 1-897809-62-X	Slavegirl from Suburbia *Mark Slade**
ISBN 1-897809-64-6	Submission of a Clan Girl *Mark Stewart**
ISBN 1-897809-65-4	Taming the Brat *Sean O'Kane**
ISBN 1-897809-66-2	Slave for Sale *J.T. Pearce* *

Silver Mink

ISBN 1-897809-15-8	The Darker Side *Larry Stern*
ISBN 1-897809-21-2	Sonia *RD Hall*
ISBN 1-897809-22-0	The Captive *Amber Jameson*
ISBN 1-897809-24-7	Dear Master *Terry Smith*
ISBN 1-897809-26-3	Sisters in Servitude *Nicole Dere*
ISBN 1-897809-28-X	Cradle of Pain *Krys Antarakis*
ISBN 1-897809-32-8	The Contract *Sarah Fisher*
ISBN 1-897809-33-6	Virgin for Sale *Nicole Dere*
ISBN 1-897809-39-5	Training Jenny *Rosetta Stone*
ISBN 1-897898-45-X	Dominating Obsession *Terry Smith*
ISBN 1-897809-49-2	The Penitent *Charles Arnold**
ISBN 1-897809-56-5	Please Save Me! *Dr. Gerald Rochelle**
ISBN 1-897809-58-1	Private Tuition *Jay Merson**
ISBN 1-897809-61-1	Little One *Rachel Hurst**
ISBN 1-897809-63-8	Naked Truth II *Nicole Dere**
ISBN 1-897809-67-0	Tales from the Lodge *O'Kane/Bridges* *

*UK £4.99 except *£5.99 --USA $8.95 except *$9.95*